WRONG SIDE OF FORTY

JANA DELEON

Paperback/eBook cover design by The Illustrated Author.

www.theillustratedauthor.net

❀ Created with Vellum

CHAPTER ONE

MARINA TRAHAN DROPPED into the driver's seat of her well-used Honda Accord and turned on the engine. Hot air blasted from the vents, making her feel as if she were in the middle of the desert rather than tucked away in Last Chance, a tiny bayou town in southeast Louisiana. The humidity, which sat at around a thousand percent, made it so hot and sticky that after even a minute outside, a person felt as if they'd gone five rounds with Mike Tyson. Young Mike Tyson. Before he'd married and lost his edge.

She put the car in Drive and grabbed the steering wheel, then cursed and let go. She'd forgotten to put that thingy on her dashboard again, and the steering wheel felt like a skillet that had been sitting on high heat for an hour. She shook her hands, silently willing them to stop burning, then grabbed a bottle of water from her purse and dumped some of it on the steering wheel. Sitting here waiting for it to cool wasn't an option. It was only August. She'd be waiting until October.

With both herself and her steering wheel now dripping, she pulled out of the parking lot of the Cut & Curl, where she'd worked as a stylist for twenty-five years, and directed her vehicle onto Main Street and then into the cute little neighborhood of historic homes that occupied three blocks behind the center of town.

Maybe that was her problem, she thought as she drove. She'd married and lost her edge. Of course, that was presuming she'd ever had an edge. And Harold wasn't all that bad. Yes, he was balding, and had a spare tire around his waist that you could drive to Mississippi, and he preferred his tax returns and spreadsheets to a spirited discussion about most anything else, but he had a good CPA practice, and along with the money she made as a stylist, they had a comfortable lifestyle.

Still, it seemed that everything she'd heard or read lately was about how to spice things up. Especially when the kids left home. They only had the one daughter, Avery, but she'd been the work of at least ten as far as Marina was concerned. Smart, bullheaded, and a raging extrovert, she'd kept Marina running until last week, when she'd driven off to the university in New Orleans. Marina had crawled into bed after she left and hadn't come out for sixteen hours.

But now, she and Harold had the house to themselves, and Marina had decided to take some of that advice she'd been hearing and ordered a slinky negligee. It was sapphire blue with black lace and of course, crotchless. When her last appointment of the day had canceled, Marina figured this was the golden opportunity to test out her new purchase. As soon as she got home, she was going to shower, style her hair, do up her makeup, slip into that silky garment, and greet Harold as he walked in the door. Just looking at the sexy nightie had made Marina flush a bit, so she was expecting great things when Harold caught sight of her in it.

She pulled into the drive and was disappointed to see Harold's shiny new Mercedes convertible already parked there. So much for the surprise. It was barely three in the afternoon and Harold wasn't usually due home for another couple hours. But then maybe he was taking a really late lunch. Maybe he'd go back to the office soon and she could still put her plan in action.

She headed inside to the kitchen, but there was no sign of her husband there. She started to call out when she heard a noise at the back of the house. Frowning, she headed down the hallway toward their bedroom. It would be her luck that the one day she'd gotten off early in a million years, Harold had come down with a stomach flu or something.

She pushed open the door to the bedroom and gasped.

Harold was indeed in bed, but he wasn't alone. His part time file clerk, a girl only three years older than their daughter, was with him. Even worse, she was wearing Marina's new negligee. Things would never be the same. Someone else's crotch had been in her nightie and unfortunately, looked better in it than hers did.

CHAPTER TWO

"I'll cut his little winkie off!"

Marina's half sister, Halcyon, ranted as she stomped across her living room. It was fairly impressive, as she managed to do so with a full glass of red wine and wearing six-inch stilettos on thick white carpet. Halcyon preferred to make a statement, even if Marina was the only one to see it. If Marina had attempted the same move, that carpet would look like a scene from *Forensic Files*.

"And I do mean little!" Halcyon continued. "I've seen that man's feet. And that slut Chastity LeDoux—someone needs to superglue her privates shut. That girl has plowed through three-quarters of the male population. The only ones that she's missed are either out of Viagra or gay."

"It does seem rather ironic, her parents naming her Chastity," Marina said.

Halcyon threw her arms in the air. "Might as well stick her on a pole as soon as she can walk. Putting a name like that on your kid is just asking to be defied."

"I don't know. Dad named me Marina and I love the water."

"Dad named you Marina because he really wanted a new bass boat and couldn't afford a new boat and two babies."

Marina stared. "How do you know that?"

"I heard him tell it to Six-Pack Steve one night when they were drunk fishing."

"Did they catch anything?"

"Hell from my mother."

"Was she upset that you overheard?"

"No. She was upset that they drank the last of the beer."

Marina nodded. The truth was, neither she nor Halcyon had won the lottery in the mother department. They'd decided long ago to just be thankful their father had died young and hadn't had a chance to subject more of his DNA to his questionable choices in women.

At least they'd had each other. Their mothers had hated each other on sight, but Marina and Halcyon had always been thick as thieves, even though their personalities were nothing alike. Marina was the calm, polite one—and if she was willing to admit it, too accommodating. Halcyon constantly nagged her for it. Her sister was only six months older but she played the wiser-big-sister role to the hilt. Halcyon was nothing like her name. Marina was certain her mother, Constance, had named her in high hopes that the baby she got would be calm and peaceful. Constance only did drama if she was the one causing it. To her dismay, what she'd gotten was a hurricane on two legs.

Halcyon stopped pacing and stared at Marina. "So what are you going to do? And why are you here? Why did you leave your house? Attorneys advise against that."

"What was I supposed to do? Give her my good robe? Cook them dinner? I really don't think I could have joined them for a cigarette and pillow talk."

"Don't be ridiculous. You should have thrown her stolen-silk-covered butt out into the street. Let everyone in town see just what kind of cad Harold is. Instead, you admitted defeat and let that witch take over your castle."

"But it's not my castle, remember? Harold inherited that house. I don't have any rights to it."

"That's just bullshit. That place was a dump when Harold inherited it. It looked like a moldy rose garden had thrown up on every wall in the house. You put your time, money, and sweat into making it a showplace. Harold never lifted a finger to help."

"He did once. But since he almost cut that finger off with the table saw, he stuck to his spreadsheets afterward."

"Why doesn't that surprise me? Look, the bottom line is that I don't care if he inherited the house or not. You're due something for all the money you poured into the place. He can't just set you out like a stray cat."

"You think I should ask him for money?"

"Damn straight! Marriage is personal. Divorce is business. So either he coughs up some equity or you and I pay a visit to Myrna."

"Why would we visit Myrna?"

"Because her daughter is the editor of the local newspaper. Harold can give you a very generous payout, or he can be subjected to any number of articles about his proclivity for sleeping with an employee who went to high school with his daughter. Trust me, in this day and age, that is *not* a good look for a man."

"There are eight hundred people in this town. Seven hundred fifty of them probably already know and the other fifty will as soon as they sober up."

"Of course they know. I'm sure some of your nosy neighbors saw you NASCAR-drive out of there and put two and two together because they probably saw slutbag and Harold going in together earlier."

"Even if no one saw, Chastity will tell. Just for fun. That's the way she is."

"True, but as it filters through the gossip train, the bunch of hypocrites that make up this town will all pretend they don't know because anything else would be crass or worse, impolite. If you put it in front of their faces, however, then they have to take sides. And I'm guessing that Harold's accounting business would be the big loser on that one."

"That's harsh."

"You saw another woman's hoo-ha in your nightie. *That's* harsh."

Marina sighed.

Halcyon narrowed her eyes at Marina. "You're not thinking of taking him back, are you? Because even if that worm came crawling naked and carrying a solid gold rose in his teeth, I wouldn't stick around long enough for anything but to kick those new veneers out."

"No. I'm just mad at myself. I mean, it's not like I thought our marriage was great but, you know...I guess buying the nightie was too little, too late. I should have done something sooner, but I was so busy with Avery and work and the house, I just couldn't find the time for anything else."

"You were busy being responsible and twice as busy as you had to be because you had no help. God knows, Harold has never been able to handle Avery, or cooking, or cleaning, or laundry, or even the smallest home repair. But here's the thing —you thought things needed a pick-me-up, so you went out and bought a sexy nightie to wear for your *husband*. Your husband, however, let his hooker girlfriend wear your nightie.

Do you see the glaring difference in how the two of you approached the problem?"

"Of course. So why couldn't he do something like me?"

"Because he's an idiot. Harold is looking for external solutions to an internal problem. It works in the short term but in the longer term, you only end up digging yourself a bigger hole. Trust me on that one. I have the permanent eyeliner and that disastrous boob tattoo to prove it."

"I just feel so stupid."

"Don't. You were the one trying to do the right thing. God knows, I'd rather be subjected to medieval torture than see Harold naked, but you made those vows and you were doing your best to keep them going. Harold, on the other hand, just picked the easiest warm body he could get a hold of so that he could feel young again."

Marina frowned. "I never understood how that worked. How does being with someone that young make you feel young? Being around Avery always reminds me of how old I am. Those kids speak an entirely different language. I have no idea what she's saying half the time, and don't even get me started on all the shorthand in texts. You'd have to be a code-breaker for the CIA to figure them out."

"It doesn't make logical sense. But this is a man we're talking about. Well, Harold, anyway. The bottom line is you can't blame yourself because this isn't about you. It's about him. When a man goes grasping at everything but his wife to solve his problems, there's nothing left but the fallout."

Marina shook her head. Her marriage was over. She'd had an inkling that was the case for a while—the veneers, the new sporty Mercedes, refusing to eat bread any longer—but with Avery getting ready to leave, she'd stuffed everything into a closet and ignored it. Now, apparently, the closet door had burst open and all the pretending she'd been doing had bitch-slapped her right in the face.

It was time for a come-to-Jesus. She was forty-eight years old and had a lackluster career, a high-maintenance daughter, a crazy mother, and a husband who'd just made her the biggest fool in town—no easy task.

Her midlife crisis had officially begun.

CHAPTER THREE

MARINA GROANED and pulled the covers over her head as the sunlight hit her face. Why hadn't she remembered to close the shades the night before?

Because you were stinking drunk, that's why.

She needed to add drinking like a sailor along with talking like a sailor to her sister's list of talents. And Halcyon definitely knew how to bring someone along for the ride. Marina had no idea how many times her sister had refilled her glass. She'd lost count—and complete feeling in her face—around midnight.

Figuring there was no way she was getting back to sleep at that point, she threw back the covers, her mind already racing with the multitude of things she needed to do, decisions she needed to make. She swung her legs over the side of the bed and popped upright, then grabbed her head and groaned. The room started to spin, and she drew in a deep breath and slowly blew it out.

She was too old for this shit.

But then, she was too old for a lot of shit she was about to face...being broke, being homeless, being single on national holidays. It was as though she was twenty years old all over again, except with forty extra pounds, wrinkles, and too many gray hairs to count. She even had the high school hangover to go along with the rest of the list of undesirable things in her life.

She pushed herself off the bed and staggered into the bathroom, almost afraid to look at herself in the mirror. The night before, when she'd changed clothes, she'd realized just how big and dark the circles under her eyes were. How puffy and loose the skin was when she poked at it. How had she failed to notice this? She looked as if she'd been ill for a long time. This morning, she was probably going to look as if she'd rolled over and died.

Quite frankly, she still wasn't convinced she hadn't.

"Think positive," she said out loud. "If your reflection doesn't appear, you're either dead or a vampire."

She flipped on the bathroom light and positioned herself in front of the sink, then slowly lifted her head. Her eyes widened, then squinted. She lifted a finger and ran it under one eye. The dark circles were almost completely gone. And the skin was firm, not even remotely puffy. What the hell? She'd always been told drinking would make her skin worse. Obviously she'd been lied to all these years. Or she was still drunk and wasn't seeing things right. Either way, she'd take it. Especially given her first order of business this morning.

She headed into the kitchen to make a pot of coffee and when she poured the first cup, Halcyon came shuffling in, looking as if she'd been to war. Her long, blond, and usually straight hair was frizzy and sticking out in every direction. Apparently, she spent her nights scooting around her silk sheets, because the amount of static electricity she was carrying could probably power the coffeepot. Maybe even the toaster.

"You want some coffee?" Marina asked.

"Nope. Just a handful of aspirin and a Diet Coke. Then I'm going back to bed until next week."

She grabbed a bottle of aspirin and dumped a pile of it in her hand. Before Marina could caution against taking that many at once, Halcyon had popped the handful into her mouth and then stuck her entire head under the kitchen faucet to get a drink. Then she stood up, hair dripping with tap water, and stared at Marina.

"What are you doing up this early?" Halcyon asked.

"Couldn't sleep any longer. I figured I might as well head over to the house and collect my things."

"You want me to come with you?"

"No. You never liked Harold on his and your best days. I don't want to have to involve the cops in this."

"Or the coroner." She narrowed her eyes at Marina and took a step closer. "What kind of cream did you use on your eyes last night?"

"Are you kidding me? I brushed my teeth this morning with my finger. I didn't stop to pack a bag when I left yesterday. I just ran out and drove here like a maniac."

"Then I must still be drunk. Because I swear your skin looks better this morning than it did last night. And I refuse to believe that God would be that unfair while handing out the symptoms of a hangover. I'm going back to bed. Call if you need me. Or something with a higher caliber."

Marina nodded and as Halcyon headed back to bed, she poked at the skin under her eyes again. Still no puffiness. Weird.

She shot back the remainder of her cup of coffee, then

poured the rest of the pot into a thermos. Caffeine and fear might be the only two things that would keep her moving today. She grabbed her purse off the counter and headed outside. It was just after 8:00 a.m. on a Saturday morning, but she didn't care. If Harold was still asleep, he'd have to get over it. She wasn't spending one more night without her toiletries and a change of clothes. Or the stash of good chocolate she kept in a frozen peas bag in the fridge. Harold and Avery both hated peas.

She circled the block twice before finally pulling into the driveway of Harold's home. The moment she'd seen another woman in her bed it had ceased being hers. But she didn't want a repeat of the day before. She didn't think Harold would be foolish enough to allow the girl to stay overnight, but then, she hadn't thought him foolish enough to have an affair with a girl who was young enough to be his daughter, much less an employee.

She had a moment of pause when she spotted a man standing next to a mailbox two doors down from Harold's house. He definitely wasn't Old Man Johnson, the owner of the home, and she was pretty sure he wasn't one of his kids, as he had three daughters. But he'd caught Marina's attention because he was just standing there. Not checking the mail. Not looking at his phone. Just staring at her as she drove past, his white V-neck T-shirt and purple skinny jeans looking completely out of place in Last Chance, where the majority of the men lived in ragged blue jeans and work boots.

Whatever, she thought as she climbed out of the car. If Harold had acquired a strange new neighbor, it wasn't her problem. She slammed her car door, angry that she had to case the neighborhood she'd called home for almost thirty years. Angry that she was forced to worry about finding a half-naked girl inside with her half-naked husband in the bed that she'd called her own just one night before. But more than anything, angry that she cared. And she *did* still care. How did someone simply erase three decades of her life?

She unlocked the front door and stomped inside. But once she caught sight of the living room that she'd spent so many nights in, all the anger drained away and sadness coursed through her as she realized she felt like a stranger. A stranger walking into a strange place. Just like that, her home had become somewhere that somebody else lived. Tears pooled in her eyes, threatening to spill over, and she struggled to maintain control. The last thing she wanted was for Harold to see her upset. He didn't deserve her tears.

"Marina." Harold's voice sounded from the hallway and she looked over to see him dressed for the office. Of course he would be dressed for work. Harold had always insisted on working Saturdays, although now, Marina wondered if it was work or play that kept him from staying home. It wasn't like *his* life had exploded the day before. For Harold, it was just another day of accounting and sneaking around with his hired help. All those pesky details such as being married didn't matter.

"I thought you'd call before you came," Harold said.

Marina stared. Halcyon had warned her that Harold would likely be on the defensive. She swore that men who were caught in the act immediately lashed out with all the reasons their wives made them do it and somehow turned themselves into the victim. Marina had listened as Halcyon had explained but she hadn't wanted to believe it.

But there stood her husband of twenty-eight years, looking annoyed that she'd had the nerve to enter her own home without calling first.

And just like that, she flipped back to angry. No. Not angry.

Mad. As. Hell.

"I wasn't aware that I needed permission to enter my home," Marina said.

"This is *my* home. My mother left it to me."

"I think you might want to check with your attorney on that one. You can't force me to leave simply because it's inconvenient for you and your whore. I have rights, Harold. I'm so sorry that the three decades we've been together has placed such a burden on you."

"This is not the way I wanted things to go."

"Really? And just how did you think things would go when I found you in our bed with a girl practically your daughter's age?"

Harold flushed and she could see his jaw clench. Clearly, he'd thought Marina was going to slink silently away, avoiding conflict as she always did. Making sure everyone else got what they wanted without regard to her own needs. Well, too bad for him. That Marina had died and gone the moment she saw him standing there in all his arrogance, questioning her for being there.

"Chastity is not part of this," he said.

"Seemed like a big part yesterday. Unless there was a town vote and every man of maturity is required to sleep with her. Oh wait, every man of maturity *has* slept with her. I suppose you got sloppy eight-hundredths."

He turned beet red and clenched his hands. Marina had never seen him this mad before, and now she simply couldn't take it seriously. He looked like an angry, yapping dog. Ineffectual. Irrelevant. And mostly just annoying.

"I'm filing for divorce," he said. "You cannot stay here."

"I'll be happy to go. Just as soon as you cough up some equity."

"I don't owe you any equity. This is my house. Inheritance is not marital property."

"A judge might see the twenty-five years of salary I put into this place differently. Not to mention all the work I did without any help from you. I'd say that gives me an equity interest. Would you like to test that theory?"

"That's blackmail."

"No. That's divorce. This is all on you, Harold. So either pony up some money or I'll drag this and your indiscretions through the court system. Loudly. But first, I'll tell my sad story of woe to the local newspaper. What will that do to your business, Harold? How many of your clients will remain with a man who makes a mockery of his wife with a girl not even half his age? And what will your daughter think? How many boyfriends did she lose to Chastity when she was in high school? She'll be thrilled to know her parents are divorcing over her."

"You wouldn't dare!" he sputtered, but she could see the glimmer of fear in his eyes.

"Try me. Either I get some money or we both explode into the fiery pit of shame called bankruptcy. Your choice."

"How much?"

Marina blinked. She hadn't expected him to cave so easily. Which meant something was up. She narrowed her eyes at him.

"You're not thinking of marrying that twit, are you?" she asked.

"That's none of your business."

"Given that you're currently married to me, I'd say it's definitely my business."

"I'm not marrying her. But she needs a medical procedure and it's going to be expensive. I might not have the cash to give you."

"Your firm carries insurance. If she needs legitimate

medical help, she's covered. So what nonsense have you agreed to—vacation to France, luxury car, boob job?"

His eyes flickered down on the last one and she gasped.

"You have got to be kidding me!" Marina yelled. "You're trying to weasel out of giving me money I damn well deserve because that hooker you took up with wants new boobs? Here's a news bulletin—I don't give a damn what she wants. I only care about what I'm due. Twenty thousand for the house, and that's a bargain. And half of your retirement account. I already transferred my half of the money in the bank into my holiday savings account last night."

He stared. "You've lost your mind. I don't have twenty thousand dollars."

"Sure you do. You can borrow against this house that you're so proud to keep. But you should double that loan amount. Chastity might need a vagina replacement soon. God knows hers has a lot of miles on it."

She shoved Harold out of the way and headed for the master bedroom. No longer her bedroom.

"I need to pack!" she yelled. "I expect you to give me two days. If you see my car here, I expect you to keep driving. If I show up here, I expect you to leave until I'm gone. Understand?"

The front door slamming was the only reply.

She walked into the bedroom and slumped down onto the bed as all the strength and energy drained completely out of her. Putting her hands over her face, she started to sob. How had things gone so wrong so quickly? She was forty-eight years old and what did she have to show for her life? She wouldn't take anything from the house except her personal belongings. A lot of the furniture had come with the house, and the rest was well worn, and she'd never liked it much anyway. Besides, given that she had exactly no place to live, she couldn't fill up a U-Haul and head out.

This was it. A couple boxes of clothes, some books, pictures, and toiletries.

Her entire life would fit in the trunk of her car.

She brushed the tears from her face and rose from the bed. It was pointless to sit here feeling sorry for herself. Especially here, where she could see the edge of the sapphire-blue nightie peeking out from under the bed. There would be plenty of time to wallow in her failure later. When she and her paltry collection of belongings had a place to live.

The savings and checking accounts hadn't yielded much, about five thousand between the two, which had given her a moment's pause. Harold had always handled the finances. It had made sense, him being a CPA, but they had never lived extravagantly. So where was the money? They'd agreed to save as much as possible for Avery's schooling as soon as she'd announced her intention to be a doctor. Her scholarship covered the university, but there was still medical school to consider. Had Harold kept school money in a separate account? Invested in the stock market, maybe?

She shook her head, mentally cursing herself for not knowing her financial status. Yes, Harold was the financial guru but that didn't mean she should have stayed ignorant about their money. She supposed she was going to have to hire an attorney to find out where all their money was in order to get her share and protect Avery's future. And she was equally as sure she wasn't going to like the details of where some of it had gone. Was Chastity the first indiscretion Harold had succumbed to? Or was she simply the first Marina had found out about?

Harold had always traveled for business. He claimed it was for workshops and continuing education that he needed to keep his license, but was it really? Marina had never asked many questions because accounting talk of spreadsheets and tax returns bored her half to death, but maybe she should have been paying more attention. Maybe she needed to go through their bank and credit card records and see if she could decipher what else Harold might have been up to besides workshops. But then, she didn't have access to the CPA firm accounts. If Harold was going to route money away from the family, she would have never known it existed in the first place.

She blew out a breath. This was going to be a mess. Halcyon had warned her it would be, and her sister would know. With four husbands in her rearview mirror, Halcyon probably knew more about ending marriages than most divorce attorneys. To be fair, she'd married her second husband only weeks after meeting him and he'd died two months later. But there had still been a flurry of legal activity surrounding his death when a woman who looked ready to birth any second showed up at the funeral claiming the child was his.

In keeping with her promise to never be upstaged, Halcyon had cut a patch of hair off his head, right there in the coffin, stuffed it in the woman's purse, and ordered her to leave. The child had turned out to be his, but since his worldly possessions consisted of a leaky bass boat and debt, the woman had never been seen again. After that, Halcyon had made a vow to never marry a poor man, and she hadn't. But she'd never quite managed to avoid losers. Still, her sister had a nice house that was paid for, a Ford F-250, and enough alimony that she could squeak by without having to work. Now, Halcyon stuck with "gentlemen callers," claiming she was done with the whole relationship thing.

Although she'd never said so, Marina had always thought Halcyon was doing it all wrong. But here she sat, staring at the hem of her used-and-not-by-her nightie, with five thousand dollars and an old Honda Accord to her name, and she realized that life held no guarantees. Especially when you'd pinned your security on someone else. Maybe Halcyon hadn't been completely wrong when she'd decided to put herself first.

Maybe it was something Marina needed to learn to do.

CHAPTER FOUR

ADELAIDE BLANCHARD HURRIED down the sidewalk, brushing cat hair from her blouse. As the town's official old maid, Adelaide found it in keeping that she should always have a cat —or eight—around her place. It gave her something to do and everyone else something to talk about. Plus, the constant layer of cat hair covering all her furniture cut down on drop-by visitors. Visitors, in general, were the bane of her existence, but drop-by visitors had a special place in hell.

Normally, Adelaide spent Saturday morning in her garden. She'd never managed to grow anything worthwhile, but Southern women couldn't shirk their duty. Any Southern woman worth her salt spent at least one day a week digging around in the dirt. So far this year, Adelaide had managed to wipe out tomatoes, green beans, cucumbers, and a peach tree. Technically, she'd run over the peach tree with her car, so it wasn't a legitimate kill, but she was still counting it.

Instead of wearing her normal Saturday outfit of comfortable jeans and rubber boots, Adelaide had on her "good" black slacks, Hush Puppies, and a bright red blouse—the one considered too racy for church—and she was walking down Main

Street. There were goings-on in Last Chance, and not the good kind. Normally, Adelaide loved juicy gossip and sordid tales of woe, but not when the fallout was on someone she liked. Since the people she liked were a short list, she didn't find herself in this state of concern often, but this time was different. She had to find out if the rumors were true, which meant visiting the one place Adelaide tried to avoid.

The beauty salon.

She stepped into the Cut & Curl and gave the owner, Patricia Martin, a wave before casting a suspicious glance at Dottie Prejean. The wife of the former mayor—God rest his soul—was the closest thing Last Chance had to royalty, and Adelaide had to admit the old biddy wore it well. No matter the season, time of day, or weather, Dottie looked as if someone had just varnished and ironed her. Not a hair out of place. Clothes that didn't wrinkle. Adelaide was convinced it was some form of sorcery.

And since Adelaide was also certain that Dottie had just been to her regular stylist in New Orleans earlier that week, she knew good and well that Her Highness was in the shop today for the same reason Adelaide was. Normally Adelaide would have been put out that Dottie had beaten her to the punch, but this time was different. This time it wasn't about getting a juicy piece of gossip that she could carry to church on Sunday. This was about making sure a good woman like Marina Trahan wasn't handed a raw deal. On that, she and Dottie could agree.

"I wondered if you could fit in a quick roll for me," Adelaide asked. "I can take it out later and style it myself—I'll return the rollers this afternoon, of course. No worries if you can't. I'll just pick and fluff and spray the heck out of it."

"Helen can handle it," Patricia said. "That shouldn't take long at all. Why are you in such a rush? Is something wrong?"

"My cousin decided on a last-minute visit and even laster-minute notification, and I can't do things up as quickly as you girls," Adelaide said.

Patricia waved her to an open chair. "We can't have you looking poorly for family. You know they pull that last-minute crap just to try to catch you at your worst."

Adelaide crossed the salon, silently asking forgiveness for sullying her cousin's character. But right now, a little bit of white lying was necessary. She gave Dottie a hard stare as she took her seat, and the other woman gave her a barely imperceptible shake of the head, indicating she hadn't gotten down to the real business at hand yet. Adelaide wasn't too late after all.

"I don't suppose Marina can do it, can she?" Adelaide asked, figuring she might as well get straight to the real reason for her false claim of a hair emergency. "She manages a really tight curl. I can't ever get it to hold as long as she does."

Patricia glanced at Helen and frowned. "I'm afraid not. Marina's had a bit of trouble. I'm not sure what her plans are."

"What do you mean?" Adelaide asked, pretending confusion.

"Well, I probably shouldn't say but her husband left her," Patricia said.

"Harold died?" Adelaide asked.

"No," Patricia said. "Why would you think that?"

"Because a man who looks like Harold shouldn't leave a woman like Marina," Adelaide said. "She was always too good for him."

Patricia sniffed. "I guess it's all a matter of taste. But I have to say I'm not really surprised. I mean, Marina was kind of cute, I guess, when she was young, but she's let herself go the last couple years."

The haughty, holier-than-thou tone in Patricia's voice made

Adelaide want to strangle her with a blow-dryer cord. But then, ever since she'd been crowned homecoming queen thirty years ago, Patricia had thought she was better than most people in town. Why, Adelaide had no idea. She still had the same squinty eyes and crooked front tooth that she'd had when Adelaide taught her in high school. And the stick up her butt hadn't moved an inch, either.

"Gaining a few pounds hardly constitutes letting yourself go," Adelaide said. "I think we've all gained a few pounds in our later years."

"Isn't that the truth," Dottie agreed. "Besides, Marina has had a lot to deal with. That daughter of hers is smart as Einstein but stubborn as all get-out and convinced she knew better than everyone else by the time she hit elementary school. And no one has ever kept Marina's mother out of trouble. Quite frankly, it's a testament to her character that Marina didn't turn to drink before she got Letitia into that assisted living facility."

"Besides, Harold's no lightweight," Adelaide said. "And the best of his hair left him years ago. Surely you're not suggesting he rates a supermodel."

Patricia drew herself up and her jaw tightened. "Of course not, but the reality is when a man has a steady job with good pay, he can score a woman who's better-looking than him."

"He already did," Dottie said. "Marina."

Adelaide gave her an approving nod.

"Some people age better than others," Patricia said.

"So despite the fact that Harold looks like a woeful toad," Adelaide said, "you're implying he has taken up with someone else because Marina is no longer pretty enough for him?"

Adelaide had already heard the rumors about Chastity LeDoux, and the fact that Patricia was her aunt and Marina's employer was exactly why Adelaide had required an emergency hair session.

"I might have heard something to that effect," Patricia said.

"Who in their right mind would take up with Harold?" Adelaide asked. "I don't care if he's as rich as Caesar. I can barely shake the man's hand without having to use that antibacterial hand gel afterward. I don't know what it would take to wash the ick off my privates. Maybe bleach."

"I don't think we need to hear about your privates," Dottie said. "But I think we can all agree that it's a woman of dubious ethics and character who takes up with a married man."

Patricia's jaw clenched and Adelaide could tell she wanted to say something but didn't dare. Adelaide had figured Patricia would side with her niece. Especially since Patricia's brother was the town attorney and gunning for mayor. The salon owner loved nothing more than throwing his name around to get faster service, tables at the local "fine" dining even when they were booked, and a host of other things she wouldn't otherwise rate if she wasn't sister to the only man in town who could sue everyone.

"Most marriages have ended long before the actual separation," Patricia said.

"For one of them that's usually true," Dottie said. "The problem is the cheater always forgets to tell his wife. Ah well, I suppose it will all come out sooner rather than later and everyone can make up their own minds. Not that it should be very difficult."

Patricia sniffed. "Well, I believe there's always two sides to every divorce."

"Sure," Dottie said. "The right side and the wrong side."

"And you don't want to be on the wrong side of things in Last Chance," Adelaide said.

Dottie nodded. "People here are long on memory and short on forgiveness."

Adelaide looked over at the clearly agitated Patricia. "What did you mean when you said you didn't know what Marina's plans were? I can't imagine they'd be much different than now except she wouldn't be living with Harold any longer. She's hardly the type to get a tattoo and leave on a Harley trip around the country."

Patricia shrugged but Adelaide could tell the salon owner had spoken too much, too soon, and now she was going to attempt to backtrack.

"A lot of people decide to make big changes when their marriage breaks up," Patricia said. "Who knows what her future might hold?"

Adelaide looked over at Dottie, who gave her a worried look. They were both thinking the same thing.

An hour later, they stood in the square in the middle of downtown, positioned behind an enormous oak tree so they weren't visible to most foot traffic. Dottie was drinking one of those snooty coffee drinks that cost a fortune and consisted mostly of foam. Adelaide was drinking straight-up black coffee from the gas station.

Dottie looked over at the church and frowned. "You did that, didn't you?"

The sign that had read "FREE FLU SHOTS" the day before now displayed "FREE F U SHOTS."

Adelaide grinned. "I'll never tell."

"I don't think you have to." Dottie sighed. "So...this situation."

"That Patricia is one big, flaming bitch," Adelaide said.

"Crude but accurate," Dottie agreed. "She's always thought she was better than she was. That's her mother's fault. And that brother of hers has just kept it all going with his pompous way of lording over anyone who'll let him."

"The problem is there's plenty in this town that let him."

"That's fear. Not respect."

"Yeah, well, I'm afraid fear is going to get him elected mayor."

Dottie shook her head. "William must be rolling over in his grave."

Adelaide nodded. William was Dottie's deceased husband and the former mayor. As far as men went, he was one of the few good ones. He and Adelaide had disagreed about some things, like whether or not it should be illegal to grow corn in your backyard and how many cats should be allowed in one home, but he'd been a good mayor.

"If that idiot gets elected," Adelaide said, "William's going to come back to haunt us. Maybe even do a curse."

"It's rumored his family descended from Marie Laveau. I suppose if anyone could be outraged enough to rise from the dead, it would be William."

"He always had an unwavering sense of propriety. One of the things I admired about him."

Dottie snorted. "That's because you don't have any."

Adelaide waved a hand in dismissal. "It's overrated. Besides, I'm too old to give a damn what other people think."

"You reached that point in kindergarten."

"Possibly even before."

"That niece of Patricia's has been brought up to be useless and aimless," Dottie said. "What she needs is a job. A real job. Not these silly part-time things Preston strong-arms locals into hiring her for since neither he or Patricia want her underfoot."

"Ha. The only thing she knows how to do isn't legal to charge for."

"Also crude."

"Also accurate." Adelaide frowned. "I'm worried about Marina's job."

Dottie sighed. "So am I. I think Patricia is going to back that oversexed niece of hers regardless of what others think. No way she's going to come out against Chastity and risk losing favor with her brother."

"If Chastity had '666' on her scalp, Patricia would still back her. She's not about to give up her perks."

"The problem is Patricia is a subpar human being but she's not a sociopath. Her conscience won't allow her to face Marina every day, knowing she's standing in the wrong corner strictly for her own benefit."

"You think she's going to fire her?"

"Or be so nasty she runs her off. Either way, the end result is the same."

Adelaide nodded. "Marina is out of a job. And at the worst possible time. No way Harold is going to play fair in a divorce. Not with that little girl hanging around waiting for daddy to hand out her allowance."

Dottie cringed. "That statement is mortifying. But you're right. So what do we do?"

"I don't know that there's anything we can do, but we have to warn her at least. God knows, she didn't have any warning before she caught her husband in the act. I don't imagine she'd appreciate another surprise."

"Surely she's already realized there might be a problem."

"When William died, how much of what was going on around you did you process completely? I know this isn't a death, but..."

Dottie nodded. "No. You're right. This is a life-altering event. At least with William, he'd been ill and we knew it was coming. I had time to prepare—as much as one can, anyway."

"Exactly. So I'm betting that Marina hasn't processed much past where she's sleeping tonight."

"I assume she'll be at her sister's."

"I think we need to pay her a visit. I don't know that we can do anything for her but at least we can make sure she's not caught unaware again."

Dottie stared at her for a bit. "I'm surprised at you. I know you love to collect and disperse gossip, but your usual policy is to remain on the sidelines flinging mud into the fray."

"This is different. I really like Marina. And I never liked Harold."

Dottie gave her an approving nod. "I think we might have more in common than we thought."

"Kinda scary, right?"

"Terrifying."

CHAPTER FIVE

Marina put her shoulder against the front door and gave it a hard shove. It flew open, and she felt her back catch and a sharp pain go through her left butt cheek and knee before she fell through the doorway, crashing onto the tile entry. As she pushed herself into a sitting position, she made a mental note to adjust the door. Tackling it like a linebacker every day wasn't an option her body could sustain for very long, probably not longer than today. The ancient tile floor probably wouldn't last very long under those conditions, either. It was already cracked.

"Good Lord, sis," Halcyon's voice sounded behind her. "Just because you're newly single doesn't mean you should throw caution to the wind. You're going to break a hip if you keep falling that way. And there is no way to make a walker look stylish."

"I didn't do it on purpose. That darn door is stuck. And besides, I don't know who I have to impress out here anyway. The mosquitoes?"

Halcyon reached down and helped her up, frowning as she

limped over to clutch the kitchen counter. "Why are you walking funny?"

"The doctor says it's because of sciatica."

"Who is this bitch Sciatica? Don't tell me Harold has two girlfriends."

"No. It's a nerve in your back. If I twist it wrong, sleep wrong, cough incorrectly, or do anything to get my back inflamed, things touch that nerve. Feels like someone's shooting hot nails into my butt and knee."

"Good God, that sounds horrible. How did you get it?"

"Standing all day? Sitting all night? Heck if I know. Apparently, it's mostly an age and usage sort of problem."

"Can't you do anything for it? Like a heating pad or something?"

"I've got heating pads in every chair I own. The only place I sit that I don't have one is the toilet, and sometimes I consider one there as well."

Halcyon shook her head. "You'd think menopause was enough to throw at us. I guess this is something else I have to look forward to. Right up there with incontinence and death."

"I'm kinda hoping to put off the second one for a while longer and the first one forever."

"We can always dream." Halcyon looked around the fishing camp that belonged to Marina's mother and grimaced. "Are you sure you want to do this? No one has used this place in years. It's barely fit for fishing, much less daily living."

"It's free, and at least I've got a view."

Halcyon stared out the back window at the bayou. "It *is* a decent view. But this place...it's filthy and you don't even know if everything works. What if the roof leaks? Or raccoons have moved in?"

"I'll clean it. If something is broken, I'll fix it. If the roof leaks, I'll call a repairman. If raccoons have moved in, then I'll have someone to watch HGTV with."

"Honey, I know you're capable of replacing a faucet and probably even conversing with the wildlife, but this place is awful. Why don't you stay with me?"

"Because although I love you to death, you know we can't live together. Besides, what would your latest catch say about having me in the way?"

"He'd probably incorrectly assume he'd hit the threesome lotto, but he wouldn't have the nerve to say it or to make any suggestions around that fact. And I know I'm not the easiest person to cohabitate with, but you're my sister and I don't want you living like a hermit out here in the marsh."

"I appreciate the offer, truly I do. But remember, I come with baggage. Hairy baggage that makes your eyes swell. You know that's not a good look for you."

Halcyon sighed. "Why can't you leave that bloodhound with Harold?"

"Because Snooze hates him. Every time Harold comes into the room, Snooze starts farting. He never does it when it's just me."

"Really? I didn't realize Snooze was so clever. Maybe I could take a Benadryl every day."

"You tried that last Thanksgiving and ended up missing the Black Friday sales because your eyes were too swollen to see. I'm staying here in the cabin. I'll make it work."

"Cabin...I was thinking more along the lines of shack. But I suppose with a good cleaning and some new furniture, a couple of rugs, some wall decor, a couple of plants— Oh Jesus, who am I kidding? It's still going to be a fishing camp and it would probably take a hazmat team to get the smell out. But if you think this is best for you, then you know I've got your back."

"Just not a scrub brush?"

Marina grinned. Her sister's aversion to all things domestic was a pretty well-known fact.

Halcyon wrinkled her nose. "I'll get Bonnie to help you tomorrow. My house can wait another week. This can't."

"Tomorrow's Sunday."

"And? I think we have bigger fish to fry than traipsing to church for the ole stare-and-whisper."

"Yeah. I'm definitely not ready for all that."

"Then we'll work on this place tomorrow. But you're not sleeping here until we're certain everything is in working order and you install a dead bolt. And you're taking one of my pistols and a shotgun. No arguing. There are things in this marsh to worry about that a dead bolt won't keep out."

Marina just nodded. Once Halcyon was in big-sister mode, it was easier to just go along and then adjust when she was focused on something else. And something else always came along to draw Halcyon's attention. Usually a new man. And as much as Marina appreciated Halcyon's generous offer to stay with her, Marina was also aware that it would never work. She and Halcyon were simply too different. They'd be at each other's throats within a week, and since her sister represented the only solid relationship she had left, it was probably best not to put unnecessary strain on it. Besides, how was Marina supposed to figure out her new adult life if she was living in her sister's spare room with Halcyon telling her what to do every minute?

"What did Letitia say when you told her you were leaving Harold and moving into her fishing camp?" Halcyon asked.

"I haven't told her," Marina said.

Letitia Comeaux was Marina's mother and before the current situation with Harold, had represented the most difficult part of Marina's life.

"When she went into the facility, I was given power of

attorney," Marina said. "I control everything of mother's, which basically means her checking account and this camp."

"Is there any money left from the sale of her house?" Halcyon asked.

"Yes, but it's paying the difference for the assisted living facility that her Social Security doesn't cover. If I don't cover it, then they'll toss her out, and trust me, they're already looking for a reason."

"Since when?"

"Since she tried to burn the place down."

"I thought she was in a locked-down wing...you know, dementia patients and all that."

"She is, but apparently, one of the employees got careless on a smoke break and Mother took advantage. They called to tell me I had to come get her but their story didn't add up so I refused. I had to make a big stink about getting camera footage before they'd admit they were liable. Having some dirt on them is the only thing keeping her there."

"She needs to be in a mental health hospital."

"There's nothing available. At least this claim of dementia got her into a secure facility."

"Only sort of secure, apparently." Halcyon shook her head. "I'm glad I got the narcissist for a mother. You can write a narcissist off and no one blames you for it but you're stuck with crazy until it dies."

Marina nodded. Halcyon didn't even know the half of it. Before Dr. Miller was convinced to declare that Letitia was suffering from dementia, Marina had been to the sheriff's department four times to deal with her mother's shenanigans. And each time, they got increasingly more dangerous. The final shot, literally, was when she took aim at the postman, claiming she thought it was a home invasion. Marina knew her mother had hated the man ever since he'd dumped Letitia for her best friend in high school, so she wasn't buying it for a second. But Dr. Miller was, and that was enough to give Marina power of attorney over Letitia's affairs and the ability to get her into the lockdown unit at the assisted living facility.

Marina had never told anyone—not even Halcyon—but the day of the transport, she'd given Letitia sedatives and convinced her they were going shopping. It was the only way she knew she could get her mother into the facility without incident. If Letitia had known where they were going, no telling who she would have opened fire on to avoid it. Marina still felt guilty for what she'd done, but she'd also decided that her mother was going to be locked up one way or another. It was simply a choice between a medical facility and prison. She'd opted for the choice that left no other potential victims.

At least, that's what she'd thought before the fire.

"Was anyone hurt?" Halcyon asked. "In the fire, I mean?"

"No. Thank God. They caught her right after she'd poured rubbing alcohol on the living room furniture. She was holding the lighter when a nurse's aide tackled her."

"Good. God."

"So anyway, all that is to say that my mother doesn't get a vote in my living here," Marina said.

"You might still want to keep it a secret. If she finds out you're here and actually happy for a change, the old witch will change her will and leave everything to someone else just to spite you."

Marina sighed but couldn't argue. Halcyon was probably right.

"To be honest, I'm more worried about Avery than Letitia," Marina said.

"Oh shit! I guess I hadn't thought that far. What are you going to tell her?"

"I have no idea. If I tell her the truth, then I'm that parent who's trying to turn their child against their soon-to-be-ex. If I don't tell her the truth, she's sure to find out and then I'll be that parent who lies. It's really a no-win situation."

"Based on what I've seen, having children, in general, is a no-win situation."

"It definitely can be at times."

"I think you're going to have to level with her. Especially since Avery has history with the slut. Didn't Avery's high school boyfriend cheat on her with that nightmare?"

Marina held up two fingers.

Halcyon's eyes widened. "*Two* boyfriends. You definitely don't have a choice. If she finds out that bit of information from someone else, both you *and* Harold will be on the permanent outs with her. So I say throw him to the wolves. This is, after all, completely on him."

"You're right. I know you're right."

"But?"

"But it feels so mean."

"It *is* mean. Mean for Avery to have to hear something like this about her father. Not mean of you to have to tell her. You owe her the truth. You're not the bad guy here and no way should you take any of the blame. If I get even a whiff of blame-accepting on your behalf, I swear to God, I'll drive to the university and tell her the whole sordid truth myself. Right down to the colors of that new nightie."

"You wouldn't dare."

"I would and I will. Look, I'm not trying to come down on you but life as you knew it just ended, which means Marina as you knew her needs to end as well. This is no time to be the nice guy. You saw how Harold acted this morning. And if you hadn't gotten mad, you'd have ended up leaving with nothing. You have to start putting yourself first. You're not a bad person for taking care of yourself."

Marina nodded. Once again, she knew her sister was right, but why did it seem so hard? Had she spent so much of her life catering to others that she'd forgotten she deserved some of her time as much as anyone else? Her mother was being cared for by professionals. Her daughter was away at university. Snooze wasn't any work. He slept for twenty-three hours out of the day and seemed as allergic to exercise as she was.

Maybe Halcyon was right. It was time for Marina.

"I'll call her as soon as we get back to your house," Marina said. "The cell phone service is sketchy out here and I don't want this conversation to be a mess of bad connections."

"Yet another reason to reconsider moving into the marsh—the lack of reliable connections to other people."

Marina just nodded. It wouldn't do to tell Halcyon that was the thing she was happiest about.

"I'm going to put together a list of supplies," Marina said. "I can probably find most of the things I need at the hardware store. If they don't have it, I can either take a drive up the highway to Home Depot or see what I can find on Amazon."

"You can find everything on Amazon except a man. But there's other sources for that."

"Don't even go there. I haven't even filed for divorce. I'm not ready to date."

"Who said anything about dating? I'm talking about sexy time."

Marina thought about her size 14 butt and all those sections that now jiggled, and grimaced. The last thing she wanted was to put all her flaws in front of a stranger.

"I'm *definitely* not ready for sexy time," Marina said.

Halcyon narrowed her eyes at her. "You're not feeling all self-conscious about a few extra pounds, are you?"

Marina felt a blush run up her neck. Sometimes she could

swear her sister could read minds. And it was never when you wanted her to.

"I could stand to tighten things up a bit," Marina said. Her sexy nightie had hung like a sack on the much younger and thinner Chastity.

"We're forty-eight years old. Things don't tighten all the way anymore. You have to get close enough and use spandex to smooth out the rest."

"Things were tight on Chastity."

"Not the one thing that needed to be."

Marina burst out laughing. She couldn't help it. No matter how dire things sometimes seemed, Halcyon had a way of breaking them all down to crude and humorous.

When she finally regained composure, Marina grinned at her sister. "Have I told you lately how much I love you?"

Halcyon smiled and wrapped her arms around Marina. "I love you too, baby. And this is all going to be fine. I promise you. I would say I'm going to be right there beside you the whole way, but that would be a damned lie. I'm going to be in front of you, blasting obstacles with my quick wit and laser-sharp tongue. If that doesn't work, I'll shoot 'em."

"Spoken like a true Cajun." Marina glanced back outside and gave her sister's arm a squeeze. "Give me a minute. There's something I need to do."

As she headed for the back door, she heard Halcyon's uncertain steps behind her.

"Out back? It's waist-high with grass and weeds and there's probably a million snakes."

Marina opened the back door and pointed to a vine creeping around an old fence post. "There's also that."

"What is it?"

"Poison ivy."

"Good Lord, you're not going to touch poison ivy, are you? Why? You'll be one red itchy blob."

"It doesn't bother me. Remember that fishing trip?"

Halcyon frowned. "I mentally blocked it."

Halcyon and Marina had sat on poison ivy wearing their bathing suits, and Halcyon had scratched her butt cheeks for weeks. It hadn't fazed Marina one bit. It wasn't until Tommy Cox got caught practicing French kissing on his hand that kids stopped teasing her sister about it.

"You know who else is highly allergic to poison ivy?" Marina asked.

Halcyon shook her head.

"Harold."

"So what are you going to do?"

"I'm going to pick a mess of it and rub it in every pair of underwear he owns."

CHAPTER SIX

MARINA CLUTCHED the phone as she sat on the edge of the bed in Halcyon's guest room. Her sister had offered to hold her hand—or a pistol—while she made the call, but Marina didn't think she'd be able to handle Avery's and Halcyon's outrage at the same time. And she had no doubt Avery's default emotion was going to be anger. Not sad. Not upset. Her daughter didn't do "useless" emotions, as she referred to them. But anger was different. Anger, Avery said, got things done.

Marina had tried to argue with Avery over that idea in the past. But ever since losing it with Harold and walking away with a promise of twenty grand, Marina was quickly discovering just how lucrative anger could be. Mind you, she didn't plan on it becoming a full-time job, as it was for her mother, but she could definitely see where it offered benefits in the right situation.

"Hi, Mom," Avery answered.

She sounded upbeat and happy, and Marina silently cursed Harold for putting her in this position. The last thing Marina wanted to do was cause hardship for Avery, especially when she'd just gotten to the university the week before. She was right in the thick of decorating her room and making friends and figuring out what clubs, if any, she wanted to be part of. Marina was about to put a dark cloud over all of that.

"Hi, baby," Marina said. "How are things going?"

"Great! Jackie and I went to a flea market yesterday and found the cutest rugs for our dorm room. They're pink and black and have sparkly gold stripes. And Jackie's mom bought us a mini fridge so we can shop in bulk at Costco and don't have to worry about getting ice or drinking stuff hot. We're going out this evening to find a cheap coffee maker."

"I wish you would have told me you wanted one. I would have been happy to find you something before you left."

"I wanted to do it myself. It's like a college rite of passage."

"I thought beer drinking was the college rite of passage."

"Women in Last Chance still rub beer on the gums of teething babies. We all moved past beer being a rite of passage before we could walk."

"Well, let me know what you end up getting and I'll put some coffee in your next gift basket."

"And sugar cookies, right? I handed out a couple and I'm pretty sure I could get people to commit a crime for seconds. I was thinking they might help if I land some crappy professors."

Marina frowned. "I don't think bribing your professors is what college had in mind for preparing you for the workforce."

"Why not? I've seen how things work, Mom."

Marina wanted to argue, but she couldn't think of a good rebuttal. Maybe it was better that Avery already understood that the world was unfair and seriously sucked a lot of the time. Her daughter was probably more prepared to deal with what Marina was about to tell her than Marina was.

"I called because I need to tell you something," Marina

said. "It's serious and I hate having to tell you over the phone, but I don't want you to hear it from someone else."

"Oh my God, are you ill? Did someone die?"

"No to the first. Not yet to the second."

"Then what? Stop worrying about how I'm going to handle things. I'm not a child anymore. Besides, I have a freshman mixer to get to and still have to finish my tinfoil dress first."

Pre-Stolen-Crotchless-Lingerie Marina would have launched into a million questions and then a plethora of unwanted advice about the tinfoil dress thing, but Post-Stolen-Crotchless-Lingerie Marina just cringed a little and moved on. She had bigger fish to fry.

"It's about your father and me," Marina said. "We're getting a divorce."

"What? Are you kidding me?"

Avery's voice had shifted from wanting to get away from the conversation to somewhat anxious.

"I wish I were kidding," Marina said. "I'm so sorry to have to tell you this way. I would have preferred to do it in person but I was afraid someone might call and tell you before I had a chance to talk to you."

"Why would someone else call to tell me anything about you and Dad? That doesn't make sense."

"It makes sense if your father was having an affair and everyone in Last Chance found out. Including me."

Avery let out a single laugh. "An affair? Dad? No way. He's too old and well, he's Dad. No offense, but who would want him?"

"That's the other really bad thing. He's taken up with Chastity."

There was dead silence on the phone for so long that Marina thought Avery had hung up on her.

"Avery?" Marina said finally. "Are you still there?"

Avery let out a string of cursing, with some phrases Marina was going to have to google later on. When her ranting finally stopped, Marina heard a huge intake of breath and then what sounded like a choked sob. Marina's heart clenched so hard she felt as if her chest would burst.

If Halcyon had been standing there with that offered pistol, Marina would have grabbed it from her hands and driven straight to Harold's house and put a round or two in him. Avery never cried. Never. She thought it was stupid and weak. Even when she'd had appendicitis, she'd waited until it was about to burst to complain about the pain. And even though surgery had been difficult and recovery less than desirable, her daughter had never once complained, much less shed a tear. She took stoic to a level that Rambo hadn't achieved.

"Avery?" Marina said quietly.

Another sniff.

"Yeah, Mom. I'm here. Sorry for all the cussing. I know you hate it."

"Given the circumstances, I'm okay with it. I said some things to Halcyon that I thought would never come out of my mouth."

"Can't you fix it?" Avery asked, sounding more like a little girl than the adult she so desperately tried to be. Marina's heart broke all over again.

"I don't think so. It takes two to make a marriage work. Three is sort of a crowd."

"You could make him dump her. I mean, maybe if you changed your hair and bought some new clothes."

Marina clenched her hands into fists and wished horrible things on Harold all over again. She hated this. Hated it for herself, but even more so, she hated it for Avery. Her daughter shouldn't have to deal with her parents divorcing before she'd even finished unpacking her dorm room. She definitely shouldn't have to deal with the fact that the same girl had taken both her high school boyfriends and her father. And to hell with society for pushing the impossibility of women looking awesome and young until they were in the grave. For creating the fantasy that being pretty somehow made your life perfect.

"I'm so sorry, baby, but it doesn't work that way," Marina said. "Your father has made it clear that his future doesn't include me, and I've got to be honest, I'm not sure I could forgive him. Not for this. Not with her."

Another sniff. "I get it. I don't think I can forgive him, either."

"He left me, not you," Marina said, hating herself for the tired comment as soon as it came out of her mouth.

"Whatever. The thing is, he doesn't get to decide what I do, right?"

"He can't force you to have a relationship with him, but he's still your father. And you got a full ride to university so you're not in danger of losing tuition or your dorm as long as you keep your grades up, but there's still your car insurance and cell phone and you'll need spending money. I think things will be a little tight for me for a while. I'll do what I can, but…"

"This sucks. And I don't mean because of the money. I don't care about the money."

"It does suck," Marina agreed.

"So where are you? Did you kick him out of the house?"

"The house was his mother's. I can't really do that."

"Are you staying with Aunt Halcyon?"

"For now."

"What about later?"

"I'll let you know when I decide."

If Avery knew Marina was planning to move into the dilapidated fishing cabin, she'd drive straight back to Last Chance just to check her temperature. It was better to leave the logistics of some things for future conversations. After Avery had time to process the bigger aspects of the situation.

"You're sure about...her?" Avery asked. "I mean, it's not just someone making something up?"

"I'm sure." No way was Marina telling Avery she'd actually caught them in the act, although she knew that bit of information would eventually filter down to her. But if there was a God, her daughter would never hear about the whole lingerie fiasco.

"I'm sorry, Mom," Avery said quietly.

"I'm sorry too."

———

MARINA CLUTCHED the sink as the cold water she'd splashed on her face dripped onto her shirt. She patted her face with a washrag and let out a big sigh. Wisps of silver hair clung to her damp forehead. She leaned forward for a closer look and squinted, running her finger over the offending locks. Maybe Avery had been right about a new hairstyle. Or at minimum, some maintenance. It really didn't do for a stylist to let her own hair go. But the gray seemed to sneak in overnight. One day it wasn't there. The next day, she was sporting more silver than a vampire hunter.

She headed downstairs, still clutching her cell phone and desperate for a glass of wine, despite the fact that she wasn't completely free of the effects of her drinking the night before. And even though she'd finally dipped into Halcyon's aspirin, her headache had lingered all day long, through packing, cabin inspection, and the trip to the hardware store. The call to Avery had made it worse.

Halcyon had heard her coming and was apparently on her mind-reading kick again, because she stood in the kitchen opening a bottle of moscato. The aspirin was already on the counter next to the bag of peas that housed her good chocolate. Basically, they were all set for round two of the commiserating.

"I thought you hated the fruity stuff," Marina said.

"I do, but it's your favorite, and this bottle is all about you."

Marina slid onto a barstool and took the full wineglass from Halcyon. "Have I told you lately that you're a great sister?"

"Maybe a time or two, but it's always nice to hear." Halcyon sat next to her. "How did it go?"

"Crappy. I mean, as good as it could. Probably better than I expected, but..."

"How much is Avery hiding her real feelings?" Halcyon finished her thought.

"She was fairly vocal about the angry feelings. You would have appreciated her cursing rant. But yeah, I worry that she keeps the other emotions bottled up."

"It's that intelligence thing. She's always been the smartest person in the room. She'll have to process everything to death before she comes to a final conclusion."

"Still doesn't mean she'll address how she feels about it. I don't care how logical Avery seems, everyone has their trigger points. I just hope this doesn't get her off-balance. Not now. The timing couldn't be worse."

"So what are you going to do?"

Marina shrugged. "Wait, I guess. See how she is when I call. If things start to sound sketchy, I'll go down there."

"If that dumbass screws up her ride, I'm going to make him pay the rest of his life."

"If this crap screws up her ride, he's not going to have much time left for you to work with."

Halcyon put her hand on Marina's arm and squeezed. "I'm so sorry. I know that had to be one of the worst discussions you've ever had. I can't even imagine."

"It was definitely hard."

Halcyon shook her head. "I don't know how you do it—being a mother, I mean. It's like you're carrying someone else's heart around in your pocket and you're always working not to trip or let someone bump into you."

"That's fairly accurate, although any honest mother would admit to tripping all the time. I know there's all kinds of books, but the reality is, kids don't come with instruction manuals. They can't because they're all different. So are mothers."

"And Avery's high IQ thing just added to the difficulty level."

Marina nodded. "It certainly made things challenging. Still does."

"I love Avery. You know I do, but at the same time, I'm so glad I never bowed to societal pressure and had one of my own. I wouldn't have been good at it. I know that."

"And I have an enormous amount of respect for you for knowing that and refusing to give on it. I wish everyone took the decision that seriously and had the backbone to go against convention if that's what was right for them."

"I will admit that the constant harping of older women got to me some when I was in my twenties. Not that I ever came close to relenting on my stance, but I did come close to punching a few for their smug 'you'll change your mind' comments. Or my absolute favorite, 'you'll never know real love unless you have a child.' What kind of bullshit is that?"

"The kind said by a very narrow-minded person. You know how to love and you *are* loved. I love you to pieces. And you're the most generous person I know."

"To you. Because you're my other half. And to Avery, because she's part of you."

"Regardless. You're an awesome woman, Halcyon. I always wished I could be more like you."

"Now's your chance. Fling all the rules out the door. It's time for a rebirth."

"I think you're right."

Halcyon rose from her stool and headed for the refrigerator. "To kick off this Era of the New Marina, we're going to eat cheese and crackers. And raspberries. I bought some yesterday. They weren't even on sale."

"You're such a bad girl."

Halcyon smiled. "I saw Preston LeDoux eyeballing them and there were only four boxes left. So I bought every one of them."

Marina laughed. Preston was Chastity's father and had been on Halcyon's shit list ever since he'd hit on her at the town Christmas gala while his very pregnant wife was giving out punch.

"I guess Chastity comes by her 'skills' genetically," Marina said as she remembered. "I'm surprised no one has called Preston on his crap."

"He learned his lesson with me and he takes all his extracurricular business to New Orleans now. I heard he's got a couple of women on tap over there. Do you really think there's that much legal work in Last Chance that requires business trips to New Orleans? Complete with overnight stays?"

"Really? And his wife docsn't know?"

"I'm sure she does. We usually do, no offense. But as long as she doesn't catch him in her bed with one of them, then she can continue her weekly pedicures and her shopping trips to NOLA and her expensive champagne drinking habit."

"No! Why don't I hear about any of this? I'm a hairstylist. We're supposed to know everything that goes on."

"People aren't going to talk about the LeDoux in the salon, not when Preston's sister owns the place. She'd run tattling to big brother and then he'd sue everyone. He loves to sue people."

"I wish Patricia didn't own the only salon in town."

"She's a horrible person. Worse than him in a lot of ways. You know her dad paid off the principal for that whole homecoming queen thing, right?"

"I always thought that was urban legend."

"Nope. I hooked up with the principal's son a couple months ago and he confirmed that Big Daddy LeDoux was the source of his father's new bass boat. Remember, we always wondered how he'd managed to swing that on his school salary."

"I wonder who should have won."

Halcyon raised one eyebrow.

"You? Oh no! I'm surprised you didn't dig up Big Daddy LeDoux and beat the crap out of him."

"It crossed my mind. I settled for setting cow crap on fire on his grave instead. I did it on Father's Day and waited until I saw Patricia coming through the cemetery with flowers. She stomped it out and totally ruined a new pair of heels."

"How come you never tell me these things?"

"Because you don't approve of some of my more colorful behavior, and I don't want you stressing about what I'm up to. You've had enough on your plate dealing with your mother."

"I would have approved of Patricia stomping cow poop in new shoes."

"Then I'll keep you in the loop next time."

Halcyon frowned and leaned over her sink to look out the window. "Good God. What are those two doing together? And coming up my walkway? Hell has officially frozen over."

"Who?"

"Adelaide Blanchard and Dottie Prejean."

CHAPTER SEVEN

MARINA STARED AT HER SISTER. "Dottie and Adelaide are together?"

The doorbell rang and Halcyon shook her head. "Nothing good can come of this."

"Probably not, but I'm dying to know what they want."

Halcyon pursed her lips. "There is that. Well, let's find out, shall we? We could make it through the apocalypse with the wine stores I have. A couple of old ladies shouldn't kill us."

She walked to the door, threw it open, and stared at the two women on her porch.

"I hope you're not about to hit me up for one of your charity things," Halcyon said.

"Please," Adelaide said. "There's not a charity in the world that would send me to your doorstep."

"We need to talk to Marina," Dottie interrupted. "It's important. Is she here?"

"The plot thickens," Halcyon said as she stood back and waved them inside.

Adelaide practically stomped into the kitchen, caught sight

of the bottle of wine, and dumped a good portion into a pink glass container at the end of the counter.

Halcyon looked at her with all the frustration that a mother has when looking at a belligerent teen girl. "That's a vase, not a cup. I would tell you to get out more among real people so you could learn normal social graces, but I'm afraid to since you might decide to come here."

Adelaide tossed back a big gulp of the wine and waved her hand in dismissal. "Tastes the same regardless. I once drank whiskey out of a rubber boot."

Dottie shot Adelaide a look that was half disbelief and half fear, then looked back at Marina. "We were at the salon earlier today having our hair done."

"Ha!" Halcyon said, choking on her wine. "You've never done your hair in Patricia's place and that one looks like she does hers with a Weed Eater."

"I have been known to trim it up with gardening shears," Adelaide said.

Halcyon stared. "Did you miss the line where they handed out girl genes?"

Adelaide nodded. "I missed the one where they handed out giving a damn, too."

"Anyway," Dottie said loudly. "We heard about your troubles with Harold and that—"

"Hoochie," Adelaide interrupted.

"Do people still say that?" Marina asked.

"We've never gotten confirmation that Adelaide is 'people,'" Halcyon said.

Adelaide gave her the finger and served herself another round of wine.

Dottie took a deep breath and started again. "The bottom line is that we were concerned, with Patricia being Chastity's aunt and also your employer, that there might be trouble for you."

A wave of dismay passed over Marina. "Oh crap. I hadn't even thought that far. I mean, I figured Patricia would side with Chastity, but I guess I didn't think that my job might be on the line."

Halcyon let out a stream of cursing and Adelaide gave her an approving nod.

"That bitch will do anything to stay in Preston's good graces," Adelaide said.

Dottie nodded. "And I'm afraid keeping Princess Chastity up on a pedestal is a priority for him."

"No way Patricia wants to lose the income Marina brings in," Halcyon said, but she didn't sound convinced.

"She'd just push all Marina's customers off to Helen," Dottie said. "I never see Helen working when I walk by the salon."

"That's because she sucks," Adelaide said. "I get a straighter cut with my gardening shears. All I had her do earlier was a simple roll, and half of them had fallen out before I was a block away."

"If Patricia forces clients on Helen, they'll go somewhere else to have their hair done," Halcyon said.

"Where?" Dottie asked. "The nearest shop is across the bayou in Double Deuces, and with the age-old feud between the two towns, no one will want to do business there. Anywhere else is going to be a thirty-minute drive or better, and that's assuming you don't run into road construction, bridge outages, and farmers moving their heavy equipment."

"Or a crawfish migration," Adelaide said.

"Might as well go to New Orleans," Halcyon said.

Dottie nodded. "Except most don't have the time to drive

all the way to New Orleans for a hair appointment or the money to pay the steeper prices it costs in the city."

"You could start a carpool," Adelaide said. "That Cadillac of yours will probably hold five people…four if you pick a bunch of wide butts."

"I have no desire to become bayou Uber," Dottie said.

"She's right, though," Halcyon said. "If the options are Deuces or driving to NOLA, then a lot of people are going to be stuck with Helen. Good God, can you imagine all the selfies on Facebook once Helen gets a hold of half the population's hair?"

Marina blew out a breath. "What am I going to do? It's not like there's other options around here for employment for hairstylists. And I wouldn't trust that old car of mine to make a commute anywhere, even if a position magically appeared in one of the neighboring towns."

"I wouldn't trust that car of yours to back out of my driveway," Halcyon said. "What about doing hair out of your house?"

"You mean the fishing camp that is soon to be my residence?" Marina asked. "How many people are going to want to drive out to the boondocks to have their hair done? The road isn't even paved. And I don't have the equipment to do hair on my own or the room to install it there even if I did."

Adelaide and Dottie exchanged worried looks.

"I'm sorry we sprang this on you," Dottie said. "But we didn't want you to be waylaid again. And we were afraid you might not have thought about that situation with everything else you have to deal with."

"No, that's fine," Marina said, her mind racing with the possibility of being broke, relatively homeless, and unemployed. "I'm glad you told me. And you're right—I hadn't made it that far in my thinking. Apparently, I'm a step behind on everything lately."

Halcyon slammed her fist down on the counter. "Someone needs to take the LeDoux down about ten notches."

"Now you're talking," Adelaide said and lifted the vase.

"Preston is a cheater, his wife is a drunk, and his daughter is a sleaze, and yet this entire town seems to overlook everything," Halcyon said. "I don't get it. He can't sue everyone."

"It's not just lawsuits," Dottie said. "This probably won't surprise you, but Preston's grandfather was an unscrupulous sort. Back when oil crashed, he bought up a lot of commercial mortgages that were in default and made some loans to people to keep their businesses afloat."

Marina closed her eyes and groaned as Dottie's words brought everything about Preston and his attitude into focus.

"How many?" Marina asked.

Dottie shook her head. "Maybe half the town. Some turned things around and paid him off, and some just closed down or sold out, but he's still got leverage on enough people to keep them from going against him. At least openly."

"Those idiots better not vote for him when he runs for mayor," Halcyon said. "That's anonymous."

"We can only hope they don't chicken out at the polls," Dottie agreed. "But unfortunately, anything Preston can see firsthand is probably off the table."

"So no one will hire me and no one will rent me space, even if I had the money to open my own shop," Marina said. "I might as well pack up and move. Well, technically, I'm already packed. One less thing."

"No!" Halcyon said. "That piece of crap you married is not going to be the cause of you leaving your hometown. If you want to at some point, that's an entirely different thing. But not like this. Not while I'm still breathing."

"I just sharpened my shovel," Adelaide said.

"What does that have to do with anything?" Dottie asked.

"In case there's a need for a hole," Adelaide said.

"Too much work," Halcyon said. "Dump them in the bayou and let the gators do the work."

Marina held up her hands. "No one is digging a hole or feeding gators. There are better solutions to my problems."

"But not nearly as fun," Adelaide said. "I'm making a new bed for roses. Just so you know."

"I thought you planted roses last year," Dottie said.

"The cats peed on them so they all died," Adelaide said. "That makes it the perfect spot for Harold...he hates cats."

"Nobody is killing Harold," Marina said. "At least, not anyone in this room. If someone else takes a shot at him, then that's another story."

"That story might be worth a fresh bottle of wine to celebrate," Adelaide said as she tipped the last of the wine into the vase.

Halcyon sighed. "As much as I hate to admit it, my sister is right. Marina's already served time being married to Harold. No use in her serving more over his death."

Dottie motioned to Adelaide and rose from her stool. She reached over and patted Marina on her arm. "This will all work out, honey. And if there's anything I can do, you let me know. I can't stand a cheater. I watched my father do it to my mother her whole life and I swore I wouldn't tolerate it for one minute. You did right by leaving. And you'll be the one to come out ahead in the end. I truly believe that."

Everyone went stock-still and Marina stared. In the forty-eight years Marina had known her, Dottie had never revealed anything private. The fact that she'd shared such a personal thing about her mother was both surprising and touching.

Marina wasn't even sure what to say. She finally settled on "thank you."

"Keep the vase," Halcyon said to Adelaide as she hopped off her stool. "I can't look at flowers in it knowing your lips were on it."

Adelaide grinned. "Cool. Next time, I'll drink out of your Waterford crystal."

Feeling restless, Marina walked to the window and watched as the two women went up the driveway, still arguing. Halcyon closed the door and shook her head.

"It's like *Steel Magnolias* filmed a follow-up right here in my kitchen," Halcyon said.

"They are an unlikely duo," Marina said. "But it's nice that they tried to help me."

She started to turn away, then noticed a man standing at the edge of Halcyon's yard, looking toward the house. It was the same man she'd seen across the street from Harold's house that morning.

"Come here," Marina said, motioning to Halcyon. "Hurry."

"Are they scrapping on my front lawn?"

Marina pointed. "Do you know that guy?"

Halcyon leaned forward and studied the man for several seconds, then finally shook her head. "Never seen him before."

"I have. This morning across the street from Harold's house. He was standing there, just like he is now. Not doing anything. Just standing."

Halcyon frowned. "I don't like it."

"You think I do? What in the world could he want? You think he's a PI or something? That Harold is having me followed?"

"For what? He's the one cheating."

"I know, but why was this guy standing around staring at

the place I used to live this morning and the place I now live this evening?"

"Let's go ask him."

Before Marina could protest, Halcyon hurried to the front door, threw it open, and strode across her front lawn.

"You!" she shouted as she walked. "Who are you and what are you doing here?"

His eyes widened and he looked a tiny bit afraid. A second later, he hurried off down the street. Marina took off after Halcyon and they half jogged, half limped to the end of the block but when they checked the streets, he was nowhere to be seen.

"I need oxygen," Marina said, wheezing.

"I need a defibrillator," Halcyon said. "How did he move so fast without running?"

"And where did he go?"

"It's like a horror movie. You know, where the cute girl is running like she's in the last leg of the 1,200-meter relay and the scary dude is just loping along but always gaining on her."

Marina frowned. "Except this guy didn't look scary."

He wasn't a big guy. Maybe five ten and thin, not muscular. His haircut was the typical corporate job. If he'd been dressed in slacks and a dress shirt instead of purple skinny jeans and a white T-shirt, he could have passed for her banker.

"Of course he wasn't scary," Halcyon said. "I would have brought my gun if he was scary. But that doesn't make him lurking around houses any less creepy."

"It's definitely a ten on the creepy scale."

"You sure you don't recognize him? His haircut didn't look like the usual barbershop hack job most of the guys around here have."

"Definitely a salon cut, but I've never seen him before. And

I took a really long look at him this time. You sure he's not one of your past admirers?"

"Please. You know my rules. If I can kick his butt and I can't fit in his pants, it's a no. And I'm betting I'd be two for two on that one. Come on. Let's get back to my house before people start wondering why *we're* standing here."

Marina took one last glance up and down the street but the strange man in the purple pants had simply vanished. She supposed he could be ducked behind a bush or a car, but why? And why hurry off when it was clear that Halcyon was addressing him? The only answer she could come up with was because he was up to no good.

Which sucked. Because this week had already had enough "no good" to last a lifetime.

CHAPTER EIGHT

MARINA HURRIED out of the bakery, carrying a box of doughnuts. It wasn't the healthiest breakfast, but it was certain to be
one of the tastiest. Her car was already filled with cleaning
supplies and items for some of the smaller repairs the cabin
needed, including the dead bolts that Halcyon had insisted she
buy. Most importantly, a shiny new coffeepot sat on the front
seat next to a bag of expensive gourmet coffee she'd picked up
on her last trip to New Orleans. No way was she leaving
Harold with the good stuff.

Halcyon was going to meet her at the cabin and her housekeeper would pop in after church to help with the deep cleaning. Marina would get on to the repairs and Halcyon would
probably spend the day ordering everyone else around and
complaining about the cheap wood paneling and lack of square
footage. When she'd left Halcyon's house earlier, her sister had
been in the garage, muttering about old lamps and carpets.
Marina had just yelled a goodbye and headed out. Halcyon's
old decor probably wouldn't match the cabin or each other,
but she'd take anything her sister was willing to donate.

The bed frame and a small dresser that were already in the

cabin were made from old pine and would still be standing after a nuclear war. She'd put the mattress out to air as soon as she got there and try to beat some of the dust out of it until the new set she'd ordered was delivered. In the meantime, she had a thick mattress cover to help with allergens. The living room furniture consisted of an old leather couch and two mismatched recliners. They were castoffs from when Marina's mother had bought new furniture for their house. The leather was cracked and worn in spots and the couch sank down on one end more than the other, but they'd do until she could manage better. Besides, there was no use thinking about buying new furniture until she knew for certain where she'd be living. The cabin wasn't a good long-term option and with her job situation up in the air, moving loomed as a more likely alternative than remaining.

As she crossed the street, Marina caught sight of Harold coming up the sidewalk. She ducked behind a shrub in the town square, then cursed herself for acting like a silly teen. It was a small town. She was bound to run into Harold more times than she wanted to. Which was another point in favor of moving.

"If you're going to stand here with that box of doughnuts for very long, I'm going to ask for one."

Marina whirled around and saw Adelaide behind her, frowning.

"I know you're not hiding from that crap husband of yours, right?" she asked.

Marina sighed and stepped out from behind the bush to stand next to Adelaide on the sidewalk.

"I did it without even thinking," Marina said. "And then I didn't even know why for sure. I mean, it's not logical."

"The heart protecting itself, I suppose," Adelaide said. "Or your mind protecting you from possible jail time. It could go either way."

"Maybe both."

Adelaide looked down the street at Harold as he scratched his crotch, a pained look on his face.

"What the hell is he doing?" Adelaide asked.

Marina started to giggle and Adelaide stared.

"I might have rubbed poison ivy in his underwear," Marina said.

The look of surprise and respect on Adelaide's face was priceless. She shoved Marina back behind the shrub.

"Stay there so he doesn't see you," Adelaide said. "I've got this."

Marina had no idea what was going on but she figured no matter what, she couldn't get in trouble for standing in the park. She inched toward the thickest part of the shrub, then stuck her free hand in it to part the leaves and allow herself to see whatever Adelaide was about to do.

Deputy Jimmy Franks, who was in his sixties and always threatening to retire, was crossing the street in Adelaide's direction. She motioned him over and he gave her a nod. Harold was almost on top of her, scratching again and glaring at his crotch, when he looked up and realized Adelaide was standing there. He came to a halt and froze. Adelaide looked at Jimmy and pointed to Harold.

"Deputy Franks," Adelaide said, "this man made a lewd sexual gesture toward me."

Harold's eyes widened. "What? No!"

"You did it twice," Adelaide said. "Grabbing your crotch. I watch the MTV. I know what that means and I don't appreciate it."

Marina tucked the box of doughnuts under her arm and

covered her mouth with her hand as Jimmy gave Harold a disapproving frown.

"I swear, I wasn't gesturing," Harold said. "I have this...this thing."

"All men have that thing," Adelaide said. "And you're not allowed to touch it in public."

Harold's face turned beet red. "Not that—it's a rash, okay?"

Adelaide and Jimmy both stared, looking disgusted.

"Lie down with the dogs, you get fleas," Adelaide said. "Lie down with sluts, you get STDs."

Jimmy cleared his throat. "Mr. Trahan, I think you need to see a doctor about that, er, situation. Until then, you need to control yourself in public or stay home. We've got kids in this town."

Harold whirled around and practically ran. Marina managed to hold everything in until Jimmy had walked off, then she sank onto the ground and collapsed in a heap of laughter. Adelaide stepped behind the bush and grinned down at her.

"Got his goat on that one," she said.

"Oh my God," Marina said, gasping for breath. "I think I might have peed."

"It's an age thing. Welcome to the last half of your life."

———

MARINA FOLLOWED Halcyon to the door of the fishing cabin, practically shoving her sister out. Between Halcyon and her housekeeper, she'd been ordered around so much she felt as if she'd joined the military. But she had to admit, the place looked better. The housekeeper had helped her scrub it from top to bottom, and Halcyon had dragged some old rugs, lamps, pictures, and some other items out of storage and told her she could have it all. It was an eclectic blend of things her sister had grown attached to over decades of decorating changes, but the mismatched items added a bit of festivity to the cabin. Made it more interesting and less gloomy.

Remarkably, one outstanding repair issue remained and that was a leak in the bathroom sink. Until the town's only plumber could fit her in, Marina figured she could just use the kitchen sink to brush her teeth. It wasn't as though anyone would be there to tell her it was inappropriate. Halcyon had raised hell over the locks until Marina made an appointment for the next week with the locksmith, but she'd installed dead bolts on the inside so that her sister wouldn't worry about her staying in the cabin that night.

It wasn't that Marina didn't appreciate everything Halcyon was doing for her. And her sister's house was better than any fancy hotel—a soft mattress, an en suite bathroom, and a store of wine that beat most of the local restaurants. She also had awesome snacks. Halcyon was a professional at treating herself well and she'd extended all of those things to Marina.

But the truth was Marina needed to be alone.

She'd kept busy with the moving, cleaning, and decorating. And having other people around meant her mind had fewer chances to dwell on pointless things that would never change. But that couldn't last forever and every night when Marina went to bed, the silence was overwhelming. Her mind raced with a million thoughts of how things could go from bad to worse to why-do-I-even-bother. And she knew that as long as she put off the serious thinking and decision-making she needed to do she'd never get past this.

She needed a plan. A long-term plan. Not just one that covered what she was doing today or tomorrow. A long-term plan meant there was a reason to get out of bed every day. Something to work toward. Something to look forward to. All that pop psychology about living in the moment was great if the moment was awesome. But if the moment was absolute shit, she didn't see the point.

It was hard to figure out the future with Halcyon hovering, trying to fix everything with wine and cursing. Not that she didn't appreciate both. Her sister's heart had always been in the right place where Marina was concerned. But Marina couldn't let Halcyon make decisions for her. That was a cop-out. She was a forty-eight-year-old woman. She'd let Harold run things for decades and look where that had gotten her. It was time to take control of her life. That way, if it stayed in the toilet, at least she had no one to blame but herself.

She opened the back door and called to Snooze, who was napping on the porch. He opened one eye and stared.

"The noisy, sneezing one is gone," Marina said.

The old hound dog opened the other eye and both of them gave her a suspicious look, but finally, he pulled himself up and strolled inside. He glanced around, as if to make sure Marina hadn't been lying to him, then apparently satisfied, lay down on the donated rug next to one of the old tacky recliners. Marina sat next to him and reached over to rub his ears.

"We're going to be fine," she said, more for herself than Snooze. The old hound appeared quite content at the cabin. Probably because Harold wasn't there.

Marina glanced into the kitchen at the boxes on the counter and felt her energy wane. Not because they needed to be unpacked but because there were so few of them, even with Halcyon's donations. Truth be told, Avery's dorm room probably contained more and better stuff than the cabin did.

It was a bunch of old, ugly furniture and questionable decor—just like the house she'd shared with Harold. Apparently, she couldn't escape that fate.

She blew out a breath. If Harold had ever given any indication that he'd be willing to get rid of his mother's things, Marina would have built a bonfire up to the heavens and lit it all up in the backyard. But he'd insisted that all the furniture was "quality" and there was no need to replace it. Marina had assumed he was just being cheap. Now she wondered if he'd been reserving that money for other things. Things that didn't include Marina. She wondered about a lot of things as far as her marriage was concerned.

But none of that mattered now. What mattered now was collecting her payout from Harold, looking for an attorney, and calling the plumber. She pulled her cell phone out of her jeans pocket. At least she could handle the last one of those items now.

She heard the movement behind her before she saw the man step into her side view. She bolted out of the recliner and threw her phone at the man in the purple skinny jeans—which probably wasn't the best idea—then ran for the kitchen and grabbed the first thing out of a box that she could put her hands on, which turned out to be a bottle of perfume.

The man slowly approached and Marina was certain she was about to be serial killed.

CHAPTER NINE

THIS WAS IT. This was how Marina's life ended. In a pair of jeans with a hole in the crotch that her thighs had caused, a T-shirt with dirt and cleaning solution on it, and no bra. She was even wearing basic white granny panties. Good God, what was the undertaker going to think?

"We need to talk," the man said.

Marina thrust the perfume bottle in front of her, determined to go down in a fight. "Stop right there."

The man looked a bit confused but continued to move toward her. "You don't understand—"

"Oh, I understand!" she yelled, and sprayed him right in the face with the perfume. It wasn't Mace but surely it would give her time to dive for her cell phone. Maybe even run out the door, because getting away seemed like a more viable option than locating a pair of silk underwear in the boxes.

She made a break to his right but unfortunately, Snooze decided that was the moment to get up and see what was going on. Her leg hit a hundred and ten pounds of immovable fur, and she pitched right into Skinny Jeans, hurtling them both onto the floor and sending the perfume crashing into the back door. Skinny Jeans screamed and she scrambled on top of him, trying to grab her cell phone. Snooze decided that it was all too much for him and took off for the bedroom.

Marina's hand locked around her cell phone and she launched herself toward the door. But even though she could clearly see that the locks weren't engaged, she couldn't pull the door open.

"You can't jam now!" she yelled at the door. "Skinny Michael Myers is after me!"

"I am not after you," Skinny Jeans said. "At least, not in the way you're imagining. Will you please stop with all the drama and let me explain why I'm here? Because I don't think either of us can take more of your attempts at self-defense or our olfactory senses will pack up and leave our bodies."

Marina had no idea why the man's words caused her to pause but she found herself turning back to look. He stood in the middle of the room, arms by his side, his nose wrinkled in distaste. But Marina was most impressed by the fact that he was glaring at her, eyes wide open, giving no indication that the perfume had bothered him at all. Which made no sense. Marina had accidentally sprayed some in her eyes one morning before work and she'd cut Mrs. Breaux's hair an inch too short in the back. It had taken a good hour before her eyes stabilized. Way longer than that for Mrs. Breaux's hair.

"Do you have something I can wipe this off with?" Skinny Jeans asked. "Before I pass out from the smell. This is so awful."

"That's Chanel!"

"No. It's not. It's a really cheap and awful knockoff."

Marina sighed, all fear slipping away from her. How dangerous could a man who recognized knockoff perfume really be?

"I should have known," she said. "It was a gift from my soon-to-be ex-husband."

"It smells like a skunk in a stinkweed patch with a hint of motor oil. Please don't tell me you've been wearing this."

"I thought maybe it smelled differently on me—you know how you don't smell it the same as other people do."

"I'm pretty sure that's not the case here."

"Of course not." Her perfume was just one more thing in a long line of failures. She shouldn't have been surprised.

She headed into the kitchen and located a dish towel in one of the boxes, then wet it and handed it to Skinny Jeans. He rubbed his face but didn't seem satisfied with the results.

"I can offer you dishwashing soap," Marina said. "But that's all I've had time to unpack."

He waved a hand in dismissal. "I'll shower later and snort coffee grounds."

Marina nodded. Shoving her nose in a jar of coffee grounds sounded really good. Why in the world had she thought that perfume smelled okay?

"So you want to tell me why you've been stalking me?" Marina asked, no longer concerned about his intentions. If he wanted to kill her, he'd had plenty of opportunity already. "Let's start with your name."

"I am called Alexios."

"But that's not your name?"

He frowned. "I just said it was."

"No. You said you were *called* Alexios. Some people call me Biscuit because it's all I'd eat for a year when I was three, but that doesn't mean it's my name."

"Why does my choice of grammar seem to annoy you?" He looked genuinely confused.

"Because 'I am called' is a really pompous way of saying it when you could just say 'my name is.' And your name being

Alexios isn't helping matters. In a place like Last Chance, it sounds uppity."

"Interesting. I suppose I could go by Alex while I'm here. Would that help me blend?"

"Not as long as you're wearing purple jeans."

"Humans are a very peculiar bunch."

Marina narrowed her eyes. He might not be a serial killer, but he was definitely walking the crazy plank. "Some of us are, certainly. I take it you're not claiming human as your species?"

"I'd love to say that's the case, but unfortunately, a part of me is. Apparently not the part that prefers purple jeans or proper speech."

"What's the other half? And I swear to God if you say you're an alien I'm going to spray you with cooking oil. It's right here in this box."

He considered this far too long for Marina's taste but finally nodded. "I suppose if you mean that a part of my lineage is not of the Earth, then perhaps I could be considered alien. But if you're speaking of the general Hollywood definition, then no."

"You know, it's been a really long day and an even longer week. And I'm going to hate myself for asking this, but where exactly is the other part of you from?"

"I'm a demigod."

Marina stared. "You really *are* into yourself, aren't you? I mean, I know a lot of men who think they're gods, but not any that just come right out and say it."

"This is the worst part of my job. The convincing."

"If you're waiting for women to believe you're a god, I can see where that would be difficult."

"A demigod. Not a god. If I were a god, I wouldn't have this horrible assignment. I'd be living it up on a cloud."

"Okay, I'll bite. What's a demigod?"

"I'm the product of the mating of a god and a mortal."

"You mean like Hercules?"

He rolled his eyes. "What is it with you humans and Hercules?"

"I don't know. Defied the gods, saved the world, that sort of thing."

"Good! That gives us some common ground. You're a Seeker and I'm here to help you save the world."

The tiny shred of patience that she'd been clinging to dissolved. "Dude, I can't save my marriage. Or myself. Hell, I can't even keep a cactus alive. If the world is depending on me, then this is the saddest day in history since God said 'let there be light.'"

"That's not really how it happened...you know what, never mind. I can see you'll need some convincing, so I'll just save some time and launch right into the dog and pony show. Let's start with how I got into your house."

"That's easy. I forgot to lock the door."

"You did not. In fact, you locked the door and pulled the shiny new dead bolt as well."

"So you're telling me you can walk through walls?"

"Not exactly. Just that human constructs can't bind me. Follow me. I'm going to step outside and I want you to lock the door. Both locks."

He headed out her back door and pulled the door shut.

Marina shrugged. What the hell? The worst thing that could happen was he was out of her house and couldn't get back in. Seemed like a win. She headed for the door and twisted the regular lock, then pulled the new sturdy dead bolt and took a step back.

"Okay, do your thing," she called out.

A second later, the dead bolt slid back, the knob twisted as if it weren't locked, and Alexios strolled inside.

Marina stared at the door as if it were going to take flight. "How did you do that?"

"I thought I had explained this."

"Yeah, yeah, you're a demigod. So is that why the perfume didn't make your eyes red?"

His brow scrunched. "I suppose so. Your weaponry can't harm me, and I suppose the perfume was being used as a weapon. Alas, my birthright didn't extend to saving me from the smell."

"Alas? That's what you're going with?"

She walked back to the recliner and flopped down, overcome by a wave of sheer exhaustion. At that point, an appearance by Jesus Christ himself wouldn't have moved her off that chair.

"You know," she said, "your Houdini trick with the door is cool and all. And probably on a different day, I'd be surprised or even remotely interested in how you did it. But I have to be honest—I don't have one ounce of energy left to give. I've pretty much decided to sit here until I starve to death or have to pee. Might not even move for the second one."

He stared up at the ceiling. "For the love of Zeus, please give this assignment to someone else."

A bolt of lightning came through the window and struck the floor directly in front of Alexios. He jumped back, looking sheepish.

"Point taken," he grumbled.

Marina pointed at the singe on her donated rug, still not ready to buy into the superhero status Alexios was pitching, but unable to explain why a bolt of lightning had appeared from a cloudless sky.

"That's going to leave a mark," Marina said. "Was that a message from your boss?"

"Yes. A very direct one."

"He seems like a dick," Marina said.

Thunder rumbled and the house shook.

Alexios cast a nervous glance upward, then stared at her, clearly confused. Finally, he sat on the couch across from her.

"Your response to all of this is somewhat odd," he said. "Definitely unlike the others."

"I imagine you get the cops called on you quite a bit. Wait...there are others?"

It figured. She wasn't even special in the musings of a crazy person.

"There have been several over the last couple centuries."

"Of course there were. Wait...centuries?"

"Yes. It's been a very long assignment. Much longer than I'd hoped."

Marina narrowed her eyes at him. "You want me to believe that you're centuries old?"

"Yes," he said, looking somewhat bored. As if all of this was completely normal.

"That's some seriously good antiaging cream you've got."

"We only age to a certain point and then that's where we remain."

"For how long?"

"Forever. Well, forever is the ideal. Unfortunately, the Seekers before you have been unsuccessful and our time is running out. I don't know that our world or yours can last much longer."

"Can they last until I soak my feet?"

"You're not taking this seriously at all, are you?"

"Put yourself in my position. Would you?"

"I have been in your position, of sorts. I was sent here with assurances that you are the Seeker, and yet I find this disheveled, middle-aged woman in the midst of some sort of personal crisis. You're going gray and have"—he covered his mouth with his hand—"a black chin hair."

She rubbed her finger across her jawline where the offender usually made its appearance. Sure enough, even though she'd just plucked it two days ago, it was sticking out at least a quarter inch. Sighing, she slumped lower in the chair. Alexios was just one more man who had issues with her appearance.

Apparently, he realized he'd offended her because he was instantly apologetic.

"I'm so sorry," he said. "I wasn't trying to insult you—I need to explain. But I have to go back a bit to do so. May I?"

"I already told you I have no plans to leave this chair and my gun is in the other room, so go for it."

"Okay. A very long time ago, the goddess Aphrodite had an affair with a demigod named Drakos and became pregnant from that union. She's been long married to Hephaestus, the god of metalworking, but he's always overlooked her dalliances. When she ended her affair with Drakos, he became angered. He loved Aphrodite and felt that she'd misled him. He insisted she leave Hephaestus to be with him and their child, but Aphrodite just laughed at the ridiculous suggestion."

"Did Hephaestus ever catch Drakos in his bed with Aphrodite and wearing Hephaestus's sexiest boxers?"

"I'm certain the answer is no. For many reasons. Why?"

Marina waved a hand in dismissal. "Doesn't matter."

"Anyway, Zeus had commissioned Hephaestus with the creation of certain items of power. Items that could harness the strength of multiple gods for the wielding of a single user."

"Why would he do that?"

"To ensure he remained in control. When you're sitting in the big chair, there are always those who wish for your seat. Hephaestus, however, had always been aligned with Zeus and set about making the objects. Somehow Drakos learned of this and visited Aphrodite one last time under the pretense of attempting to win her over. While he was with her, he cast a spell on their wine. That night, when Aphrodite and Hephaestus were unconscious, he sneaked into Hephaestus's workshop and stole the objects of power. But he was caught by guards before he could get away. Knowing that his fate was sealed, he summoned all of his power to fling the objects down to earth before the guards killed him."

"So why didn't one of the gods just pop down here and retrieve them?"

"Because Drakos cast a spell on them so that they are invisible. He thought in the absence of those objects, some of the dissenters he'd aligned with would be able to overthrow Zeus."

"But that didn't happen."

"Not yet."

"Well, if these magic things are invisible, then I don't know how you think I can help. Seeing invisible objects isn't my superpower."

"You have a superpower?"

"Bad decision-making."

Alexios frowned. "The objects are only invisible to gods. We believe humans can see them."

"You believe...but you don't know."

"No, but Hephaestus put a spin on the objects of his own. He'd worked Aphrodite's blood into the creation of the objects, creating a link between the objects and some who share Aphrodite's bloodline. That's where you come in."

Marina blinked. "You're saying I'm a descendent of Aphrodite?"

She let out a single laugh, then the longer she thought about it, the more ridiculous it sounded. So she laughed more and more until she was headfirst in her knees, practically sobbing. Alexios waited silently and clearly annoyed until she regained self-control. Finally, she sat back upright and wiped the tears from her face.

"And because Aphrodite was a great beauty and I have a chin hair, that's why you were confused?" she asked, and started to laugh again. "I'm sorry. I'll stop. But jeez, you have to see the hilarity in all of this, right?"

"I assure you this is very serious business. End-of-the-world serious. And yes, your appearance did give me pause. The others have been considered great beauties of their era and have derived power from their appearance alone."

"Like who?"

"Cleopatra and Lady Godiva to name two. And in more recent times, Marilyn Monroe."

"Cleopatra, Lady Godiva, Marilyn Monroe, and me? Did you ever watch *Sesame Street*? You remember that song 'One of These Things Is Not Like the Others'?"

"Which is why I observed before approaching, so the recordkeepers had time to double-check everything. But all the signals are correct. You are the next chosen."

"So you're saying I'm related to those people—Cleopatra and company?"

"Yes, but perhaps hundreds or even thousands of times removed. Aphrodite had children with multiple partners and those children had affairs and children and so on. The record-keepers finally came up with a potential explanation for the uh, variance, between you and those before you, which also explains why not every woman who shares Aphrodite's DNA comes into power."

"I can't wait to hear it."

"The beauty is part of the power that comes with the DNA, but in the case of the others, there was a childhood trauma that seemed to have triggered the gene. Apparently, you were bereft of this trauma, as were many before you who never came into power."

She stared. "No childhood trauma? Have you met my mother?"

He wrinkled his nose. "Unfortunately, yes. Observing her was part of my investigation when it appeared as if we'd made a mistake. She's a most disagreeable woman. And a visit with her did further confuse me, but we finally decided that you must have been stronger as a child than the others. So your power wasn't triggered during your formative years, which is usually the case. For you, it appears that a lifetime accumulation of stress, culminating with finding your husband in bed with another woman, was the catalyst. It's the first time anyone has come into power at this advanced age."

Marina raised an eyebrow at the word "advanced" but didn't feel like arguing. "So I got cheated out of being a supermodel or a world ruler because I was raised to 'suck it up'?"

"I suppose you could look at it that way, but I do find it interesting that despite the lack of power in your earlier years, you were still drawn to the profession of beauty."

"Yeah, but it's too late for me to be a *Sports Illustrated* swimsuit model or have an affair with a president."

"The first is not entirely out of the question as your society is becoming more focused on aging. As for the second, would you really want to?"

"That's a whole different discussion, but I'm still calling bullshit on modeling."

"Why? The power is already making a difference. Did you not notice the change underneath your eyes? And the gray in your hair has diminished by about 30 percent over the course of today. I predict by tomorrow morning you won't have any left."

Marina touched her face under her eyes and the skin was still tight and firm. It wasn't possible, right? Alexios was just some nutjob with a bizarre notion that she was part of his fantasy. But then, there was the singed carpet, and her eyes did look better than they had in decades. Even Halcyon had noticed.

She reached up and touched her hair but didn't feel like going to the bathroom to look. "I wish I had a mirror on me."

Alexios reached into his jeans pocket and tossed her a glittery pink compact.

She narrowed her eyes at him. "Did you conjure this into your pants with magic?"

"Of course not. I don't have that ability. I carry that everywhere. You never know when you'll need to check your teeth or the size of your pores."

"Are you..." She shook her head. Was that even possible?

"If you're asking if I prefer the company of a hot male, then yes, we have the same inclinations where that's concerned."

"Not me. My inclination is to remain alone."

He gave her a wistful look. "Yes. I'm afraid I feel the same at the moment. The dating scene has been particularly rough this century."

"So tell me more about these magical items," she said. She'd seen that look before and the last thing she wanted to do was listen to Alexios launch into his dating woes. She was certain she didn't have enough alcohol to endure centuries of relationship failures.

He looked a little disappointed but then put on his business face and got back to the job at hand. "There were three total, but the only one that Hephaestus has ever gotten a signal from is a ring."

"Signal? Like GPS?"

"No. More like a brief pulse, kind of like a heartbeat."

"And he got this signal how?"

"He felt it. It was faint, but he's certain the ring is still intact."

"So why doesn't he tell us where it is?"

"The only thing he can tell us is that it's on Earth. We believe those of the bloodline are born near the object."

"There it is, that 'you believe' again. But you don't know. So this ring could be in Russia or at the bottom of the ocean."

"That's not what we chose to think."

"Ha! You *are* gods. Because you want something to be a certain way, you decide to believe it is."

"We believe this way because the alternative is the end of our lives and yours. Would you prefer to go the other route?"

She must have hesitated too long for his taste because he waved a hand in dismissal.

"Anyway, we need to find this ring now. Zeus has to be able to harness the power of the other gods in order to defeat our enemy."

"A ring, huh? That holds the power of many and can only be carried by one. I've seen this movie. And if you're saying I'm Frodo, we're going to have big problems."

"This is *not Lord of the Rings*. Although someone with a predilection for purple jeans might have gotten drunk with Tolkien back in the day and exchanged tales."

She frowned. "Why don't you just send Aphrodite down to find the ring? I mean, it's her blood. Wouldn't she have a stronger connection than descendants born centuries down the line?"

"She's tried. For thousands and thousands of years she's roamed the earth trying to find the ring. But for whatever reason, she's never felt the draw. And since we can't see it..."

"Did you ever think that maybe she never felt a draw because it isn't here? Everything you've just told me is based on speculation. Let's just say for a minute that I buy any of this—how am I supposed to find this ring if Aphrodite can't?"

He hesitated. "We're not quite sure. Our hope is that now that you've come into your birthright, you'll be drawn to it."

"But none of the others before me were."

His shoulders slumped. "I know. It's a failure I've carried with me for a long time, and trust me, the boss does not let me forget it."

"Surely you've gleaned something from centuries of trying to find this thing."

"Only the side effects of beauty. Nothing that helps us determine the location of the ring."

Marina blew out a breath. It was ridiculous, of course. The belief that she was descended from a goddess and possessed the ability to find a magical object that would save the world. That was the sort of thing that got you a long visit in a padded room. But there was something about his story that stirred her deep inside. Like a tiny tickle at the bottom of her stomach. Something that made her believe he might not be crazy after all.

"What's in it for me?" she asked. "I mean, the earth not ending isn't really a good selling point for me. Not today."

"Of course. Because you came late to the party, so to speak, and didn't benefit financially from your bloodline as others have, we're prepared to make you a monetary offer. If you are successful in your pursuit, we'll arrange for one million dollars to appear in your bank account."

"The IRS will love that."

"They'll never know it happened. Neither will the bank. As far as humans are concerned, it will have always existed, so no red flags."

"And if I'm not successful?"

"Then no amount of money would make a difference."

"How long do I have?"

"Our best estimate is a week."

"You want me to solve a centuries-old puzzle in seven days."

"Give or take." He gave her a hopeful look.

Marina stared out the window at the slow-moving tide on the bayou, the last few days rolling around in her mind. Then the last twenty-eight years with Harold. Then her childhood with Mother of the Year.

Could she make things any worse?

CHAPTER TEN

MARINA BOUNCED out of bed the next morning, feeling better than she had in forever. Which was amazing given the amount of physical labor she'd endured the day before and the amount of wine and Cheez-Its she'd consumed that night. But when she went into the bathroom that morning and looked into the mirror, the exhausted, stressed face that she was used to seeing wasn't there. Instead, tight skin with no wrinkles stared back at her, not a single gray hair at her crown. The offensive chin hair had even disappeared.

She leaned forward to take a closer look at her chin but couldn't even see a pore, much less a hair. This entire charade might be worth it for the elimination of that hair alone. She'd showered the night before, so she ran a brush through her hair, which was unusually untangled and glossy. But at the point where she normally would have reached the end, she kept brushing. She pulled a lock of hair from her back to her front and realized that it was a good two inches longer than the day before.

Marina had always wanted long luxurious hair, but no matter what product she tried, her hair started to break and thin out once it got past her shoulders. Now she had thick, soft, shiny auburn hair as you only saw in commercials. She stared into the mirror several seconds longer, the reality of the situation sinking in.

"Alexios was telling the truth," she said out loud.

Because there was no other explanation for the changes. People didn't get younger—at least, not naturally. Getting younger required a serious investment in a plastic surgeon. And you could still only push it so far before you started looking like the Joker. But no plastic surgeon made gray hair turn back to brown and grow two inches overnight. And her skin didn't have that slightly stretched look of surgery or Botox. It simply looked the way it had fifteen years ago, before all of life's BS had finally registered and she'd started dangling off the aging cliff.

She headed for the kitchen and set coffee to brew. Then she pondered. Was she really going there? Was she really going to believe that she was descended from a goddess and had some magical ability? Her appearance certainly suggested she should give it serious consideration. The day before, she'd thought Alexios was moderately interesting and ridiculously creative, but even the door opening and lightning strike hadn't completely convinced her. Of course, she *had* been exhausted. Maybe she wasn't able to fully process everything because her mind and body were operating at half throttle.

Or...!

She whipped around, looking at the front and back doors, but both dead bolts were in place. So unless Alexios could lock the door after leaving, he hadn't sneaked in during the night to dye her hair and inject her with Botox. Also, even though she had been beyond tired, surely she would have woken up if he'd shoved a needle in her face.

This is it. You're one-billionth goddess.

She'd made up her mind. She was going to believe Alexios, and if that meant playing Frodo, then so be it. What was the worst that could happen? She ran around looking for a ring that didn't exist? At least she'd burn off a few pounds. But if all of this was true and she found the ring, then she'd cash in some serious money. Assuming Alexios came through on that end of things. It's not as if he'd offered a down payment.

She frowned. Maybe she should ask for one. If the world only had a week left, then shouldn't it be worth it to cough up some incentive money now?

Snooze strolled up and sat, staring up at her with that sad expression that only a hound dog could manage. He'd hidden under the bed, pouting, after she'd tripped over him the night before, so she hadn't been able to get his take on her purple-clad friend. That was unfortunate because Snooze always seemed to know when someone was bad news. He showed his displeasure by peeing on their leg.

She reached down to scratch his head.

"What do you think? Should I ask Alexios for money?"

Snooze let out a single bark, which made her jump. Barking was rare unless he was upset about something. Even hunting, it was more of a bay. Not the piercing sound he'd just emitted. She stared at the hound and realized he was staring right back, a very intent look in his eyes. If she didn't know any better, she'd swear he understood what she was saying and was trying to answer.

"What the heck—let's play a game. I'll ask a question. You bark once if it's a yes and twice if it's a no."

Snooze tilted his head to one side.

"I'll take that as you're in. We'll start with something easy. Is your name Snooze?"

One bark.

"Do you like Harold?"

Two barks.

Marina stared.

"Do you like sweet potato?"

One bark.

"Do you like apples?"

Two barks.

Un-friggin'-believable. He'd gotten every question correct.

Marina pinched her arm in case she was still asleep or had died. But it hurt just as it should have and she released the skin. Things were so incredibly weird. Her life was the very definition of chaos and now, she was convinced the dog was communicating. It was definitely time to call Alexios. He'd given her his cell number to get in touch.

She grabbed her cell phone off the counter and sent him a text. A couple seconds later, a gust of wind hit the back of her house and Alexios strolled inside. He must have listened to her on the whole purple pants thing because today, he wore plain blue jeans and a polo shirt. The shirt was bright fuchsia, but it was still progress.

Snooze walked over and sniffed his tennis shoe, then plopped down on the rug and promptly went to sleep. A good sign.

"Did you spend the night on my porch?" she asked.

"Of course not. My bosses aren't that cruel."

"Then how did you get here so fast?"

"When I'm not on earth, I reside in between worlds. Think of it as an invisible, moving condo."

"That's convenient."

"Very. Nothing is more comfortable than your own bed. Centuries of travel can be hell on the back." He took a step closer and scrutinized her. "I see all the gray is gone."

She nodded. "And I don't have pores. I mean, I have pores, but they're so small now my skin looks fifteen years younger.

Plus, I think I can talk to the dog. I mean, I've always been able to talk to the dog, but I think he understands what I'm saying. Is that possible?"

"I suppose it could be. Aphrodite is crazy about dogs. She always has one."

"And she can communicate with her dogs?"

"Of course. She's a goddess."

"Interesting. Okay, so I was thinking and after a discussion with Snooze, I've made a decision. I'm going to try to find your ring, like I said last night, but it's going to cost you. And not after I do all the work. I want a down payment. Something that proves to me that you are on the up-and-up. I can't do good work if I'm worried about money. And since I'm pretty sure I'm going to be fired when I go into work today, that's a viable concern."

"Perfectly reasonable. I'm authorized to advance you ten thousand as long as you promise to legitimately launch a search for the ring."

"I take it by your tone and the use of the word 'legitimately' that someone before me took the money and ran?"

"A particularly long and expensive vacation, in which she was eaten by sharks, thus starting our wait for a Seeker all over again."

"Did your boss have anything to do with that shark thing?"

"He says no."

"Hmmmm. Okay, well, since I have no intention of hopping on a plane to film a sequel to *Jaws*, I think I'm good."

"Then consider it done."

She looked around. "Is it in a bag under my bed?"

"Of course not. It's in your bank account."

Marina grabbed her phone and accessed her account. Sure enough, her balance had increased by ten thousand, but there was no sign of a recent transaction.

"That is a really cool trick," she said.

"We think so."

"Okay, so I have to go to work this morning. I expect that's going to be a mess, but I have a client first thing and I won't let her down unless I have no option. I will do everything possible to find the ring, but I can't take a complete hiatus from my life. I've got a job—today anyway—a divorce to get processing, a house that needs serious attention, a crazy mother in lockdown, and a college-student daughter that could explode into drama any second. If I let all of that slide for even seven days, the world won't be worth saving. Not for me, anyway."

"I get it. You have responsibilities. The fact that you stand by your word is actually encouraging. I am sure you will commit your best to procuring the ring. So do you have a plan?"

She blinked. "Well, I'm going to put on clothes meant for public and go to work. Beyond that, I haven't thought about it. But I will. Can we meet later so I can get more details?"

"You know where to find me," he said and headed out the door.

She hurried over as the door closed and yanked it open, but Alexios had already vanished. She glanced around, wondering if his invisible condo was hovering over her yard and if he could see her. Just in case, she waved at nothing and headed back inside.

It was time to face the kraken.

―――――

AT FIVE MINUTES TILL TEN, Marina walked into the Cut & Curl with her shoulders back and a smile on her face. She looked and felt better than she had in years. And why the hell not? She had enough money in her bank account to cover her small expenses for months and with nothing tying her down anymore, she could consider options. She'd never thought about leaving Last Chance before, but if that was where her future lay, then it was going on her list. And the best part was, she didn't have to make any decisions right away because if Alexios was telling the truth, then all of this was going to hell in a handbasket in a week unless she found a magical ring that no one for centuries before her had managed to find.

Patricia was going to be very disappointed when she realized Marina had no fucks left to give. The entire drive into town, every insult, slight, and sneer that had come from her boss had replayed in her mind like one big, never-ending sea of crap, starting from kindergarten and going right up to three days ago.

For the life of her, Marina couldn't think of a single good reason why she'd taken it. In the early years, things would have been tight without her paycheck, but in the last ten years, there really hadn't been any motivation for her to endure the continued abuse. Over the last two days, her somewhat blurry past had slowly come into focus. And Marina didn't like what she saw.

Patricia was at her station, rolling the hair of Barbara Cormier, one of the stuffy old women who ran herd over all the local Baptist church events, making them pretty much miserable for everyone. Marina's mother used to have a go at her every time she had an opportunity, just for sport. When she'd finally gotten her mother into the assisted living center, the old crow had the nerve to tell Marina that she was glad she'd finally seen fit to lock the "menace" away. It had taken all the energy Marina could muster to keep walking and not respond. It was one thing for Marina to call her mother a menace. It was completely another for Barbara Cormier to do it.

Both Patricia and Barbara frowned at her as she walked in. Marina's ten o'clock appointment sat in Helen's chair, her flaming red hair dripping onto the collar of her blouse. Helen froze as soon as she saw her. Ms. Kitty, the client, turned in the chair and gave Patricia a look that should have turned her to stone. Ms. Kitty was sixty years old and had owned and managed the local honky-tonk for thirty-five years. She did not suffer fools.

"I thought you said Marina wasn't coming in today," Ms. Kitty said.

"I said I needed a day," Marina said, giving Patricia a hard stare, "and that's what I took. Surely you can still count to one."

A blush ran up Patricia's neck and onto her face, and Marina could tell her words and tone were completely unexpected and had angered the salon owner. Patricia sputtered a bit, then collected herself.

"With everything that has happened, I assumed you'd need more time to get your life together," Patricia said.

"You mean 'everything' like catching your slutty niece in bed with my husband? That kind of 'everything'?"

Patricia's eyes widened and the color fled from her face.

Barbara glared at her. "Normally, I would say your mother raised you better when I hear a comment like that but in this case, it would be a lie."

"You're right," Marina said. "My mother raised me to believe that most people were assholes who were out to get me. Guess what? Turns out the crazy woman had it right."

"'Crazy' is a relative term," Ms. Kitty said.

Patricia cleared her throat, clearly trying to regain control.

"I don't think your kind of talk is appropriate, especially to me. That's my family you're talking about."

Marina shrugged. "I don't think it's appropriate that half the men in town and at least one woman—me—has seen her privates. The fact that she's your family is unfortunate, but not my problem."

Ms. Kitty burst out laughing, giant tears streaming down her face. "Maybe there's a flaw with the genetics. You know, some behaviors are inherited."

Rage flashed across Patricia's face.

"I won't stand for this," she said.

Marina smiled. "Then sit down, because I'm not about to shut up."

My God, Marina thought, *that felt great.* Why had she waited so long to do it?

"People have danced around you for years because they don't want your brother to launch a million frivolous lawsuits in their direction," Marina said. "Well, I for one am done playing stupid where your family's bad behavior is concerned. I plan on telling the entire world what I saw. This time, no one in Last Chance will be able to talk about it behind closed doors and play dumb in public. They'll be forced to pick a side. Any bets on how that one lines up?"

Ms. Kitty rose from Helen's chair and moved over to Marina's. "Ha! I see that bit of fluff leaving with a different man every week in my bar. A different *married* man. I'm pretty sure I know where the women in this town are going to stand."

Patricia dropped the brush she'd been holding on her stand, and Marina could tell she was a second away from losing it.

"A man's marriage vows are *not* my niece's responsibility," she said.

"Never said they were," Ms. Kitty said. "Still doesn't change the fact that the girl's a sleaze."

Patricia's face turned beet red and her jaw flexed. "If the women in this town bothered to take care of themselves, then maybe their husbands wouldn't go seeking the company of someone who keeps themselves up."

"Are you saying Marina's let herself go?" Ms. Kitty asked. "Because I can see your gray hair shining from here and that mustache on your lip is going to rival the drummer in my band if you let it go another couple hours. The bags under your eyes look like you just went shopping with them and you could redirect water flow with the creases in your face. I don't see any of that on Marina. According to your theory, I guess you best start checking up on *your* husband, right?"

Patricia whipped her head around and flung her arm out at Marina. "She does too have—"

Then she stopped short and stared. "That's not possible. You had gray hair all over your crown, and dark circles and wrinkles around your eyes. I know what I saw."

"You're absolutely right," Marina said. "And in the two days since you saw me last, I moved out of my home, dyed my hair, and had plastic surgery. I also recovered from that surgery and that's why you can't tell I had any."

"You did something!" Patricia screamed, coming completely unhinged.

"Yep, she sure did," Ms. Kitty said. "She looked better than you."

"Get out!" Patricia yelled.

"With pleasure," Ms. Kitty said. "I'll send you a bill for my blouse. This is silk."

Patricia looked horrified. "I wasn't talking to you, Ms. Kitty. I was talking to her."

Marina grinned. "I thought you'd never ask. Come on, Ms.

Kitty. I'm happy to give you a blowout and curl at my house. And we'll see what we can do about that blouse."

"You'll be sorry," Patricia said as they were walking out. "There's not another job in this town for stylists and without Harold's money, you'll be destitute in a week."

"I'll take destitute over prostitute any day," Marina said, and gave them the finger on her way out.

Ms. Kitty followed her to the parking lot, chuckling all the way.

"What the hell got into you?" she asked as they stopped by her hot-pink dually.

"I don't know. I guess I got to that point where I just can't be bothered to care anymore, you know?"

"Oh, I know it well. Welcome to the club. And don't worry about my hair. I'll do it myself. I should have left as soon as that witch pointed to Helen's chair. I know that sister of yours is probably setting up to wage a war on your behalf, but if you need anything, you come by the bar. I've dealt with my share of cheating men."

"Thanks. I really appreciate you standing up for me in there."

Ms. Kitty waved a hand in dismissal. "That was just me telling the truth. Something I'm guilty of a lot."

"I wish I was. It still feels a little uncomfortable."

"Keep trying it on. It stretches to fit real quick-like."

Ms. Kitty climbed into her truck and Marina waved as she drove away. She turned around to look back at the salon and saw the three remaining women looking at her through the blinds. She waved and grinned and the blinds snapped shut. Laughing, she climbed in her own car. Alexios had no idea the gift he'd given her. Her only regret was that it took forty-eight years to happen.

She pulled out of the parking lot and directed her car

toward her cabin, dialing Halcyon's number while she drove. If she was going to find the ring, she needed help. And the one person who'd always had her back was Halcyon. It would take some convincing to get her sister on board with the whole magical, mystical, descended-from-a-goddess thing, but even if her sister never believed it, she'd still help if Marina asked.

Thank God, because Marina needed all the help she could get.

CHAPTER ELEVEN

THIRTY MINUTES LATER, Marina was perched on a stool in her kitchen, attempting to explain her newfound power to her more-than-skeptical sister. When she finished, Halcyon stared at her for a while, then finally frowned.

"This is the emergency you had me rushing over here for?" Halcyon asked. Clearly her sister had expected something else.

"What did you think I called you for?"

"To celebrate your newfound attitude or commiserate your nervous breakdown...I wasn't sure which direction you were going to take things. That's why I brought champagne *and* Xanax."

"You know about what happened in the salon already? How is that possible?"

"My current booty call—sorry, 'gentleman caller'—is the drummer for Ms. Kitty's band. She was still laughing when she walked into the bar earlier and couldn't wait to tell them about you going off on Patricia. I'm pretty sure you can get free beer for life if you want it."

"Not right this moment, but I'll keep that in mind."

Even though it wasn't noon yet, Halcyon looked somewhat disappointed.

"You don't think there's an, uh, hereditary component to this, do you?" Halcyon asked.

"Of course," Marina said. "That's what I've been telling you."

"I don't mean the whole Aphrodite thing. I was talking about your mother."

Marina blinked. "You think I'm crazy?"

"Honey, you know I love you and if you really believe this and want to go on some scavenger hunt for a magical ring, then you know I'm in with whatever. It's not like I have lines in the sand about anything except underwire bras and getting married again. But you've got to realize how this sounds."

"Alexios said getting people to believe him was always the hardest part."

"His wardrobe isn't helping matters."

"He's not wearing the purple jeans anymore. I told him he wouldn't blend here."

"So he's dressed more appropriately, but he's still pitching this outlandish tale."

"Yes, but what about the money in my bank account? I am positive it wasn't there before. It's not like I'd forget about ten thousand dollars I had sitting around. And look at my hair and my skin. I didn't even put on moisturizer last night and I haven't had a dye bottle near my head in months. And I certainly didn't spend my night putting in extensions."

Halcyon stepped closer to Marina and scrutinized her face. Marina could tell her sister was confused. On the one hand, there was absolutely no way Marina could have gone through a procedure to get her skin to that state—if a procedure even existed that would accomplish it. And definitely no way she'd gotten it done and recovered overnight. But still, it was a lot to take in.

Unfortunately, Marina didn't have a lot of time. She needed Halcyon on board quickly. Her sister would help her no matter what, but if Halcyon believed, then her focus would be greater. And once Halcyon was focused, she was like a dog with a bone. Marina needed some of that spirit right now.

"Does it work on other people?" Halcyon asked.

"What do you mean?"

"You said you touched your face and the next morning it was beautiful again. So if you touched my face, would the same thing happen?"

"I don't know. Alexios didn't say anything like that and surely he would have mentioned it."

"Maybe he doesn't know. Maybe the others before you were too egotistical to try to help someone else."

"I suppose that's possible. Do you want me to rub your face?"

"Why not?"

"Okay, but take off your makeup first."

Halcyon headed to the bathroom for makeup wipes and came back looking several years older. Something Marina wasn't about to mention. Apparently, they'd both inherited their father's bags and dark circles. Marina had always thought his were due to being perpetually drunk, but she and Halcyon both had the same thing, no matter what they drank or how long they slept. Maybe there was more to this DNA stuff than people knew.

Marina reached up and swiped her finger under her sister's eyes. "Let's start with something small and that will be the easiest to see a change. Let me get a pic."

She grabbed her cell phone and took pictures of the offending dark puffy circles.

"How long will it take?" Halcyon asked. "Do I have to wait until tomorrow?"

"I don't know. I always messed with my face and hair at night, so when I woke up, the changes were there. Maybe sleeping activates it. Or maybe it's just time. It's not like there's an operating manual for this."

"No worries. So let's assume I believe all of this—what do you need from me?"

"I need help finding the ring. You've been reading Nancy Drew and Agatha Christie since third grade. Surely you have some ideas on how to go about this. I can't even locate a missing sock from the dryer."

"That's true, and I do love a puzzle."

"Okay. So I bought cinnamon rolls from the bakery before I went into work and I have a stash of Hawaiian coffee."

"Jesus, why have you been holding out? I'd commit murder for a bakery cinnamon roll."

Marina put the coffee on to brew and pulled out the cinnamon rolls, which were still warm. "So how do we start?"

Halcyon took a bite of one of the rolls and sighed with pleasure. "We start with what we know."

"Which is basically nothing."

"Not true. We know a little. We know that no one has found it before you, so either they all sucked, or didn't try, or the ring is elusive. I'm going to bet it was a combination of all three. Then there's Alexios's theory that the ring will be located near the—what did he call you—the Seeker?"

"But that doesn't make sense. How can it relocate without people noticing a ring appearing?"

"Money appeared in your bank account and no one noticed. But it might be simpler than that. Let's say the ring gravitates toward those from Aphrodite's bloodline. What's the easiest way for a ring to move around?"

"On a finger."

Halcyon sighed. "You are *really* bad at this."

"We've already established that."

"Okay, so here's my thinking. Unless the ring can change its appearance, then it looks like it did when this metalworking god made it. So that means old."

"Like an heirloom! That makes total sense. So nothing that looks modern. A collector's piece."

"Exactly. Although that presents a few problems."

"Yeah, the breaking-and-entering kind of problems," Marina said.

"Here's an idea—why can't we just have this Alexios walk through a locked door and steal the ring after we locate it?"

"Because he can't see it, remember?"

"Oh, right. I bet it really chaps their godlike asses to have to depend on us lowly humans."

"Probably, but it wouldn't be polite to point it out."

"You know me—I'm all about being polite. So we're back to potential breaking-and-entering charges."

Marina nodded. "Not to mention grand theft if the ring is worth a lot by our standards. I don't know if Alexios can make an arrest go away. And that's assuming we'd steal from people anyway."

"If the world is really going to end, I don't think we have a choice. And I'm sure something could be done if we were caught, but it sounds like the boss is a hothead, so we might not like his take on things. It's probably better if we don't get caught."

"That sounds good in theory but we're talking about me here. In forty-eight years, I've never even managed to walk around the edge of the fountain downtown without falling in. Do you really think I can climb in windows and sneak around dark houses without someone noticing?"

"So you were a clumsy kid. That can change."

"I fell in it three months ago."

Halcyon stared. "Why were you walking around the fountain three months ago?"

"I don't know. Because I keep thinking this time will be different? I usually manage to dunk myself once a year."

"I do not understand this town. I know that Old Lady Richard woke up this morning with a blister on her heel from her new shoes, but I don't hear about you flinging yourself into the fountain every year."

"I do it in the middle of the night."

"Sometimes you surprise me. Maybe there's a sense of adventure in you after all. If so, we're going to pull it out, even if it's kicking and screaming."

"Even if it means falling in a fountain?"

"As long as I'm wearing cotton, we're good."

"Black cotton if we're planning on cat-burgling on the regular."

"The upside is most people in Last Chance don't have alarms. The downside is most *do* have dogs and guns."

"You'll have a sneezing fit and blow our cover."

"I'll take Benadryl and wear a mask. We should both wear masks. I'll order some off Amazon. Not like we're going to find ski masks in south Louisiana."

"Okay, so we get ski masks and then what—start roaming through people's houses every night? Do we go alphabetically? By street would probably be more efficient. But what about everyone who lives out in the bayou? We've only got a week and we can't exactly stroll around in black ski masks during the day."

"You're overthinking this. We can eliminate a lot of people simply because some wouldn't have an heirloom. Take Six-Pack

Steve, for example. If he had anything of value, he would have already sold it for beer."

"So add pawnshops to the list."

"Definitely. So I guess the first thing we need to do is ask this Alexios what the ring looks like."

"Oh yeah, right! I can text him."

"Let me have another cinnamon roll first. Those skinny guys are the worst. They can pack away more than any two regular guys."

Marina nodded and passed the box of baked goods. And that's when she realized that the circles under Halcyon's eyes were lighter. She grabbed her phone and clicked a picture, blinding Halcyon with the flash.

"A little warning, please!" Halcyon complained. "Now I can't even see to find the cinnamon roll."

"Blink a few times." Marina scrolled back and forth between the before and after photos, to make sure she wasn't seeing things, but the evidence was right there. Halcyon's bags were disappearing.

"Look!" Marina turned her phone to show Halcyon the pic.

Halcyon winced. "Good Lord. That's worse than I thought."

"It was. But look at it now."

Halcyon blinked a couple times and leaned forward, studying the photo, then flipped the images back and forth. Finally, she jumped off her stool and ran into the bathroom.

"Holy shit!" she yelled. "You're right. The circles are fading and the skin isn't as puffy. That's amazing."

She came back into the kitchen, shaking her head in disbelief. "I didn't want to believe you. Not about any of this. I mean, I wanted to believe you but it was too far out there. Then my face changes in a matter of thirty minutes and all you did was touch it."

"It's kinda overwhelming."

"It's awesome!" Halcyon grabbed her by the shoulders. "Can you put my boobs back up where they used to be? Because that would be some magic I'd be seriously interested in. Hell, if you can do that, you could open your own shop and become a billionaire. You'd have to look at more boobs than a straight woman ever wants to see, but still."

"I don't think I can lift body parts except with my hands, and I'm pretty sure no one is going to pay me to do that."

"You'd be surprised." Halcyon scrunched her brow. "What about hot flashes? Can you make them go away? Or whip up a cold front?"

"If I could do that I wouldn't be standing here sweating and wearing only a tank top."

"I thought you'd taken a shower before I got here and didn't bother drying before answering the door."

"No. I stripped off my bra as soon as I got in the car, but the rest of it came off when hellfire and brimstone converged on me while getting the coffeepot set up. I thought I was going to spontaneously combust. I stood in front of the refrigerator so long I'm afraid my lunch meat spoiled."

"So you can't solve the world's biggest problems, but you can give people a facelift and find magical objects. Hey, maybe the ring can lift boobs."

"It sounds like a bit of a stretch. Besides, if we find the ring and these gods come through on their promise, then I'll have a million dollars. We could lift our boobs up to our chins with that kind of money."

Halcyon shook her head. "Have you seen what they do? They cut your nipples off! I looked it up online, thinking it can't be that bad and I'd really love to wear a tank without a bra again—outside of the house, I mean. Horror story! I couldn't eat for two days."

"Oh my God. That's awful. Custom-made tanks then. Even if they weren't good enough for public consumption, I'd be happy just to not roll over on one while I was sleeping."

"Deal. Okay, so we have a sort of plan. Do you want to call this Alexios? I'm dying to meet him."

Marina reached for her phone and Halcyon grabbed her arm.

"Aren't you forgetting something?" her sister asked.

Marina stared, confused.

"Pants," Halcyon said. "Unless you've undergone a complete personality change, I'm assuming you don't want to talk to a man wearing a tank and your underwear. Especially that underwear. Basic cotton is not a sexy look."

"Alexios swings the other way."

"Interesting. Then he's probably got on better underwear than you. I still recommend pants."

"Of course I'm going to put on pants. I just forgot."

"Maybe a sports bra!" Halcyon yelled as she hurried into the bedroom.

Marina pulled on a sports bra, then grabbed the first pair of capris she could find in a clothes box, which left her wearing a bright red tank and turquoise pants. At least all the important—or potentially embarrassing—things were covered.

She sent Alexios a text as she was exiting the bedroom and seconds later, he walked into the cabin. He gave her an up-and-down look and his nose twitched a bit, but he wisely kept his mouth shut.

"Are those cinnamon rolls?" he asked.

"Yes," Marina said. "Do you want one?"

"More than life itself," Alexios said and leaned over the box before inhaling. "But I'm doing keto."

"Were you lurking on the porch?" Halcyon asked.

"There's this condo thing," Marina said. "I'll explain later.

Anyway, Alexios, this is my sister, Halcyon. I've brought her in as a consultant of sorts."

"More like a partner in crime given the situation," Halcyon said.

"What do you mean?" Alexios asked.

Marina explained their theory about how to find the ring and the potential legal fallout that could arise. He nodded.

"Yes, the laws of your world are often a hindrance to our business here. Humans seem to cling to rule-following."

"Have you ever popped out of that condo and into a prison?" Halcyon asked. "There's a reason we cling."

"Anyway," Marina said. "We're going to be careful, but there's a possibility of trouble. I was hoping you had a way to handle anything that might crop up on that end."

"I'm sure I could figure something out if needed," he said. "If I can't, my boss would be willing to help."

"He'll just strike everyone with lightning," Marina said. "The point of looking for the ring is to avoid the apocalypse. I don't want a small one right here in Last Chance."

Halcyon raised her hand. "But if he was interested in a mini apocalypse, I could provide a short list. Well, maybe not too short."

"Zeus would like you," Alexios said. "Your theory about the ring being an heirloom is interesting and something I hadn't considered."

"What we need to know is what it looks like," Marina said.

He nodded. "I can show you the original design, of course. But we believe that Drakos disguised the objects as he sent them to earth. We tried the usual things with an actual rendering—posted signs with big rewards, even got it onto television once—but we never got so much as a thin lead."

"Crap," Marina said. "Nothing like making things more difficult."

"If it was easy, we wouldn't be talking," Alexios said. "I'd be happily wearing my purple jeans somewhere that I wasn't judged for such fashion choices, and you would be dealing with your personal problems without the benefit of an extra ten thousand dollars in your bank account."

"Touché," Marina said. "Okay. Well, show us the original. It could be that some things about it remained the same."

"Almost certainly so," Alexios agreed. "Aphrodite's blood was woven into the gemstone, so that's the most likely commonality you'll find. And, of course, the quality of the silver would be the same, but that's not as easy to test."

He pulled out his cell phone and accessed photos.

"Really?" Halcyon said. "You can't just conjure up a hologram? Even Iron Man can do that."

"Sometimes streaming service doesn't work all that great from our world, so we ditched holograms in favor of your phone system," Alexios said. He turned the phone around and they both leaned in to look.

The ring was beautiful, but then Marina hadn't expected anything less from a piece of jewelry made by a god. The silver was fashioned into tiny threads, wrapped around one another like vines, that formed the band. In the center was a single huge ruby, the color so bright and clear that it looked as if it had a light in it.

"Wow," Halcyon said. "That's seriously pretty. I don't suppose Hephaestus takes commissions. I've got a couple wedding rings I'd like to do something with."

Alexios frowned. "I'm certain that falls outside of his normal fare."

"It wouldn't have to be magical or anything," Halcyon said. "And I'd really prefer it if no one bled on it."

"It's still a no," Alexios said, then looked at Marina. "I'll text this photo to you along with the specifications for the ruby and the silver."

"Thanks," Marina said, but she was feeling far less optimistic now that they'd talked to Alexios.

"You look disheartened," Alexios said. "Please don't give up so soon."

"I'm not giving up," Marina said. "I'm just trying to figure out how I'm supposed to find something when I don't know what it looks like."

"We believe that when you see the object, you'll know," Alexios said. "Hephaestus thinks you might even feel the pull of the ring when you're near."

"This one thinks. That one believes," Halcyon said. "After all this time, you don't know crap, do you?"

Alexios straightened, looking mildly insulted. "Magic is a difficult thing to pin down, especially when we all have different abilities. There's no historical consistency to draw from. Drakos was gifted in the art of deception, and that came through in his ability to make objects appear differently than they were. No one else has had a similar ability and with Drakos dead, we can't exactly ask him how it works."

"So what happened to Aphrodite and Drakos's love child?" Halcyon asked.

"Is this relevant to the search for the ring?" Alexios asked.

"No," Halcyon said. "I just love a good Jerry Springer drama as long as it doesn't involve me."

Alexios frowned. "The child was raised by Aphrodite and is now languishing in a super easy position that requires next to no skill and very little of his time."

"So he got a better job than you," Halcyon said.

"Way better," Alexios said, then looked at Marina. "If I've answered all your inquiries about the ring and provided your sister with a suitable amount of drama to mull over, I'd like to take my leave. There's a Hallmark *Golden Girls* marathon on."

"Really?" Halcyon perked up.

"Not now," Marina said and nodded to Alexios. "I think we're done."

He headed out the door and Halcyon raced after him, but even though she yanked the door open the second it closed, he was nowhere to be seen.

"I wish I could do that," Halcyon said as she closed the door. "Especially after church when all those committee women are just lurking on the back row, waiting to pounce."

"They're mercenary."

"I was claiming heavy water consumption, then leaving five minutes early, figuring they'd all think I was going to the ladies' room."

"I wish I would have thought of that."

Halcyon sighed. "It only worked twice before one of them started following me out and accosting me in the bathroom."

"She didn't talk through the stall door, did she?"

"Good Lord, no. This is the South, not prison."

"So what should we do now? Hit up pawnshops?"

Halcyon nodded. "After that, I think we should walk the neighborhoods. See if you get a twinge or something passing one of the houses."

"I guess I have to change clothes, right?"

"Unless you want everyone in town staring at us. You're already going to be the subject of speculation given the situation with Harold. There's no point in making yourself easy to spot."

"I'll grab a ball cap and sunglasses," Marina said. "And a set for you as well."

"I've never worn a ball cap in my life."

"Then I'll get you my floppy beach hat. But it does me no good to disguise myself if you're strolling around as you."

"Fine, then, I'll wear the stupid floppy hat, but you're going to have to style my hair afterward. I have a booty...uh, gentleman caller tonight."

"Isn't the drummer working tonight?"

"Yes. Which is why the petroleum engineer is on the books."

"You know what? I don't even want to know."

CHAPTER TWELVE

THERE WERE two pawnshops in Last Chance on the outskirts of town and across the street from each other. Marina supposed it cut down on travel time for the shoppers and the sellers of secondhand items. She'd never been in either, but Halcyon, who'd had a couple of weird experiences trying to sell things herself, had sold a few items of value that her last two husbands had left behind when she'd booted them out. The only things she'd held on to were the wedding rings, and she'd claimed she was saving them for the creation of an individual piece. She'd just never found the craftsman or decided what she wanted.

Since Halcyon had experience with pawnshops, they decided she would take the lead and Marina would follow along, hoping to feel a twinge or tickle or whatever the heck was supposed to happen if she was close to the ring. The whole thing was still unbelievable and bordered on slightly ridiculous, but she supposed it didn't hurt to go look. And she did take their money. That singed spot on her carpet was enough to push her out of her comfort zone. Pissing off the boss didn't appear to be a good option.

Halcyon pushed open the door and motioned to a glass counter in the back that held jewelry. A guy who looked like an extra on *Sons of Anarchy* stood behind the counter and gave Halcyon the up-and-down as they approached.

"Haven't seen you in a while," he said. "You ditch another man who left power tools behind?"

"I've moved on to musicians," Halcyon said. "Maybe next time I'll have a guitar."

"If you ever want to move on to bikers, I've got an opening on the back of my Hog," he said.

"I *am* a bitch," Halcyon said. "I don't ride bitch."

He chuckled. "What can I help you ladies with?"

"We're looking for a present for an elderly cousin of ours," Halcyon said, giving him the cover story they'd cooked up. "She loves old jewelry and had a piece years ago that she lost during the Civil War or whatever. We can't pay her a visit without her harping for hours about that ring so we thought maybe we could find her something to replace it."

He nodded. "I got an old uncle like that except his gripe was about a fishing reel he probably got from Moses. I have to tell you, though, I've taken him seventeen different reels over the years, and not a one has stopped his complaining. But if you want to give it a shot, I've got a couple older pieces you can look at."

They followed him to the end of the counter, where he pulled out a tray of rings and set it in front of them. "Anything here look like what she lost?" he asked.

Marina studied the rings. Two had a red stone. She wasn't an expert, so she didn't know if they were rubies or garnet, but only one had a silver band, so she picked that one up and studied it.

"What do you think?" Halcyon asked.

Marina shook her head. "I don't think it will work. The

band is too narrow and the stone too small. It's pretty, though," she said, and put it back on the tray.

He gave them a nod and slid it back into the display.

"I don't suppose you know anyone in Last Chance who has some old jewelry," Halcyon said. "You know, the heirloom type? If people have something just sitting around, they might be willing to sell."

"Most of the older pieces that run through here were kids and grandkids selling off things after a parent or grandparent died," he said. "But I imagine Dottie Prejean has some good pieces. Her mother-in-law used to wear more rings than Liberace and I think she inherited some of them."

"Anyone else?" Halcyon asked.

He frowned. "The LeDoux probably do, but I don't figure you'd go talking to them, given the situation."

Marina felt a blush creep up her neck. She knew there was little to no chance that news of her misfortune hadn't reached every resident of Last Chance, and probably plenty of people who didn't even live there. But having to face those people every day, knowing that they were all aware of the worst thing that had ever happened to her, was going to be hard.

"Thank you for your help," Marina said and practically ran out of the building. Even though the other pawnshop was across the street, she jumped into her car and clenched the steering wheel, trying to slow her racing heart. Halcyon climbed inside and gave her a worried look.

"Are you all right?" she asked.

"I can't do this," Marina said. "The looks of pity. The talking around me. That guy is scary as hell and he was trying not to hurt my feelings. Everyone knows what happened. I'm either going to get pity or blame wherever I go, depending on whose side people have taken. And they've all taken sides."

Halcyon reached over to squeeze her arm. "I know they

have, honey. People always do. They just don't necessarily let you in on which way they went."

"But I'll know. I'll know every time I talk to someone. Every time someone looks at me. How long does this last? You've been cheated on. How long did the pity party go on? Or the gleeful celebration behind your back?"

"I don't know."

"How can you not know? You were married to three cheaters and the one who died had that whole baby-mama-at-the-funeral thing. You're telling me you never noticed all the side glances and sympathetic looks?"

Halcyon shrugged. "With a mother like Constance Dumont, I've gotten those looks my entire life. I decided long ago to simply stop noticing. The kindest thing you can do for yourself is stop caring what other people think."

Marina stared at her sister, her final sentence sinking in.

"If only it was that easy," she said quietly.

"I never said it was easy to get there, but once you've arrived, it's forever. If anything, I care even less as time passes. Whenever you see someone giving you a look, tell yourself their opinion doesn't matter. That *they* don't matter. Unless you have a lot of respect for someone, why bother to care what they think?"

"It sounds so logical."

"It *is* logical. And when you can stop thinking with your heart and start thinking with your head, everything will be smoother."

Marina nodded but she wondered, would it really be smoother? Was closing off her heart how Halcyon had dealt with all the disappointments life had thrown at her? And if you closed yourself off to pain, didn't that mean you were also closing yourself off to joy? Was it really possible to turn your emotions on or off based on who was standing in front of you?

And how did that work when she was handling people like her mother, whom she loved but didn't really like much?

She started the car and pulled across the street to the other pawnshop. Now wasn't the time for delving too deep into her psyche. And Lord knew, she wasn't going to figure out in the next couple minutes something that had escaped her for forty-eight years. She just needed to focus on finding the ring. That was something tangible and not emotional.

It was something she could handle.

———

SIX HOURS LATER, Marina stumbled into her cabin with Halcyon close behind. They'd been to the two pawnshops and walked at least ten miles. And they'd come up with absolutely nothing. They both flopped onto the couch and Halcyon closed her eyes and let out a whining sort of gasp.

"Are you all right?" Marina asked.

"I'm on hour twenty-four of an eighteen-hour bra."

Marina stared.

"After my shower last night, I got dressed to go to the gas station and get a hot dog but I fell asleep on the couch before I made it out the door."

"Well, you won't need it tonight with the plans you've got. Do you want me to do your hair?"

"No. I got a text earlier. They were held up leaving the rig so he's still out in the Gulf."

"Maybe tomorrow then. I owe you."

"The drummer doesn't have a gig tomorrow night. And he'd still be on the hook if I shaved my head, so I don't see the point."

Marina nodded. All day, she'd tried to focus on the search for the ring, but Halcyon's words and the way her sister lived kept creeping back into her thoughts. She'd always wondered how her sister made it work but had never wanted to ask. She'd been afraid Halcyon would tell her that everything about Marina's life was wrong, which was something she didn't want to hear. Especially as she hadn't been willing to change anything. Ultimately, she figured the conversation would have only served to make her feel worse, so she'd never gone there.

But given everything that had happened in the last couple days, maybe it was time to open up that dialogue, especially now that Marina was going to have to figure out how to negotiate the single life. Halcyon never seemed upset about things. Angry, sure, but not upset. Anger didn't last. And her attitude couldn't exist only because she'd stopped caring what people thought.

Or could it? Was peace of mind really that simple?

And if that was the case, then why wouldn't her sister settle on one man? Was not caring keeping her from forming lasting relationships? Was surface-level okay with Halcyon? Did it make her happy? Marina couldn't wrap her mind around being involved, especially sexually, with someone she didn't have deeper feelings for. Was she old-fashioned for thinking that way? Would she be better off to avoid romantic relationships forever, as Halcyon seemed to do? At the moment, she couldn't imagine trekking down that path, but one day she might feel differently. Would she be too scared to try it? Would everything she'd gone through close her heart off to anything in the future?

"I've never asked you this before because I figured it was none of my business," Marina said. "It still isn't, and if you don't want to tell me I'm fine with that, but I really want to understand what you're doing with these men. The drummer sounds like a nice guy. The commercial fisherman before him was a nice guy. I'm sure the engineer is nice as well. So why the revolving door?"

Halcyon squinted at Marina before closing her eyes again. "It's easier to remain unattached that way. Can't get used to having someone around if they're not around for long."

"And that's what you want? A never-ending parade of men that you have no feelings for?"

Halcyon looked at Marina and smiled. "Oh, I've got plenty of feelings."

"Not those kind. You know what I'm talking about."

"You mean the big *L*. Let me ask you something—where has love gotten you?"

"I love you."

"And I love you too, sweetie. But I didn't make vows with you. I can love you and still do who or what I want without repercussions, at least where our relationship is involved. Our relationship isn't about compromise and it will never be about betrayal."

"Most people would argue that family is all about compromise and betrayal."

"Not me and you. We've shared a heart since we were born and that's never going to change. We trust each other completely. That has never and will never come into question. Tell me who else you have that with."

Marina considered the question. Clearly, she'd never had that kind of bond with Harold and if she was being honest with herself, she'd always known that. And while she loved Avery with every ounce of her being, the relationship between a mother and daughter—especially when the daughter wasn't really an adult—was an entirely different kettle of fish.

"I guess if you never develop feelings you don't have to worry about being hurt," Marina said.

Halcyon nodded. "And if you have no expectations of people, you can't be disappointed."

"But is that enough? These men are like a commercial slot in between your regular show. Does that really make you happy?"

"I was in love once...twice if you count my first marriage. Looking back, I see that it was the infatuation of a starry-eyed teen but I thought it was real at the time."

"Then it still counts. The feelings are the same whether you have the maturity to understand them well or not. And the second time? Danny?"

Of all of Halcyon's husbands, Danny was the only one that she'd kept photos of.

"Danny didn't choose to leave me," Halcyon said. "I know there was that baby-mama drama after he passed but she was a fling that he had months before he ever met me. And the woman even admitted that Danny never knew she was pregnant. Didn't want her husband to find out. Then he found out anyway and dumped her, so she came looking for a payout."

Marina nodded. She already knew the facts. "It's not optimum, but what happened before you didn't have any bearing on your relationship."

"Exactly. And I know we didn't have much time together before he died, but I honestly don't think he ever would have stepped out on me. What we had was so much more than I had with anyone else. It was pure. There was never a moment with him where I didn't know how much he loved me and how much I loved him. It was a certainty I've never felt with anyone else and I don't think I ever will. I just wish we'd had more time together."

"So no one else will ever measure up."

"No. I tried twice after him but I knew both were wrong. I was grieving...trying to fill that huge hole that Danny left in my heart, but another person can't do that. I had to heal myself."

"But is refusing to ever give love another chance healing?"

"It's closer to healing than breaking all over again would be."

Sadness coursed through Marina. She'd never realized just how deeply Danny's loss had affected Halcyon. Marina had guessed that Danny was the one Halcyon used to measure everyone else against, and it had been easy to see how much they loved and enjoyed each other. But she had just realized that Halcyon was still in love with him. Eighteen years he'd been gone, and her sister still hadn't gotten over his death.

Could that one true love sustain her forever? Certainly, her sister never appeared to be unhappy. In fact, Halcyon mostly exhibited two sides—upbeat or pissed. Even her sarcasm was funny as hell. It had never occurred to Marina that all of that might be masking her sister's real heartache. And was it even worth pointing out that had Halcyon had more time with Danny, things could have gone south just like her other relationships? It couldn't be healthy for her sister to compare all relationships to the one that hadn't even covered a three-month period. No one would ever measure up long-term.

As soon as all of this was behind them Marina and Halcyon were going to talk more. About Halcyon's life. For so many years while dealing with Avery and her mother, Marina had always had Halcyon to lean on. And her sister had never wavered, nor was she wavering now. It was time for Marina to be that rock for Halcyon, whether her sister wanted her to or not. Because no matter how put together Halcyon appeared, she couldn't possibly be satisfied with a life that never cracked the surface.

It was time for both of them to figure out what they wanted the most and go grab it.

CHAPTER THIRTEEN

EVERY INCH of Marina's body ached as she headed to the shower. Halcyon had trudged to her car earlier, swearing she was going to soak her feet the entire night. Marina pulled off her clothes, struggling a bit to bend over far enough to get her yoga pants off, then she yanked off her tank and sports bra. Her boobs slid down on her chest and flattened like balloons filled with sand.

She looked in the mirror and sighed. At one time, she'd had awesome boobs. The kind of boobs that other women wanted and surgeons worked hard to create. But one morning when she was thirty-eight, she'd gone into the bathroom and found that they'd fallen and couldn't get up. It was the beginning of the end—that dreaded day when gravity came to visit and refused to leave.

She grabbed them with both hands and lifted them back into place, then shifted them from side to side, trying to remember what they looked like in sweaters before Gravity Day had come calling.

What the hell.

"I order you to stay perky like you were in my twenties,"

she said out loud then climbed into the shower.

Maybe she *could* lift boobs. And maybe if she was really specific about what she wanted, the magic would understand. Despite a bitch of a day, the puffiness and dark circles under Halcyon's eyes had disappeared altogether by that evening. She'd made Marina rub every square inch of her face and scalp before she left and had threatened to demand a foot rub since she hadn't had time for a pedicure that week. Marina had politely declined. She loved her sister but massaging someone's sweaty feet was one of those lines she wasn't interested in crossing. Her professional interest was solely on the other end of the body.

She looked down at her feet and frowned. They could use a pedicure. In fact, she couldn't remember the last time she'd had one, but that was typical. Pre-Crotchapocalypse, Marina had been so busy with everyone and everything else that she had stopped making time for herself. And no one had even seemed to notice. Or care. She supposed that's what happened to most women with families, but from her new perspective, she could see the imbalance.

But really, who was to blame? Not Avery. Her daughter was self-involved, but most teens were and besides, she'd been trained to believe that Mom took care of everything, mainly because Mom always had. Harold could share some of the blame but then, his mother had been one of the old-school, non-career women who canned vegetables, made homemade bread, and stitched her own hideous place mats. Harold had been raised to believe the mom took care of everything as well.

So that left her, and that was a hard pill to swallow. Why hadn't she ever advocated for herself? Why had she let her family take her for granted? And they *did* take her for granted. Because in all the years of giving and doing and sacrificing, not once could she remember anyone telling her thank you. Once, recently, she'd complained about the weight of her responsibilities to Harold and how no one seemed to appreciate them. He'd made some nasty comment about her wanting credit for things she was supposed to do.

If he were standing in front of her right now, she'd kick him right in that rash.

Every day at work, Marina received money for styling hair because that's what she was supposed to do, but a customer never left her chair without thanking her for her work. Why should family be an exception? Was it really so hard to occasionally utter two words?

It was too late to demand respect from Harold. He'd clearly crapped the bed on that one. But at some point, she needed to work on her relationship with Avery. Her daughter was hyperintelligent and funny and a genuinely good person, but she was also headstrong and tended toward selfish a lot of the time. Marina hoped as she got older their relationship would mature into something more like what she and Halcyon had, but that was a lot of years off.

The water started to shift from steaming hot to mildly warm and Marina took that as her cue to get out. She toweled off and pulled on a clean tank and boy shorts and strolled into the kitchen to rummage for dinner. She still hadn't had a chance to make a real grocery store run, so her options mostly consisted of cheese, lunch meat, bread, Goldfish, a bottle of wine, sodas, and her secret chocolate stash. Since Halcyon had given her a toaster oven she didn't use, she opted for grilled cheese with wine and chocolate. She popped the bread and cheese into the oven and poured a glass of wine, then went to the back door to let Snooze out since he was whining.

"Do not get in the bayou," she said as he headed off the porch. "You don't want a bath and I don't want another one."

He gave her a long-suffering look, then headed down the

steps and into the yard-slash-field of weeds. Another thing on the long list of items she needed to address. She had no intention of sodding the yard, but mowing around the house would cut down on bugs and the snake potential. The snake potential was a real fear. Marina hated snakes.

She headed back into the kitchen to check on the grilled cheese and that's when Snooze started to bark. Loudly. And this wasn't his I-found-something-interesting sound. This was his I-found-something-I-don't-like sound. Marina grabbed a flashlight and the pistol Halcyon had lent her out of a kitchen drawer and headed outside.

At the edge of the back porch, she stopped to figure out what direction she needed to go. Sound carried over water and sometimes it was hard to pinpoint exactly where it was coming from. Snooze barked again, sounding more agitated than before, and she shifted to the left, locking her gaze on the row of cypress trees that lined one side of the property. She shone the flashlight in that direction, but it didn't reach far enough for her to see anything. When she was unpacking, she'd put her rubber boots on the porch, so she pulled them on and headed into the yard.

The weeds rubbed the bare skin on her legs and made her itch. If this turned out to be a rabbit or a raccoon, she was going to cut off that dog's treats for a week. She hadn't even unpacked everything and had no idea if she had calamine lotion. And since the drugstore closed hours ago, she was looking at a long night of scratching.

She crept toward the cypress trees, following Snooze's wailing. The brush was thick and with a thunderstorm building overhead, the moon was hidden completely. The only light was the thin beam from her flashlight, and it wasn't enough to see a very large patch. At the edge of the trees, she called for Snooze and he let off three shrill barks. She frowned and chambered a round, then inched into the woods, pistol in firing position.

Snooze's barks grew louder—more insistent—and she could tell he wasn't far away. She moved faster now, worried that the old hound had come across an alligator. Snooze was no match for an angry gator. Even on land they could really move. She burst into a clearing, gun leveled and ready to fire. Snooze stood at the far edge of the clearing, barking at a thick set of brush. As soon as she moved forward, the brush shook as if something large had moved it and then she heard the sound of retreating steps.

She commanded Snooze to stay put, but in keeping with everyone else in her family, he completely ignored her and launched into the brush in pursuit. Yelling at him to stop, Marina bolted through the brush, tripped over a tree root, and slammed into the ground.

"I'm going to kill you, Snooze!" she yelled as she rubbed her angry back.

Thunder boomed overhead and it started to rain. Actually, it was more of a monsoon as only Louisiana can produce in the blink of an eye. The hard Louisiana mud beneath her got wet and slick within seconds, and between her back and the growing mudhole, she struggled to push herself up. When she finally got into a somewhat upright position, a spotlight hit her right in the face and she threw up her arm to block the light, almost falling again.

"Don't move!" a man's voice commanded, and just like magic, the rain stopped.

"I'm hardly going anywhere now that I'm blind," Marina said. "Either shoot me or get that light out of my face."

He chuckled and the light dropped down to the ground, illuminating the area surrounding the mudhole.

"Sorry," he said. "I thought you were someone else."

She looked up and saw a man with longish dark brown hair and green eyes smiling at her. A man she was certain she'd never seen before. She glanced down and realized he had a gun holstered at his side and her pulse jumped. Twice in one week was at least once too many times to think you were going to be serial killed. Her pistol was somewhere on the ground, but there was no way she'd be able to grab it and shoot him before he could shoot her. And with her back now protesting loudly, there was no way she was going to outrun him either.

"Who did you think I was?" she asked. Maybe if he'd been looking to serial kill someone else, he'd just continue on his merry way. And she could grab her purse and relocate out of Last Chance as soon as she could find her keys.

"An alligator poacher, but clearly I was wrong."

Relief flooded through her. He wasn't a serial killer. And since she wasn't a poacher, this would end well. Except for the backache and all the mud.

"Why can't I be an alligator poacher?" she asked. "I have a gun...somewhere. And a hunting dog, also somewhere."

"Both of those present a compelling argument, but in my experience, poachers wear pants."

For the love of everything holy!

She pulled at her tank, hoping to get it past anything that could get her arrested, but that only exposed her bustline to the point that things got sketchier.

He grinned at her and a blush ran up her neck and onto her face. Damn it. He was sexy as hell.

"I would tell you not to worry about it because I've seen everything," he said, "but I have to admit, this one is a first."

"And hopefully a last—at least where I'm concerned. And just who the hell are you and why are you lurking around my property?"

"Sorry, I should have introduced myself. I'm Luke Abshire,

130

the new game warden."

He extended his hand and Marina stared at it for a couple seconds before placing her muddy hand in his. He didn't seem to mind.

"Marina Trahan," she said. "I live in a cabin just the other side of the tree line."

"I thought that place was empty."

"It was until yesterday."

"That explains my confusion. I saw lights on and thought maybe the poacher was squatting there. Then I heard the dog and thought I'd caught him."

Marina frowned. "Wait. So the dog wasn't barking at you?"

He shook his head. "I never saw the dog. He sounds like a doozy though. Bloodhound?"

"Yes. And he doesn't signal like that unless something is wrong. Hence why I ran out half dressed."

He bent over and lifted her pistol out of the mud. "But fully armed."

She took the gun and spun around as something rustled in the brush to her right. A second later, Snooze came trotting out. He walked up to Luke and the game warden crouched down and let the hound smell his hand before lifting it to scratch his ears. Snooze closed his eyes, enjoying the petting for a bit, then licked him and went to sit next to Marina.

"That pitiful look is not going to get you out of a bath," Marina said as she stared at Snooze.

Snooze sighed and flopped down in the mud.

Luke chuckled. "It's like he understood everything you said."

"Yes, well. We're going to go home and have that bath now. I would say it was nice meeting you but that would be a lie. So I'll just go with it was interesting meeting you. Good luck catching your poacher."

"Thanks," he said and pulled a card from his back pocket to hand to her. "If you or your dog see someone lurking around, give me a call. I'd really like to catch this guy."

"No problem. Good night."

Marina tromped back through the marsh to her cabin, muttering the entire way. Why did Snooze pick tonight to be ambitious? Why did a poacher have to pick her property? Why didn't someone come up with a solution to menopause so she could wear more clothes to sleep in? Why did the game warden have to be good-looking?

Once inside, she herded the reluctant hound into the bathroom and hauled him one half at a time into the tub. Then she climbed in with him and began dousing him with shampoo.

"I don't have the energy or enough hot water to do this two times," she said as he gave her a woeful stare. "Next time, don't go chasing poachers. And especially not if it's going to rain. I'm going to have to mop the floors again. And my grilled cheese is cold. And what's with licking that game warden? You never do that."

Snooze let out a single bark.

"Don't tell me yes. You know that's not true."

He barked again.

"What? Are you trying to tell me you liked him?"

Another bark.

"You're just Mr. Congeniality lately."

He shook his entire body, flinging shampoo all over her and the walls.

"Or do you just not like Harold?"

Single bark.

She directed the shower onto his back and began rinsing the shampoo off of him.

"That makes two of us."

CHAPTER FOURTEEN

IN HER EIGHTEEN years on earth, no one had ever accused Avery Trahan of being extra. In fact, some had questioned whether she had feelings at all. But Avery never paid them any mind. Nothing could shift her from her focus. She was going to graduate premed with honors, then be accepted to the medical school of her choice, then become a surgeon. She'd spent three years working as a vet assistant and one day when the surgical tech had gotten into a car accident, the vet had asked Avery to help out on an emergency surgery.

Avery had been fascinated with medicine—surgery specifically—ever since. But she had no desire to practice on animals. She loved them too much and knew she'd never be able to develop the detachment necessary to focus 100 percent on the job. People, on the other hand, often ranked low on her list of things she loved, and almost never occupied a spot higher than dogs.

Now was definitely no exception.

When she'd first gotten off the phone with her mom, she'd sat shell-shocked for so long that her roommate asked her what was wrong. No way was Avery repeating the horrific drama to the person she was going to be sharing close space with for the next four years. At least, not until she was certain it was true.

Not that she thought her mom was lying. Her mom never lied except about things that didn't matter, like Santa and telling someone they looked nice when they looked awful. So at best, someone had convinced her mom that this nightmare had happened. At worst, it was all true and her dad had officially become that gross, creepy old man.

As soon as her roommate left for the swimming pool, Avery had called her bestie from high school. She'd gone off to college in California, but her mother was one of the town's biggest gossips. If anyone could verify what had happened it would be Simone. Unfortunately, her phone call with Simone hadn't gone the way she'd hoped it would. Her bestie had not only verified that what her mom told Avery was true but that her mom had actually caught them in her own house. Her own bed.

Which left absolutely zero chance that it was a lie.

Her entire life, Avery had considered her parents average, boring people and her own life less than fascinating. And there were times she'd desperately wished for something interesting to happen. But this wasn't what she'd had in mind at all. This was horrifying and embarrassing, and she'd never been this upset before. Not ever.

How could her dad do this to her mom? To her?

And those two questions were exactly why she was barreling down the highway to Last Chance, hoping to talk some sense into her dad. Because no way could the nerdy guy who loved spreadsheets more than life blow up their family over that thot. Something was wrong. Maybe he was on drugs or having a nervous breakdown. Either way, she was going to get to the bottom of things and stop this train wreck before it got worse.

She exited the highway and made the drive into Last Chance at twice the posted speed limit. If she got stopped, she'd tell them it was an emergency. Everyone at the sheriff's department knew her family and Avery was certain the gossip had made the rounds. They would understand.

It was barely 8:00 a.m. when she drove down her block and spotted Chastity's bright red convertible in their driveway. Rage and shame coursed through her. It was bad enough to have a romp with the town ho, but being so blatant about it was beyond gross. She pulled into the driveway, making sure she didn't block Chastity's car since she'd be leaving, and let herself into the house, slamming the front door as she entered. The last thing she wanted was to see anyone naked.

She heard footsteps hurrying down the hallway and a couple seconds later, her dad came into the living room, looking around frantically for the source of the noise. When his gaze landed on her, he let out a breath.

"Avery," he said. "I thought you were someone else."

"You mean Mom? The woman who lived here for a million years until you threw her out? That someone else? The one who cleaned and decorated and repaired everything in this broken piece of crap that you refused to sell or even update because Grandmother might roll over in her grave?"

His face flushed with anger. "I will not have you talking to me that way. Your mother chose to leave."

Avery stared at him, dumbfounded. How did that even make sense? The entire drive to Last Chance, she'd hoped that everyone had been wrong. That some sort of shared psychosis was what was really going on. She'd seen it in a movie once. It was totally possible. At least, that's what she'd wanted to believe. When she'd seen Chastity's car in the driveway, all hope had fled on that end of things, but she couldn't believe her dad was standing there all indignant, insisting that this was her mom's fault. What the hell was wrong with him?

"Seriously?" Avery said. "Mom caught you in bed with that whore. The same one whose car is parked in the driveway right now. And you're actually going to claim that leaving was her choice? Everyone says Grandma Letitia is crazy but I think they've got the wrong person locked up."

"I will not listen to this. Your mother and I are getting a divorce. I'm not happy with her and I refuse to live the rest of my life that way. Chastity is part of my life now and you just have to deal with it."

Avery gasped. How could he be so cold? This was her dad. The man who was supposed to love her. The man who...and that's when it hit her...the man who went to work.

It was her mom who walked her to school and cooked the meals. Who read her bedtime stories and slept with her when she was sick. It was her mom who'd tried to help her learn baseball when she'd gone through her tomboy phase and wanted to make the middle school team. And it was her mom who'd taken her out for ice cream when she didn't make the cut. It was her mom who helped her fill out her college and scholarship paperwork and went on campus visits. It was her mom who helped her pack her things and stood in the driveway crying as she drove away a week before.

"Fine," she said. "So I choose to deal with it by not dealing with you."

"You don't have a choice in the matter. I'm your father."

"A real father wouldn't do this."

"What's wrong, Pookie Bear?" Chastity's voice echoed down the hall. "Is that little girl of yours giving you problems?"

Chastity walked into the living room and circled her arms around Harold's waist and kissed him on the cheek. And if that wasn't enough insult, the whore was wearing Avery's clothes.

Avery blinked as blood rushed to her head, causing the room to spin. She thought she'd been angry in the past, but those times were nothing compared to that moment. If there were a way she could have killed Chastity with her thoughts, the bitch would have dropped on the floor that very second.

"Now, Bunny," her dad said, casting nervous glances between Avery and Chastity. "Let me handle this. You just head on to work and I'll catch up with you."

"Not in my clothes, she's not!" Avery yelled. "Take my clothes off now, bitch, or I'll rip them off of you."

Her dad's expression shifted from nervous to Oh Shit.

"I live here now," Chastity said. "I can use whatever I want here. Right, Pookie Bear? What's wrong, Avery? Afraid I'll take your cheap wardrobe *and* your daddy?"

An explosion went off in Avery's head and any sliver of control she might have been holding on to fled completely. She launched into Chastity, tackling her to the ground. Chastity clawed her arms with her pointed hooker nails and Avery screamed in pain. Her loosened grip allowed Chastity to get up and run for the door, yelling at her dad to do something.

Her dad stood completely still, his face pale. What a shock. And all Avery could think as she ran by him and out the door after Chastity was how it was no surprise that her dad stood by doing nothing.

She caught Chastity as she made it to her car and yanked her backward by the collar of her bright blue shirt. This time Chastity didn't have a chance to get away. Before she could regain her balance, Avery punched her dead in the face. Blood exploded from Chastity's nose and she screamed in pain, throwing her hands up in front of her and trying to flee. Avery ran forward, arm cocked and ready to finish the job.

Chastity stumbled backward into her car and huddled there, wailing.

"Avery, stop!" her dad yelled.

Avery paused and looked back at him. All the bravado he'd worn before had fled and now he just looked scared. Good.

"I didn't know she was wearing your clothes," he said.

"All the more reason to keep hitting her," Avery said as she moved toward Chastity again.

"Help," Chastity said, and Avery turned to see her on her cell phone.

She snatched the phone from Chastity's hand and threw it into the street. "Take off my clothes right now or I will throttle you to death."

"We're outside," Chastity said, sniveling.

"Everyone in this town has seen you naked. Now!" Avery lifted her fist again.

Chastity looked at her dad, obviously expecting him to intervene, but Harold had always been allergic to actually doing something.

"Now!" Avery repeated.

Chastity undid the skirt and let it drop, then pulled the shirt off and tossed it in Avery's face. Avery wrinkled her nose at the streetwalker undergarments Chastity had on. God, those panties were nothing more than strings.

"Satisfied?" Chastity yelled. "That shirt's ruined, you know."

Avery smiled. "It was ruined the second you touched it. And yes, I'm very satisfied."

A siren sounded behind her and Avery whirled around as Deputy Kyle Pitre stepped out of the patrol car.

Crap! Kyle was Preston's cousin and only had his job because Preston had something on the sheriff.

"Chastity?" Kyle looked confused as he approached. "Are you all right?"

"What the hell, Kyle!" Chastity yelled. "Do I look all right? She broke my nose and took my clothes."

Kyle looked over at Harold, who still hadn't moved. "Jesus Christ, Harold! What the hell is going on here?"

"They got into a fight," Harold said.

"And you couldn't handle two little girls?" Kyle asked.

Harold winced at the phrase "little girls" but didn't even bother to answer.

Kyle shook his head in disgust and went back to his car. A minute later, he returned with a jacket and handed it to Chastity.

"Put that on," he said. "I called your dad. You need to get home now."

Kyle pulled out a pair of handcuffs and motioned to Avery. "Turn around. Hands behind your back."

Avery stared. "You're arresting me? She started it!"

"I did not!" Chastity yelled. "She jumped me. I was just trying to leave."

"Trying to leave wearing my clothes," Avery said. "That's theft. Are you going to arrest her for stealing?"

"That's bullshit!" Chastity said.

"Go home now, Chastity," Kyle said.

Chastity gave him a dirty look but stomped off to her car and squealed out of the driveway, giving Avery the finger as she went.

Kyle turned Avery around and grabbed her wrists. "You can take everything up with the judge."

"You're such a loser, Kyle," Avery said, struggling to maintain control. "Maybe while I'm locked up I'll tell the sheriff how you kept hitting on me when I was a minor...while you were on duty."

"Tell him anything you want," Kyle said and yanked her. "We both know who he'll choose to believe."

He shoved her in the back of his car and she slumped onto the seat, trying to position her arms where she could sit upright. It was a lot harder than it looked, especially if you had no experience. He slammed the door and stomped back over to her dad. Avery saw him pointing to her and wagging his finger in her dad's face. Her dad never said a word.

Coward.

Avery felt the tears rushing in and sucked in a deep breath, not about to let Kyle see her cry. He'd tell Chastity and they'd have a good laugh over it.

And Avery was done being Chastity LeDoux's laughingstock.

CHAPTER FIFTEEN

MARINA SCREECHED to a stop in Halcyon's driveway. Before the car had even ceased swaying, her sister bolted out her front door and jumped inside. Marina glanced over at her, wondering how she managed to do it. Regardless of the amount of notice, Halcyon never appeared outside without her hair styled and makeup on. Marina, on the other hand, had run out the door in green shorts and a purple shirt, hair looking like a rat's nest up in a clip, and not even so much as a swipe of lip balm.

"What happened?" Halcyon asked as Marina threw the car in Reverse and flew out of the driveway.

"I don't know exactly. I just got a call from Adelaide, who said she saw Kyle Pitre at Harold's house, shoving Avery into the back of his deputy car in handcuffs."

"Where the hell was Harold?"

"Standing there doing nothing."

"What a surprise. I'm going to say something now that I should have said twenty-eight years ago. I don't like Harold. He's a useless, sniveling piece of crap. I didn't tell you before because that's the man you chose and I always have your back.

But now that I don't have to pretend anymore, I'm going to call it like I see it."

"I wouldn't have it any other way. And I agree. I'm seeing a lot of things differently lately."

Halcyon nodded. "Which we can discuss at length as soon as we get your daughter out of the clink, save the world, and get you changed into matching clothes."

"I haven't exactly finished unpacking yet. These were the first things I pulled out of a box."

"I'm sure you were wiped out after yesterday."

"I was, and then I had this ridiculous run-in with the new game warden while I was chasing Snooze."

"Why was a game warden on your property?"

"He said he was looking for a poacher."

Halcyon frowned as Marina pulled into the sheriff's department parking lot. "Sounds like a good story. You can tell me all about it just as soon as we straighten these idiots out."

Marina took a deep breath and slowly blew it out.

Just stay calm. Calm will accomplish more.

She nodded to Halcyon, who was waiting for her cue, then they got out of the car and headed for the front door. As soon as she stepped inside, Kyle Pitre, who was sitting at a desk up front, smirked.

"Guess you're here to see about your little angel," he said.

"Why did you arrest her?" Marina asked.

He shook his head. "I'm not even getting into that with you. Take it up with the sheriff." He rose from his desk and headed out the door. "Good luck," he called over his shoulder as he left.

Halcyon's face flashed with anger. "Kyle Pitre has always been a—"

Marina put her hand in front of her sister's mouth. "Whatever you're about to say I totally agree with, but there could be cameras and recording devices and God knows what else in here."

They headed to the door with "Sheriff" stenciled on it and knocked.

"What do you want?" the sheriff barked from inside.

Marina opened the door a bit and poked her head in. "I need to speak to you about my daughter."

Sheriff Randy Owen looked up in surprise, then his expression changed to one of frustration. "Sorry. I thought you were Kyle. That boy can't so much as date a form without asking me a damn question."

Since the "boy" in question was almost forty years old, his statement was both unfortunate and revealing. But then, everyone in Last Chance had always known that Kyle only had his job because of Preston. The long-running suspicion was that Preston had something on Randy that he was desperate to keep quiet. Marina had never heard any gossip about Randy for the fifteen years he'd been in Last Chance, but he was a Texas transplant. It would be just like Preston to go poking around the man's past to ensure he had leverage. None of that boded well for Avery but Marina had to get this sorted.

"Come in and sit," Randy said.

"Why was Avery arrested?" Marina asked as she sat down. "Can I see her? What do I have to do to get her out of here?"

"Slow down," Randy said. "Let's take one thing at a time. Avery is locked up in the back."

Marina gasped. "She's in a cell?"

"Yes, ma'am," Randy said. "I'm sorry, but I have to follow protocol."

"It's protocol to put children in jail?" Halcyon asked.

"In the eyes of the law, she's not a child," Randy said.

"But why is she there?" Marina asked.

"She attacked Chastity LeDoux this morning," Randy said. "I'm waiting to hear from the doctor, but Kyle seemed to think her nose is broken."

Marina clasped the top of her head with both hands. "I don't understand. Avery is supposed to be in New Orleans. How could this happen?"

"You'll have to get the details from her," Randy said.

"Can I take her home?" Marina asked.

Randy hesitated a minute and she could tell he wasn't happy about what he was about to say. "I'm afraid not."

"Because?" Halcyon asked, leaning forward in her chair.

Randy shot Halcyon a nervous look before turning back to Marina. "Chastity is pressing charges. I'm trying to get Avery in front of the judge today so he can set bail. If everything lines up, you should be able to get her out by this evening."

"Pressing charges?" Marina felt as if she were going to be sick. "You can't be serious. She could lose her scholarship. Surely something can be done. I'll pay the medical bills."

Randy squirmed in his chair, looking miserable. "I'm really sorry about this, Marina. Truly, I am. But Preston is involved..."

"So your hands are tied," Halcyon said. "Because in all the years you've been here, you still haven't figured out how to stand up to the biggest asshole in town. What the hell does he have on you? Is it so bad you're willing to be the devil's puppet and ruin a girl's future?"

Randy stared down at the desk. "Leave me your number, Marina. When I get a court time, I'll call so you can be there. You should probably find a lawyer."

He never looked back up and Marina knew that was as far as things would go with him. Preston held all the cards. Again. She grabbed a pad off his desk, jotted her phone number on it, and practically threw it back at him. How the hell was she supposed to find a lawyer when the only one in town was Preston? And on such short notice. Was there even such a thing as a public defender for a place like Last Chance? Good Lord, she was so far out of her territory that she wasn't even on the map anymore.

"Can I see her, at least?" Marina asked. "Unless Preston has video cameras in the sheriff's department, he'll never know. His spy left when we came in."

Randy blushed and grabbed a set of keys from his desk. Then he headed out of the office without so much as saying a word and they followed him to the end of the hall where the holding cells were. As he unlocked the metal door that led to the cells, Marina grabbed Halcyon's hand.

"I've never seen a jail cell before," she whispered. "Randy never put Letitia in one."

"I have," Halcyon said. "Don't worry. We've got this."

But for the first time in as long as Marina could remember, her sister's voice didn't hold the same confidence that it usually did.

Randy pushed the door open. "I'll be back in ten minutes."

Marina walked through the door and into a space in front of the two holding cells. The instant Avery saw her come in, she jumped up from the cot she'd been sitting on and ran for the bars.

"Mom!" she said.

Marina put her arms through the bars and tried to hug her daughter. She could tell Avery had been crying and her heart broke all over again. Damn Harold. She didn't even care about the affair anymore but why did it have to be Chastity? Why did he have to pick the one person that would make his daughter even more miserable than Marina?

Marina released Avery and studied her face. Her daughter

was clearly stressed and upset but there was still a bit of anger lurking. Good. They hadn't broken her spirit. If that had happened, Marina didn't think she would have been able to handle it.

"What happened?" Marina asked. "Why aren't you at school?"

Avery sniffed. "I didn't want to believe it. I mean, you never lie and I checked with Simone, but it just all sounded so f...messed up."

"So you came here to confront your dad?" Marina asked.

Avery nodded. "But she was *there*. Mom, you know I'm not extra, but she started flexing on Dad and that thot was wearing my clothes!"

"Jesus H. Christ!" Marina's carefully contained control flew out the window. Just when she'd started to believe that nothing about the situation could surprise her anymore, Harold sank to a new low.

"I didn't understand any of that," Halcyon said.

"I'll explain later," Marina said and looked back at Avery. "Tell me what happened."

"I told her to take off my clothes and she refused, so I jumped her," Avery said. "She ran out the door with them on. That's stealing, right? Dad can't give her permission to take something that belongs to me, can he?"

"I don't think so," Marina said, but she really had no idea. Even more reason to need an attorney. "So you followed her?"

"Yeah, I grabbed her by my shirt when she went for her car door."

"Did you hit her in the face?"

"Damn right I did! Just like you taught me."

"That was meant for if you were being attacked," Marina said.

"I was being attacked. And robbed. Don't forget that part."

Marina's stomach rolled. This was bad. So incredibly bad. Avery didn't stand a chance in Last Chance. Kyle and Randy were both beholden to Preston and the judge was his second cousin. Even if she could get a jury trial—which Marina had zero idea about—how many locals were also obligated to Preston in some form or fashion? And if the university even got wind that Avery was being charged, they could revoke her scholarships, or worse, kick her out if she was convicted. Good God, what if she was convicted?

"Okay," Marina said, trying to hold it together in front of Avery. "Randy didn't give us much time so I'm going to have to leave soon. He's trying to get you in front of the judge today. I'll see what I need to do. But I don't want you to worry, okay? This isn't your fault."

Avery looked down at the floor. "Yes. It is. I lost it. I'm so sorry."

"Baby, you have nothing to be sorry for," Marina said. "Just try to stay calm and let me handle this, okay?"

Avery nodded and looked back up at Marina, her eyes filling with tears. "I love you, Mom. I know I never say it, but I do."

Marina reached through the bars and squeezed Avery's hand. "I know you do. I'll be back as soon as I know something. Just hang in there."

The door opened and Randy stuck his head in. "Time's up."

Marina practically ran out of the sheriff's department. As soon as she slammed the door on her car, she burst into tears. Halcyon reached across the center console and wrapped her arms around her.

"Let it out, honey," Halcyon said. "Upset always comes first but mad is on the way, I promise you."

"I'm pretty sure it's arrived," Marina coughed and choked out a few more cries before stopping. She pulled back and looked at Halcyon. "I can't believe this. Everything I've spent my entire life working for is falling apart."

"I know it feels that way, but we can handle this."

"No. It doesn't just feel that way. It *is* that way. If Chastity doesn't drop those charges, Avery will lose her scholarship. I can't afford to pay for the university and even if Harold could, why would he? He didn't even care enough to keep that tramp out of Avery's closet."

"We'll find an attorney, okay?"

But Marina could tell that Halcyon was as worried as she was. "Where? Do you have a gentleman caller with a law degree? Because the only one in Last Chance is siding with the enemy. Along with the deputy, the sheriff, and the judge. We're in big trouble here. I don't even know where to start."

"Start with explaining what the hell happened. I feel like Avery was talking in another language."

"She was. Teen. Basically, Avery isn't extra, which means overly dramatic."

Halcyon stared. "Avery doesn't think she's overly dramatic?"

"She certainly appears to have been in this situation, but in regular teen world, she's not. Trust me, I went into an online forum for teens to see if I could figure out lingo and stuff, and I almost had a heart attack at what those kids were up to. Avery is high-maintenance but she's not regular teen drama."

"Okay, so what was the rest of that?"

"Chastity was flexing about Harold, which is showing him off. That, combined with the clothes thing, set Avery off."

"And rightfully so. Why doesn't Preston give his daughter a bigger allowance so that she can get her own clothes? So what's this 'thot' thing?"

Marina sighed. "Shorthand for that ho over there."

Halcyon stared at Marina for a couple seconds, then burst out laughing. "Oh my God. That's awesome. I'm so sorry. I don't mean to laugh. Actually, I do."

Halcyon took a minute to pull herself together, then blew out a breath. "Okay. So the first order of business is a lawyer, right?"

"No. The first order of business is Harold. He needs to get his sidepiece to back off pressing charges."

"You can try, but I wouldn't expect much. Harold is deep in the new-nooky fog. My guess is that Little Miss Chastity can't do any wrong."

Marina started her car and pulled away. "He better get out of the fog before he loses his daughter."

She drove by the CPA office but Harold's car wasn't in his parking space so she headed for the house and pulled in behind his shiny new Mercedes. She stomped up to the front door and banged on it.

"What the hell are you doing?" Halcyon asked. "Open the door."

"I threw my key in the bayou the day I moved out."

"Good grief." Halcyon dug in her purse and pulled out a key, then unlocked the door. "It's Halcyon and Marina," she called out. "I suggest you get out here where there are multiple escape routes because you don't want me to corner you."

There was a noise from the master bedroom and a minute later, Harold shuffled into the living room. He didn't bother to say anything. Just stood there looking impotent.

"Avery is in jail," Marina said. "Locked up in a cell like an animal. You let them take her."

"What was I supposed to do?" Harold asked. "Deputy Pitre arrested her. I couldn't stop him."

"You didn't even call me," Marina said. "I had to hear about this from Adelaide. That's our daughter! I know you don't care about me, but how could you abandon her?"

Harold stared at the floor, shaking his head. "There was nothing I could do."

"Maybe not then, although I doubt it," Marina said. "But you can certainly do something now. You can call off your little girlfriend. If this goes to court, Avery will lose her scholarship. Her future. She's already lost her father. How much more should she pay for your bad decisions?"

"Don't you think I tried?" Harold said. "I've been begging Chastity all morning to drop the charges. But she won't back down. And the truth is Avery *did* attack her."

"Completely and totally unprovoked, right?" Marina asked. "Because sweet Chastity would never do anything to rub salt into a wound. Especially to Avery, who she's always had a problem with."

Harold's shoulders slumped. "I can't change her mind. Avery should have never come here."

"Shouldn't have come where? Her home?" Anger coursed through Marina. "You shouldn't have cheated! And definitely not with Chastity LeDoux. You picked the worst person possible and you know it. The least you can do is get your little pet in line. Clearly, she has daddy issues, so tell her to drop the charges or you're going to ground her."

Harold's jaw tightened. "I already told you there's nothing I can do."

"Unbelievable," Halcyon said. "I always thought you were a limp dick. Turns out that body part went missing right along with your common sense and your backbone. The least you can do is cough up money for the attorney we need to find. Your daughter is in jail, Harold. Jail!"

"There's no money," he said quietly.

Marina and Halcyon looked at each other, then back at Harold.

"What do you mean, there's no money?" Marina asked. "We've lived well beneath our means our entire lives. Where did it go?"

"I made some bad investments, okay?" Harold said.

"Like hair plugs, and veneers, and your new Mercedes?" Marina said.

"Don't forget Chastity," Halcyon said. "How much have you wasted on her?"

"What does it matter now?" Harold asked. "Marina already took half of everything in our accounts."

Marina felt the blood drain from her face. "That was it? That was every dime we had?"

Harold nodded.

"Oh my God," Marina said. "What have I done with my life? All that time spent working until my hands ached, then taking care of this house and Avery and you. And I have nothing to show for it except a daughter who will have a record and no college education and a husband who pissed our entire life's work away on a whore. Everything I've done is a failure."

She whirled around and ran out the door.

"Marina, wait!" Harold yelled after her, but she didn't slow.

As soon as Halcyon climbed into her car, Marina shot backward out of the driveway while her sister struggled to get the door closed. As she tore off down the street, Halcyon buckled her seat belt and made the sign of the cross.

"We're Baptist!" Marina yelled.

"I'm nervous, okay?"

The genuine fear in her sister's voice made her immediately lift her foot off the accelerator. As the car slowed to a stop in

151

the middle of the road, the breath Halcyon had been holding came out in a whoosh.

"I'm sorry," Marina said. "I don't even know what I'm doing anymore. I don't know what to do next. Do I pull over and use my phone to try to find an attorney? Do I drive home? Or maybe into the bayou?"

"You drive to my house," Halcyon said. "And we'll use my computer to find an attorney. Maybe there's one in Double Deuces that can handle something last-minute."

Someone knocked on Marina's window and she yelped. She looked up and saw Adelaide staring down at her, her normally dour expression full of concern.

"Adelaide," Marina said as soon as she lowered the window. "Thank you so much for calling me."

"Of course," Adelaide said. "Is Avery all right?"

"Not really," Marina said and gave the older woman a quick rundown of the situation.

Adelaide let out a stream of cursing that Halcyon gave a nod of approval, then she sucked in a breath and blew it out.

"Somebody has got to do something about the LeDoux before they ruin this town," Adelaide said.

"That would be awesome," Marina said, "especially if they could accomplish it today. But no one has the clout or the nerve or whatever it would take."

"Balls," Adelaide said. "And this town is running short on those as well."

"Except for some of the women," Halcyon said.

"Goes without saying," Adelaide said. "Is there anything I can do?"

"Not unless you have an attorney in your pocket," Marina said.

Adelaide frowned. "I just might. I've got a distant cousin who just moved here. He has a law degree, but he didn't like it so he quit. But as far as I know, he's still licensed."

"What didn't he like?" Halcyon asked.

"From my understanding, he hated the politics and all the shady stuff," Adelaide said. "He had some high ideals about making a difference and found out quick-like that it wasn't possible with all the corruption and red tape and stupid laws."

"Sounds like just the experience we need," Marina said. "Do you think he'd help?"

"I think he might," Adelaide said. "He's a good sort. I'm sure he'd be hacked off about the situation, given all the shadiness. And he definitely wouldn't want a young girl paying for bad adult behavior. His father was no prize."

"Who is he?" Halcyon asked. "I can't recall seeing anyone new lately."

"He's a bit of a loner, from what I understand," Adelaide said. "Went back to school and got a master's in forestry after he dropped the lawyering gig. He's the new game warden."

Marina sucked in a breath and Adelaide stared down at her.

"You've met him?" Adelaide asked.

"Sort of," Marina said. "We had a bit of a run-in last night when he mistook me for a poacher."

"Good, then he owes you," Adelaide said. "I'll give him a call and explain the situation."

"I don't..." Marina started. "I'm not sure..."

"Do it, Adelaide," Halcyon said, then looked at Marina. "We don't have many last-minute options here. Actually, more like none. Anyone is better than Marina and me trying to handle it ourselves."

Marina blew out a breath, trying to wrap her mind around the many exploded pieces of her life. "You're right. And thank you, Adelaide. For everything. I owe you big-time."

"I'll collect later in hair rolls," Adelaide said. "I'll go call right now. You girls might want to make some notes for Luke. He won't have much time to get up to speed."

"That's a good idea," Halcyon said. "That way, we're not emotionally rambling and getting off course ranting about the LeDoux."

Adelaide gave them a wave and headed toward her house. Marina put the car in gear and headed down the street, wondering if her life would ever be normal again.

CHAPTER SIXTEEN

HALCYON PACED BACK and forth across her kitchen as Marina typed notes onto her laptop. Adelaide had been right about jotting things down. Putting them in writing had forced her to be succinct and detailed at the same time. And time was something they couldn't afford to waste. Unfortunately, her sister's pacing was interfering with her scattered mind's ability to think clearly.

"Can you please sit down for a minute?" Marina asked.

"If I sit, I'll want to start smoking or eating," Halcyon said. "And since I gave up the first years ago and need to give up most of the second, this is my new way of dealing with stress."

"And normally, I'd agree that it's an awesome option, but it's distracting and I'm only one step away from a room next to my mother's."

Halcyon perched on a stool next to her. "Why don't you text Alexios? He's part god. If this treasure hunt is so important, surely they'd be willing to help."

Marina stopped typing and nodded. "I've been thinking about it, but what if Zeus's idea of fixing things is wiping out all the LeDoux?"

"Then we'd all wear red for a month?"

"Stop joking. I don't want them dead. I just want them to leave Avery alone. And in the big scheme of things, to stop riding herd over this town."

"But who's to say the gods can't make that happen? It doesn't hurt to ask."

"I suppose you're right." She pulled out her phone and sent Alexios a text. A couple minutes later, he knocked on Halcyon's front door.

"Why didn't you just come in?" Halcyon asked as she let him inside. "It's not like the lock would have stopped you."

"Yes, but it's rude to enter a person's home without permission, especially if you've never been there before," Alexios said.

"You came into my home without permission," Marina said.

"Because you wouldn't have let me in otherwise," Alexios said. "But this is your sister's home. Not yours. So I'm back to rude. I abhor rude."

"Good," Halcyon said. "Then you'll be first in line to help with our current predicament. The people involved take rude to a professional level. Actually, they've progressed so far beyond rude that if they could just get back there, everyone would probably celebrate."

Alexios frowned. "I take it your world has produced problems of a personal level, somehow involving these beyond-rude people?"

Marina nodded and gave Alexios a rundown of the situation with Avery. He listened intently but without a change in expression, and when she finished, he sat in silence for so long that Marina wondered if he was in some sort of trance.

Finally, he sighed. "I'm afraid there's nothing I can do."

"Why the hell not?" Halcyon asked. "Your boss is a god.

And not just any god—the head god. Seems to me that something like this should be a snap for him."

"And under normal circumstances, that would be the case," Alexios said. "But I'm afraid the circumstances right now are anything but normal."

"What do you mean?" Marina asked.

"I've lost contact with our world," Alexios said. "I tried to transport home last night but I was blocked. All channels of communication with them are cut off."

"Is that normal?" Marina asked.

"It's never happened before," he said.

"Then how can it happen now?" Halcyon asked.

"Two ways that I can think of," he said. "Either Zeus closed everything down to prevent an invasion there and anyone from tracking me here, or the invaders have gained control. I'm really hoping it's the first one."

"Invaders?" Marina asked.

"From another world," Alexios said. "We think the faction from our world that is attempting to take control has aligned themselves with some group from another world."

"Holy crap!" Halcyon said. "How many other worlds are looking to knock off another species?"

"You probably don't want to know," Alexios said. "It would just make it harder to sleep at night."

Marina threw her hands in the air. "Then what good does it do to find the ring if you can't even get it back to them?"

"If Zeus closed everything down as a preventive measure, he'll get word to me somehow," Alexios said. "And he'll arrange a way for me to communicate any success with the search so that the ring can be safely returned to our world."

"And if your world was taken by the enemy?" Halcyon asked.

"Then your personal crisis won't matter," he said quietly. "Nothing will matter."

Marina's thoughts whirled as his words sank in. If she chose to believe the ring existed and that she had some sort of special calling, then she didn't have the luxury of ignoring the negative aspects of the situation. Very negative aspects. And his expression left no doubt that Alexios was seriously worried. In fact, he looked stressed out of his wits.

"Isn't there something you can do?" Halcyon asked. "You're half god, right? Doesn't that count for something?"

Alexios frowned. "I'm afraid my godly abilities only extend to not being killed by your weaponry, walking through locked doors, and living in an invisible condo. I can't see that those would help."

"They might," Halcyon said. "If we need to spring Avery from prison and stash her somewhere, I'd say you're first on our list to call."

"No one's going to prison," Marina said, her breath catching in her throat. She looked at Alexios. "Okay. All of this sounds really, really bad. What do I need to do?"

"What you've already agreed to do," he said.

"How the hell is she supposed to bop around playing *Lord of the Rings* when her daughter is sitting in jail?" Halcyon asked. "Do you understand what kind of stress that places on a mother? Mothers have killed people because their daughters didn't make cheerleading teams. I think this is a bit worse."

"I suppose killing this woman pressing charges is an option," Alexios said. "Unfortunately, I can't do it."

"Why not?" Halcyon asked. "You could do the job and whisk away in your magical condo. No harm. No foul. Unless you don't have the stomach for such things."

"It's not my stomach that's in question," he said. "It's against our rules for any of us to kill humans. There were too many using your kind as entertainment and Zeus didn't like it. Except in the case of self-defense, if we kill a human, we go to the gods' equivalent of prison. And trust me, what you have here is the Ritz-Carlton compared to where Zeus sends you."

"What?" Halcyon asked. "Does he send you to Hades?"

"Yes, actually." Alexios glanced up, clearly uncomfortable.

"Jeez," Halcyon said. "I was joking."

"Yeah, well, Zeus isn't big on jokes," he said. "Not unless he's the one making them."

"Typical," Halcyon said.

"No one is getting killed," Marina said. "Not by us, at least. I'll figure something out."

"Find the ring," Alexios said. "With a million dollars, you can buy Avery's way into any university she wants to attend."

Halcyon raised an eyebrow. "You don't watch the news in our world, do you? Buying your kid's way into a university isn't a good look for parents right now."

"It wouldn't matter," Marina said. "If this gets to a conviction, no medical school will accept her anyway. A doctor is all she's ever wanted to be."

Alexios nodded, looking sad. "I understand. And I'm so sorry I can't help. Despite your questionable wardrobe choices, I really like you, Marina. And these LeDoux sound like they could use a karmic adjustment. If anything changes on my end, I'll let you know."

He shuffled out and Halcyon checked the porch before turning back to Marina.

"That still freaks me out a little," she said.

Marina nodded but her thoughts weren't on Alexios and his invisible condo.

"What if Luke won't help us?" Marina asked. "There's no way we can find an attorney who will come here today. And you and I don't know enough to keep Avery from being railroaded."

"You mean our last name isn't LeDoux."

Marina's cell phone rang. Adelaide.

"I talked to Luke," Adelaide said as soon as she answered. "I told him it was an emergency and to get to Halcyon's house now. He should be there in a couple of minutes. I still have that sharpened shovel."

Adelaide hung up before Marina could even reply.

"Well?" Halcyon asked.

"Luke will be here in a few minutes and Adelaide's shovel is still sharpened."

"Good God, I'm going to have to start liking that old broad." Halcyon looked over at her and narrowed her eyes. "What's that constipated expression for? I haven't seen it since high school, when you had a crush on Mark Walker and had to partner with him on a science project."

Damn Halcyon and her mind reading. Or face reading.

Marina sighed. "When Luke thought I was a poacher, I might have been wearing my pajamas when I ran out of the cabin after Snooze."

Halcyon stared. "Post-hot-flash pajamas or pre?"

"Pre, but I'd just gotten out of the shower. A very hot shower."

Halcyon put her hand over her mouth but she couldn't stop the laughter that was intent on coming. It started with a giggle, then went on to full-out chortling.

"Oh my God," she said when she finally caught her breath. "You were totally rocking a tank and undies. Were they sexy undies at least?"

"Does it matter?"

"It does if this Luke is good-looking."

Marina sighed. "Bright pink boy shorts."

"Nice. This is going to be interesting."

Marina shook her head. She'd had enough interesting to last a lifetime. What she desperately wanted right now was boring.

Absolutely. Stunningly. Boring.

———

MARINA WAS ALMOST to heart attack point when Luke knocked on Halcyon's door. She was strung so tight she actually snapped the handle right off the coffee mug she'd been holding. Fortunately, it was empty, although she had no idea when she'd actually drunk the coffee her sister had poured her. Maybe she should cut back on the caffeine.

She shook her head. Who was she kidding? Death was the only way to decrease her current level of stress.

Luke introduced himself to Halcyon, who pointed to the kitchen and strolled behind him, mouthing to Marina, "He is *so* hot!"

Marina ignored her completely. Unless Judge Leger had started batting for the other team, Luke's hotness wasn't going to make a bit of difference to the job ahead of him. Marina hopped off her stool and extended her hand as he walked into the room.

"Thank you so much for coming," she said. "I'm sure Adelaide told you how desperate the situation is."

He nodded. "She gave me the highlights reel. I'm really sorry you're going through this—all of it. Can you tell me what happened?"

Marina relayed what Avery had told her, deviating occasionally to throw in some backstory when he asked questions to clarify. When she was done, he shook his head.

"And this girl's father is the local sue-happy lawyer, whom half the town is in debt to?" he asked.

"I'm afraid so," Marina said. "And it gets worse. Judge Leger is his second cousin."

A flash of anger passed across his face and he shook his head. "This is exactly the sort of thing that sent me into the woods, away from people."

Marina felt her chest tighten. "If you don't want to help, I completely understand."

"No," he said. "That's not it at all. I definitely want to help. I'm just trying to figure out the best way that I can, given all the things stacked against you. How long has this Judge Leger been in office?"

"I don't know," Marina said. "Twenty years? Maybe longer?"

"And when is the next election?" he asked.

"Next year," Halcyon said.

"And can I assume he's not interested in retirement any time soon?" he asked.

"No way," Marina said. "He'd die in that chair if the state would let him."

"Besides," Halcyon said, "there's no one to run against him. That's why he's still in the seat. Young blood doesn't want a career out here in the sticks, and the older ones couldn't beat him or they already would have."

"Sounds familiar," he said. "But it's not entirely unworkable. People like Leger act like they're untouchable but if he's not interested in giving up his seat, then he'll be constantly watching for any challengers and avoiding anything that might sway a vote to new blood. It's possible to find someone younger who'd live out in the sticks. Trust me, a lot of us grow weary of bigger-city politics and hassle after a few years."

"Unless you can whip up a threat by this afternoon, I'm not sure how much good could come of it," Marina said. "What do

I need to do? What's going to happen? I'm sorry for all the questions, but I've never done this before."

"Most decent people haven't," Luke said. "First, I need to see Avery."

"But the sheriff—" Marina started.

"Don't worry about him," Luke said. "The sheriff is legally bound to let me see my client. I'll talk to her and prepare her for her appearance in front of the judge. She'll plead not guilty and we'll ask for bail. Given that it's a first offense, I would normally say it wouldn't be high, but in this situation, he might push the envelope. You be prepared to post bail and we'll have Avery out by this evening."

Marina let out a breath of relief. "Really?"

"I can't imagine him denying bail," he said. "Even given the circumstances. There's simply no grounds. Your daughter is not a threat to anyone but Chastity and she's hardly a flight risk. He will probably issue a restraining order for her to stay away from Chastity, though."

"How is she supposed to do that when Harold has that thing living in Avery's house?" Halcyon asked.

"Unfortunately, that's where your husband comes into the equation," Luke said. "If he kicks Avery out of the house, then she can't return there, and it doesn't sound like he's interested in being a good parent at the moment. Avery lives on campus, right?"

"Yes, but she still has a room full of things at Harold's house," Marina said. "It's not like she left for college expecting her entire life to explode back in Last Chance."

"Of course not," Luke said. "But to prevent Chastity from inciting any more violence, it might be a good idea to get Avery's things out of the house."

"Unbelievable," Marina said. "It's bad enough I find myself

homeless at forty-eight, but now Avery is homeless at eighteen. None of this is right."

"She can live here," Halcyon said. "You've only got one bedroom at the cabin. I have the spare room and plenty of storage for Avery's stuff. Not like she's going to be here much anyway, but she'll have a safe place for her things and won't have to worry about coming to visit and seeing things that put her in the red. At least, not in the place she's calling home."

"I think that's a really good idea," Luke said. "Unless you have any more questions for me, I'm going to try to negotiate something with the DA first. Then I'll head up to the sheriff's department and get Avery ready. I need you to document everything you can about the LeDoux and Avery's history with Chastity. It would also help if I knew which players were beholden to Preston."

Marina gave him a grateful look. "I don't know how to thank you, much less repay you."

He shook his head. "I wouldn't take payment for this. Besides, I've owed Adelaide a favor for a long time."

He gave them both a smile and headed out. Halcyon closed the door behind him, then went back into the kitchen to give Marina a hug.

"This is going to work out," she said.

"How is this going to work out?" Marina asked. "Unless Chastity decides not to press charges, which we both know isn't going to happen, Avery is going to trial."

"They might offer a plea deal," Halcyon said. "Something that isn't a felony. Remember, that's not Judge Leger's decision. If the DA wants to make a deal, then he will. And as far as I know, the LeDoux don't have a connection there."

"As far as you know."

CHAPTER SEVENTEEN

Two hours later, Avery got her opportunity to stand before the judge. Luke had attempted to bargain with the DA, but he'd held firm on felony assault. Chastity's nose was broken and had been set. Her father had beaten Luke to the DA's office and provided pictures of the nose, complete with all the blood on her scantily clad torso, and her eyes, which already had dark marks circling them.

It wasn't really surprising, as Halcyon had done some poking around and found out from a friend of the drummer that the DA had a young girlfriend his wife didn't know about. If Halcyon could get that information with a couple of phone calls, so could Preston LeDoux. The DA wasn't going to be any help.

Luke was waiting for them at the courthouse when they arrived. He'd exchanged his jeans and T-shirt for a suit and dress shoes and Marina had to admit he looked the part. He'd even attempted to comb his slightly long locks into a more professional look.

"This shouldn't take long," he said as they walked inside. "All Avery will have to do is plead not guilty, then I'll ask for bail. This part is easy so please don't worry. You'll have Avery home this evening."

Marina felt somewhat reassured given his confidence. Halcyon, who'd remained insistent that everything would be fine, relaxed a bit, and Marina knew her sister was far more worried than she was letting on. They went inside and took seats. Judge Leger glanced at them as they sat and he frowned. Preston LeDoux sat directly behind the DA and shot an openly hostile look at Marina. It was all she could do not to give him the finger.

"I'd love to slap that smug look right off his face," Halcyon whispered as they sat.

Marina nodded. Slapping him did sound more satisfying than the finger. Unfortunately, neither option helped Avery. A door on the side of the courtroom opened and the sheriff walked through with Avery.

In handcuffs.

A wave of nausea passed over Marina and she felt herself sway in her seat. Halcyon put an arm around her shoulders to steady her, but Marina could feel her sister shaking as she squeezed. Marina had never seen her daughter so scared. So defeated.

The nausea fled and anger coursed into its place. If Harold were in sight, Judge Leger would be hearing a plea on two assault charges. Marina was so mad that her chest and head felt as if they would burst. She clenched her jaw, grinding her teeth together to keep from screaming. Her hands formed fists so tight that her nails dug into her palms. The pain barely registered.

Harold, the life ruiner and coward, hadn't even bothered to show his face.

If Marina had felt even a moment of doubt about her marriage ending, it was gone. Nothing he could do would ever make up for not being in this courtroom, supporting his daughter over the situation he had created. Marina was certain she'd never hated anyone more in her life.

Avery looked over at her and Marina gave her what she hoped was a reassuring nod. Avery didn't need her anger right now. She needed support. If Avery could sense that Marina thought everything would be all right, then Avery would think everything would be all right. Despite all her noisemaking about being an adult, Avery still wasn't mature enough to handle this. Not on her own.

The bailiff called them to session and Judge Leger rapped his gavel. He motioned to the sheriff, who had Avery stand, then to the DA, who rose and presented the charges against Avery. When the DA was done, the judge looked at Luke.

"Please introduce yourself to the court," Judge Leger said.

Luke rose. "Luke Abshire. Counsel for the defendant."

"I don't believe I've had you in my court before, Mr. Abshire," Judge Leger said. "I was under the impression you were the game warden."

"That's correct, Your Honor. But I hold a law degree and am licensed to practice in Louisiana. I'm representing Ms. Trahan."

Judge Leger looked somewhat confused and definitely displeased but he turned to look at Avery. "Ms. Trahan, how do you plead?"

"Not guilty," Avery said, and Marina's heart clenched at how scared she sounded.

"Your Honor," the DA began, "we're asking that bail be denied. Even though this is her first offense, Ms. Trahan is an adult, not a child. Given that Last Chance is a small town and Ms. Trahan's attack on Ms. LeDoux produced some horrific injuries, we feel she's a danger if released."

Marina started to bolt up and yell, but Halcyon grabbed

her arm and kept her from making a huge mistake. For the first time, Halcyon was the one holding Marina back. It was usually the other way around.

"Your Honor," Luke said, "Ms. Trahan attends the university in New Orleans. Once she meets bail, she'll be returning there to pursue her studies."

"I don't think she should be allowed to leave town," the DA said.

"Why not?" Luke asked. "She's hardly a flight risk. She doesn't even have a passport. Besides, the alleged victim was in the process of stealing Ms. Trahan's property when Ms. Trahan accosted her. If she'd returned the stolen items without hesitation, all of this could have been avoided."

The DA's eyes widened as he realized this was not going as he'd intended. "Ms. LeDoux had permission from your client's father to borrow the clothing. That hardly represents a robbery."

Luke smiled. "But as you've already pointed out—Ms. Trahan is not a minor. So her father can't give permission concerning her property. Even though the domicile is deeded in her father's name, it's still my client's residence. She has rights."

Halcyon reached for Marina's hand and squeezed the life out of it. Marina was fairly certain she'd stopped breathing. Luke had put the DA firmly in his place.

Luke looked back at the judge. "I'm sure if this goes to trial and the extenuating circumstances are all presented, you'll see that Ms. Trahan was well within her rights and that charges against Ms. LeDoux are in line. In the meantime, I'm certain you wouldn't want to upset your constituency by condemning a young woman to sit in jail over a catfight."

Judge Leger looked as if he'd sucked on lemons. Luke's implication was clear, punish Avery for what her father did and the voters might turn against him. And now that Luke was in Last Chance, and waving a law degree around, there was always the lingering possibility that he might run against the judge in the next election.

"Bail is set at one hundred thousand," Judge Leger said. He banged his gavel and immediately jumped up from his seat and headed out of the courtroom before anyone could protest.

Marina sucked in a breath. "A hundred thousand? Are you kidding me? I don't have that kind of money."

The sheriff grabbed Avery's arm and motioned for her to leave. She gave Marina a pleading look before heading out the door. Luke hurried over and Marina could tell he was mad.

"What am I going to do?" Marina asked. "I don't have a hundred thousand dollars."

"Do you have ten thousand?" he asked.

"Yes."

"That's what a bail bondsman will require. There's one just down from the courthouse." He handed her a piece of paper. "Give him this information and have him bond her out.

"Marina?" he looked at her, clearly waiting for a response.

"Yes," she said. "I'm sorry. Yes, I'll take the paper to him and get him the money. Thank you so much. I don't even know what to say...there's no way I could have..."

"I'm glad I could help, but if this farce goes to trial, you're going to need a stronger attorney than me. Preferably one with better connections than Preston LeDoux."

Marina nodded but she couldn't think about that now. Right now, all she could think about was getting the bail bondsman the money so that Avery wouldn't have to spend the night in jail. Luke gave her shoulder a quick squeeze and nodded to Halcyon before heading out. Marina turned around and saw Adelaide shaking his hand before he left. She shook her head as Marina approached.

"I ought to put a load of buckshot in that Leger's butt," Adelaide said.

"I'd shoot for the front," Halcyon said.

Adelaide looked at her and nodded. "One day, you and I are going to have drinks and plot our takeover of this town."

"Count on it," Halcyon said.

"Go get your girl out of that jail," Adelaide said. "I've got spies all over this town. If the LeDoux try something, I'll let you know what they're up to."

Adelaide hurried off and Marina stared.

"That woman is full of surprises," Marina said.

"So was Luke," Halcyon said as they headed into the parking lot. "I thought Leger was going to pop a vein."

"He didn't think we'd find representation. And he likely figured even if we did, it would be someone who would kowtow to him."

"Good thing we sprang Luke on them last-minute. They didn't have time to dig up some dirt on him."

"You're assuming there is some."

"Everyone has some dirt, even if it's just something embarrassing."

"I suppose you're right. Still, he seems like a nice guy."

Halcyon's eyes narrowed. "You like him."

Marina felt a blush creep up her face. "Of course I like him. He just kept Avery from sitting in jail until trial."

"That's not what I meant and you know it."

"I don't know him well enough to like him that way."

"Okay. I'll give you that, but you're attracted to him. Why is that so hard to admit?"

"Because I don't do instant attraction. That's your field of expertise. And I just left my husband three days ago, and my daughter is looking at a felony conviction over Harold's dumbassery, and none of this insanity matters at all if I don't find the ring before the bad guys take over the universe."

Halcyon shrugged. "So the timing's not great."

Marina stared at her sister for a couple seconds, then laughed. "You are really something."

Halcyon grinned. "That's what they all tell me."

CHAPTER EIGHTEEN

THE BAIL BONDSMAN, Mike Thompson, was a guy Marina and Halcyon had gone to school with. He'd also managed to coax Halcyon into a couple of dates. He was rough around the edges and would scare the crap out of someone in a dark alley, but Marina supposed that was what made him good at his job. People were afraid to cross him. In reality, he'd always been nice and polite when Marina had run into him in town. His expression when they entered his office was one of surprise, but pleasantly so.

He waved them to two chairs in front of his desk. "I can't imagine what I could do for you two. Are you collecting for some local charity?"

"I wish that were the case," Marina said and handed him the paper Luke had given her. "I need to bail my daughter out of jail."

His eyes widened as he unfolded the paper. "Avery's in jail?"

He scanned the document and Marina could see his jaw flex.

"What is this about?" he asked. "If you don't mind my asking."

Marina gave him the short version of the fight, figuring he already knew the prequel part. He spent the entire time shaking his head in disbelief.

"I'm so sorry," he said. "Avery is a good kid and neither of you deserves this. I gotta be honest, I never liked Harold and always wondered what you saw in him, but I don't pretend to understand women all that well. My wife tends to agree that I'm clueless."

"Don't worry," Halcyon said. "You've got plenty of company."

He nodded. "I can't stand the LeDoux and could give you all kinds of reasons on that one. I'm not alone there either."

"You're not," Marina agreed. "But since most of the town is financially obligated, hiding something, or otherwise scared of a lawsuit, the LeDoux have the upper hand."

He tapped on his computer and entered some things into a form. "This will take me an hour or better to get processed. I have to get the money transferred and the paperwork filed."

"But you can get her out today?" Marina asked.

He nodded. "But you gotta keep her away from the LeDoux. If they even catch sight of her, I wouldn't put it past them to accuse her of threatening them just to get her tossed back in."

"I can't afford another round of bail," Marina said. "This one is taking most of what I have."

He gave her a sympathetic look. "I'm sorry I've got to take your money, especially for this. But you'll get it back, less a bit of a fee, once it's all over."

"Please don't feel bad," Marina said. "You have to follow the rules and this is your business. You're not responsible for any of this."

"No, but Harold is," he said. "Why isn't he here taking care of this? He's the money man."

"That's a long story," Marina said.

He stared at her for a second, then gave her a single nod. "I see."

Marina got the impression that he had read in between and beyond the lines. She supposed he'd seen and heard most every tale of woe in his line of work, and they probably weren't all that unique. It bothered her more than she'd ever admit that her entire existence had become a cliché.

"If you don't need us to stay," Halcyon said, "we can go collect her things from Harold's now. That way, when we pick her up, we can go straight to my house."

"And ship her back to college first thing tomorrow morning," Marina said.

"I think that's a really good idea," Mike said. "Can't nothing else be put on her if she's not here. And I'd tell her to make darn sure she's always in someone else's company back at college."

Marina stared. "You think she needs to have an alibi for every minute of the day?"

He shrugged. "It doesn't hurt. I've seen some things..."

Marina blew out a breath. Thank God there were people who knew how to handle these things, because that was something that never would have crossed her mind.

"All I need is your phone number and you two can get out of here and take care of your other business," he said. "I'll call when everything's been processed and meet you down at the sheriff's department with the paperwork."

"Oh, I don't want to put you out," Marina said. "I can stop and pick up the paperwork."

He shook his head. "The sheriff's beholden to that dick Preston LeDoux, one of the deputies is a relation, and the other has one foot out the door. If I'm there, no one will even think about causing problems. They won't try anything in front of a witness."

"Thank you." Marina stood and reached across the desk to shake his hand. "I really appreciate everything you're doing. I wouldn't even begin to know..."

"'Course you wouldn't," he said as he rose. "You're good people. You're not supposed to know how to do any of this and it's a damned shame you're having to do it now."

They headed out and Marina drove straight to Harold's house. Avery's car was still parked at the curb and his was in the driveway, so Marina strode onto the porch and banged on the door as hard as she could. A couple seconds later, Harold opened the door a crack and stared out at her.

"What do you want?" he asked, his voice wavering.

Unbelievable! He was actually scared of her.

"I'm here to collect Avery's things," she said as she shoved the door open. "Since you've decided to be no help with the devastation you've caused, what I *want* is for you to get out of my way."

"I want him to drop dead where he's standing," Halcyon said.

"Maybe tomorrow," Marina said. "We're too busy today. Halcyon, there's some boxes and packing tape in the storage space under the stairs."

Harold's eyes widened as she pushed past him and she heard him retreating down the hall as she stomped up the stairs to Avery's room. Most of her summer clothes had gone with her to college but as she didn't have the space there that she had here, some summer items remained, as well as her cooler-weather stuff. And then there was her personal stuff—ribbons and trophies and pictures of her friends. Stuffed animals, books, and other dust collectors.

Halcyon came in with an armful of boxes and the tape and

they went to work. Marina removed entire drawers from the dresser and dumped the contents in a box. Halcyon gathered all the clothes hanging in the closet and did the same. Then they used the sheets and pillows to cushion the breakables. It wasn't neat work, but it was efficient. In forty-five minutes, they had everything in boxes and started the cumbersome process of carrying them downstairs and stuffing them into Marina's and Avery's cars. Harold never appeared again.

By the time they had dumped all the boxes in Halcyon's living room, Marina's phone rang and Mike let her know that everything was in place for Avery's release. Marina clutched the steering wheel as she drove to the sheriff's department. Would Mike being there prevent a confrontation? Would Preston show up just to make things miserable? Would Avery have a meltdown? She'd never had one before. Not the emotional kind. Marina wasn't even sure she knew how to handle one if she did.

Mike was waiting for them outside the sheriff's department and gave Marina a reassuring nod before opening the door for them to enter. Randy was at the front desk and stood when they walked in. Marina was relieved that he appeared to be the only one in the office. Mike handed Randy the paperwork and he scanned it and nodded.

"I'll go get her," Randy said and left.

Marina pulled nervously at the end of her shirt, worried that something could happen to prevent Avery from leaving. Worried that Preston might show up and send things over the cliff. Or even worse, Chastity. But after a couple minutes, Randy opened the door and Avery walked out.

As soon as she caught sight of Marina, Avery ran over and threw her arms around her mother, squeezing her like she was the only life preserver in an endless sea. Marina hugged her daughter, fighting back the tears. This was never supposed to happen. Avery was not the kind of kid who had this brand of trouble. She was not the kind of mother who had to post bail. And yet here they were.

"Sign here, Avery," Randy's voice cut into their moment.

Avery shot over to the desk and scribbled her signature where Randy indicated. Then she whirled around and almost ran to the door.

"Let's get out of here!" she said before hurrying outside.

"Thank you again for your help," Marina said to Mike. She barely glanced at Randy before leaving, but the sheriff didn't even look up as they exited. Another coward.

Avery was already slumped in the back seat of Marina's car when she and Halcyon climbed in. Marina checked the rearview mirror and could see her daughter glancing around as they drove, probably worried that someone was going to see them and say something. Marina's heart clenched again for Avery. She didn't deserve this. Should never have to be going through this.

Before the car even came to a complete stop in Halcyon's driveway, Avery jumped out and practically ran to the front door. Halcyon hurried after her and opened the door so Avery could get inside. When Marina came in, Avery was standing in the middle of the living room, staring at the stack of boxes.

"What's all this?" she asked.

"It's your things from your father's house," Marina said. "Halcyon and I packed them up earlier."

"We'll get everything set up in my guest room," Halcyon said. "Consider it your room now."

"But where will Mom sleep?" Avery asked.

Crap! Marina had completely forgotten that she'd never let Avery in on her current living arrangements. Avery had assumed she was living with Halcyon.

"I'm not staying here," Marina said. "I moved into the fishing cabin."

Avery's eyes widened. "That dump! Good God, Mom. It's not even safe, much less hygienic. You can't live there."

"Your aunt and I got it cleaned up and decorated," Marina said. "It's a lot nicer than what you remember."

"But why don't you just stay here?" Avery asked. "Aunt Halcyon has a nice house and it's close to your job. The cabin isn't close to anything but weeds and bugs."

"I'm not working for Patricia any longer, so the commute isn't an issue," Marina said.

Avery stared at Marina for several seconds, then glanced at Halcyon, who was unusually quiet. Then tears formed in her eyes and she flopped down in the middle of the couch.

"You lost your job, didn't you?" Avery asked. "Because of me."

"No," Marina said, and sat next to her. "I quit that job yesterday because I didn't want to deal with Patricia any longer. She was never a good person to work for. You know that."

"She's a total bitch," Avery said. "But it never stopped you from working there before. This is Dad's fault. All of it. And where is he? I didn't see him in court."

"He wasn't there," Marina said.

"Did he at least give you money for bail?" Avery asked, tears pooling again.

Marina hesitated before answering. This was one of those times when she had to choose between lying to protect Avery's feelings now and risk the fallout when she found out the truth or tell her the truth and risk being accused of trying to turn her against her father. She glanced over at Halcyon, who frowned and shook her head. Her sister knew she was considering the lie and didn't think it was a good idea.

"No," Marina said quietly.

"I hate him," Avery said, her voice so cold that it made Marina's heart clench.

"You don't mean that," Marina said. "He's made some bad decisions but he's still your father."

"No. He's not," Avery said. "Father is an action, not a noun. And you can't force me to like him. I'm an adult, right? Isn't that what they established in court? My car is paid for and titled in my name, and since I have scholarships, I don't need him for money. I'll get a part-time job for spending and the other things I need. But I will never speak to him again."

Marina looked up at Halcyon, at a complete loss for how to handle this. What she wanted to say was probably what she shouldn't say. But what *should* she say? The universal "they" who wrote all the books on parenting didn't have a chapter covering this sort of thing.

"Good for you," Halcyon said and sat on the other side of Avery.

Avery's eyes widened. Marina started to talk but Halcyon waved a hand at her.

"You know you were thinking the same thing," Halcyon said. "I don't blame Avery for hating him. I hate him too. Maybe one day that will be different, but today, it's a perfectly reasonable thing to feel, and no one should have to feel bad about it."

Realization ripped through Marina. This is exactly how she'd felt about her mother at one time, but everyone had insisted that she act and believe a certain way. That she was obligated to endure the bad behavior of the woman who'd given birth to her simply because she was her mother. And Marina, being Marina, had gone along with it even though her resentment had grown every time her mother lashed out at her and treated her poorly. She'd spent the first twenty years of her life afraid of her mother. She'd spent another twenty-seven trying to convince herself that one day her mother would change. It was only in the last year that she'd finally accepted that her mother was toxic and was going to remain so until the day she died.

And Marina had been about to push Avery in the same direction she'd been pushed.

"She's right," Marina said.

Avery whipped around to stare at her, her mouth open slightly.

"I mean it," Marina said and squeezed Avery's hand. "You have a right to be angry and disappointed and you should feel that way for as long as you want to. All I ask is that you don't let it take over every second of your thought, because you have great things to accomplish, and I don't want his crap interfering with the awesome life you're building."

Halcyon nodded. "That's it exactly. Get angry. Throw things. I used to go out into the bayou and shoot stuff when I was fed up with my mother. But I learned how to partition her off, for lack of a better expression. That way, my feelings about her didn't taint everything else."

"How did you do that?" Avery asked.

"I started by distancing myself from her until I could get healthy," Halcyon said. "Being around her kept me riled up. I didn't have time to establish boundaries and learn how to separate who she was from how I needed to be. I had to accept that she was a narcissist. I didn't do anything to cause it and I couldn't do anything to change it."

"How long did you go without speaking?" Avery asked.

"Eight years," Halcyon said.

"Really?" Marina asked, surprised. She'd known that Halcyon had ceased involvement with Constance for a chunk of time but hadn't realized it had gone on for that long.

"What made you cut her off?" Avery asked.

Halcyon looked out her back window, a sad expression on her face. "Four days after Danny died, she showed up at my house, asking for money. She was having a stressful week and needed to take a trip to Mexico to recharge. She got angry when I refused to give her any. Not that I had any to give. I'd just buried my husband the day before. She hadn't even come to the funeral."

"Oh my God," Avery said. "That's awful."

Marina felt tears well up and she struggled not to break down in front of Avery. She'd known, of course, that Constance hadn't been at the funeral, but Halcyon had never told her why or what had happened after. No wonder she'd restructured her life to exclude her mother.

"It was awful," Halcyon agreed. "But it also made it very clear to me that I would never matter to Constance. It was something I had to accept in order to let it go. Does that make sense?"

Avery nodded. "But you see her now."

"Yes, but it's very surface-level," Halcyon said. "She blows into town three or four times a year and we have lunch, then she heads back to New Orleans, and we return to our regularly scheduled lives."

"If she's not capable of caring for other people, why does she come see you?" Avery asked.

"Honestly? I think it's because she doesn't want to look bad to her friends when they ask if she's seen her daughter lately," Halcyon said. "Appearance is very important to Constance. Maybe the only thing that's important. She might *be* an unfeeling bitch but she doesn't want to appear that way. At least, not to other people."

"Wow," Avery said. "I'm really sorry, Aunt Halcyon."

Halcyon leaned over to hug Avery. "You'll get through this,

baby. And your mother and I will be right there to give you an arm any time you stumble. Just take your time with it. You don't have to make decisions about your relationship with your father today. And even if you do, that decision doesn't have to be forever. But for now, you do what is best for you and don't worry about anyone else."

Avery sniffed. "If it's okay, I think I'll go take a nap. I didn't sleep much last night."

"Of course," Marina said. "And when you get up, we'll fix some dinner."

Avery nodded and rose from the couch, then headed silently upstairs.

"You think she's okay?" Marina asked.

"As okay as she can get for now. But try not to worry. She's strong. Probably stronger than either of us at that age."

"I'm pretty sure she's stronger than me right now."

Halcyon slid over and gave Marina a hug. "Honey, you are the best person I know. And spending all those years taking care of your husband and Avery and your home doesn't make you weak. It makes you the caring, loving person you are. Just think about the things that have been hurled at you the last couple days. If I'd told you last week that you could handle all of that, you'd have said I was crazy. You've always been strong. You just had to believe it."

Marina sniffed. "Would I ruin your opinion of me if I told you I desperately need a glass of wine?"

"I would have worried more if you didn't."

CHAPTER NINETEEN

THE NEXT MORNING, Marina gave Avery a hug before she climbed into her car. Dinner the night before had been a pleasant affair. They'd all agreed that no talk of anything to do with Harold or the arrest was allowed, and Avery had spent most of the night telling them about her dorm room and the other students she'd met. It was obvious to Marina that Avery was making a concerted effort to appear upbeat, but she also knew her daughter had enjoyed the simplicity and comfort of eating pizza on the living room floor while MTV played in the background.

"Are you sure you're going to be all right in the cabin?" Avery asked.

"I'm positive," Marina said.

"I still don't understand why you won't live with Aunt Halcyon. You know she'd be happy for you to."

"There's Snooze to consider. Your aunt is allergic to him and he's allergic to your father."

"Aunt Halcyon could take a pill or something."

"I know. But more importantly, I need to be alone. There's a lot of things I have to work out, and it's hard to do the kind of thinking I need to do with someone trying to help me every second. If I was living with your aunt, she wouldn't be able to keep herself from trying to fix everything for me."

Avery gave her a pointed look.

Marina smiled. "So if I'm smothering you at eighteen, how do you think I feel at forty-eight? This is something I need to do for myself by myself. It's time I decided how I want things to be instead of just accepting the way they are."

Avery nodded. "I get it. Just promise me that you'll be careful, and if there's ever a serial killer loose or some other horror movie thing going on, you'll move in with Aunt Halcyon."

"I promise not to be serial killed."

"Aunt Halcyon said you already went running into the woods half naked."

"I prefer half dressed."

Avery laughed. "I love you, Mom."

"I love you too."

Avery backed out of the driveway and Marina stood there watching until the car went around the corner and out of sight. Then she shuffled back inside and poured a cup of coffee. Halcyon trudged into the kitchen a couple minutes later.

"Is Avery gone already?" she asked as she peered out the window.

"Yeah. She wanted to get back to campus for some event today. I'm not sure that was the truth, but I don't blame her for wanting to get out of Last Chance. With the way things have gone down, she probably won't be back unless she's compelled to return by the court."

Halcyon gave Marina's shoulder a squeeze and headed for the coffeepot. "Give her some time. She's had a lot to process in only a few days. And she's young."

"I'm old and I need time to process everything. I can't even imagine how hard this is for Avery. It's one thing to be betrayed by your husband. It's completely another to be betrayed by your father."

"She'll figure out how to tuck it away until she's ready to deal with it. She has college and her new friends to fill her time."

Marina blew out a breath. Now that the crisis with Avery was handled, at least for the moment, she could no longer ignore the even bigger crisis looming.

"I have to find that ring," Marina said. "Or none of this is going to matter. All of this angst and sacrificing will have been for nothing. I have to tell you, if the world ends after I kept myself from punching Harold dead in the face, I'm going to be super pissed."

"Me too. My list is a little longer, but Harold's right up there on top. So what do you want to do? We could try some pawnshops across the bayou, I suppose."

"I was thinking about talking to Dottie Prejean first. She's bound to have some older items and even if she doesn't have the ring, she might know someone I can ask."

"And what's our angle? Because you can hardly waltz into the home of the First Lady of Last Chance and tell her you're on a magical quest for power."

"Yeah, that's where I get stuck on things. We can't go with the elderly cousin thing because Dottie knows all our relatives. You're the creative one. Can you come up with a backstory and sell it?"

Halcyon, who'd had a talent for painting, singing, and acting, had attended art school in New Orleans after high school. Marina had always hoped her sister would find a way to pursue some sort of career in the arts, but she'd never made a move in that direction. She ran the local theater group, but that was strictly volunteer. Last Chance didn't have the budget to pay someone and the work was only seasonal, when they were either preparing for or doing a production.

"A friend of mine maybe?" Halcyon suggested. "Looking for a family heirloom for her grandmother?"

"That could work. Can we make the grandmother ill?"

"We can put her on her deathbed if you think it would help. I have no qualms about killing off a made-up person. I just won't play that game with real people."

"Superstitious?"

"Bet your ass I am. This is Louisiana. You don't go around wishing people dead here unless you mean it."

"You do it all the time."

Halcyon gave her a pointed look.

"Okay, then we'll go with your friend's half-dead grandma, but be prepared to improv in case Dottie asks."

"Improv is how I live."

"True. Now, for the next problem—even if we locate the ring with Dottie or with someone else, I still have to acquire it. I'm not going to steal it, which means I need cash. And since two-thirds of my bank account balance just went to our illustrious judicial system, I might be running short on funds for a ruby of that size."

"I've got some investments," Halcyon said. "But it would take at least a week to get them converted. I've got maybe a thousand in my checking until I get my next round of alimony checks."

"I'm not going to take your money."

"Why the hell not? I can't use it if I'm dead. Besides, you can pay me back with that super support custom bra, remember?"

"But will it be enough?" Marina asked. "I figure a ruby that big is going to cost serious money and then if it's someone's heirloom, we'll probably have to offer even more than market to get them to part with it. And as much as I hate to think about it, I've got five thousand in my checking account and zero job. If I don't find the ring and the world doesn't end, things aren't looking good for me."

"You need cash and you need it fast. I have an awesome idea."

"What?"

"You sell beauty cream for an incredibly ridiculous price."

"And just how would I manage that? I can't whip up some awesome beauty cream that actually works and get it packaged and up for sale in a matter of days. And wouldn't the FDA or some other government pay-us-kickbacks sort of entity have a problem with that?"

"You don't have to go through production and the FDA is not lurking in the bushes in Last Chance. What we do is get the cheapest crap we can find at the drugstore and you stick a little in a tiny plastic container. Then you schedule one-on-one appointments with people, claiming you make the formula specifically for them. When you apply the cheap lotion, you swipe your fingers across their wrinkles and voila!"

Marina stared. Why hadn't she thought of that? If she could reverse wrinkles with no surgery, she could be rich as Caesar. The million dollars wouldn't matter at all. Why hadn't any of the Seekers before her figured that out?

Then she took a closer look at Halcyon. The skin under her eyes, which had been smooth and evenly pigmented the day before, was slightly elevated and the color a tiny bit darker than her cheeks. The laugh lines that Marina had erased were back. Much smaller, but back.

"What's wrong?" Halcyon asked.

"It's going away. Your skin is returning to normal."

Halcyon jumped off the stool and ran to a mirror hanging in the living room.

"Shit!" she yelled. "What happened?"

Halcyon clutched her cheeks and got inches from her face, scanning it. "Yours is still perfect," she said. "What gives?"

"I don't know. It's not like I got an instruction manual. Maybe the effect doesn't last on other people because it's not in you. That, and I touch my own face every day."

Halcyon flopped onto the stool. "Well, that just sucks. And totally honks my super special beauty cream idea."

"I suppose I could still do something like it, but it would have to be only done by me, none to take home, and would only last for a special occasion. Do you think anyone would be interested in that?"

"Probably, but not at ten grand a pop, which is what I was figuring you could charge for permanent changes."

"Wow. That's a lot."

"It's still cheaper than Botox for forty years. And a lot more comfortable." Halcyon sighed. "But I guess the dream is over before it even began. And the average household income in Last Chance doesn't support a healthy income stream for a temporary situation. If you were in New Orleans..."

"It might work there," Marina agreed. "But I can't exactly move, open a business, and get customers in the time frame we're working with."

Halcyon shook her head, rubbing her finger under her eyes. "And either you have to lay hands on me every day or I have to suffer like the rest of society."

"If it makes you feel any better, I told my boobs to stay upright night before last and they haven't shifted so much as a millimeter."

"Then I guess we best find this ring so you can collect your retirement."

"More like my current than my retirement. If the world

doesn't end, this thing with Avery could end up costing a fortune. Before and after the trial."

"I'm pretty sure a hit man would be cheaper than a trial."

"Not if my list keeps growing."

"God, isn't that the truth. Okay, what about this—we put together what money we can, but if we find the ring and know we won't be able to swing the cost or, God forbid, it belongs to someone like the LeDoux, we steal it."

"But what if it's someone nice and we're taking a very valuable item from them?"

"Then you'll pay them back after you collect the million. Unless it's the LeDoux. Leave a bag of money on their doorstep if it makes you feel better. But the reality is if we're going to buy into this tale then we have to buy into the ending. Taking the ring in exchange for a future payout is better than the alternative where we're all dead or worse—slaves to some invading douchebags."

"I've already done the servant thing. I'm sorta over it."

CHAPTER TWENTY

SNOOZE GAVE Marina a woeful look when she walked into the cabin.

"Don't give me that crap," she said. "I let you out last night and I brought you pizza. I had a situation with Avery that had to be taken care of. You do like Avery, right?"

Single bark.

"Okay, then we're in agreement. It's not like you needed me here to listen to you snore anyway. Besides, I have kolache."

His ears perked up and he did a regal sit.

She laughed. "You know, I kinda like this whole communication thing we have going. I wonder if I could teach you to type so we could have a real conversation. You might be the best guy I know."

Single bark.

Marina took a kolache out of the bag and tossed it to Snooze, who caught it neatly then trotted off to the living room. She popped one in the microwave for herself, then headed into the bedroom to rummage some matching clothes out of the boxes she still hadn't unpacked. She'd just started digging through the first box when Snooze started barking.

His angry bark.

She hurried into the living room and saw the old hound standing in front of the back door, almost frozen in place. And he did not look happy.

"Good God, are those hackles? You never get hackles. What's out there?"

She grabbed the shotgun off the rack next to the back door and peered outside. Maybe it was a bear or a gator. Snooze wasn't all that active, but his nose and his ears worked as well as any other bloodhound. And something had set him off.

"You stay here," she said and opened the door to slip outside.

She walked from one end of the porch to the other, scanning the weeds, the tree line, and the bayou for what might have upset Snooze, but she didn't see anything. She was just about to chalk the whole thing up to Snooze hearing a butterfly flapping somewhere in the woods when she saw something move in the trees. She lifted the shotgun and pointed it toward the area of movement. She'd only seen a shadow but whatever it was, it was tall. At least six feet.

A bear on his hind legs, maybe?

But then it took off and the bear theory flew out the window. It took off fast—on two legs. A bear couldn't maintain that kind of speed unless on all fours.

The poacher, maybe? But why would he be lurking around her cabin during the day? He hadn't been squatting here. They would have found evidence of someone living here, and the layers of dust had been a clear indication that no one had set foot inside in a long time. So why all the interest in the cabin now?

She blew out a breath and headed back inside. Snooze was

still standing guard at the back door and she reached over to scratch his ears. "At least you'll let me know if someone is out there. Between you and the guns Halcyon lent me, we've got this covered, right?"

But all the same, she made a mental note to call Luke when she got a chance. It might be nothing, but if the poacher was still on the loose, it could be that he was camped somewhere nearby. Maybe he was hoping for an opportunity to steal food or supplies.

"Okay, back to the clothes hunt," she announced.

Snooze, apparently deciding the crisis was over, headed for the rug and flopped down. A couple seconds later, he was snoring.

Marina returned to the bedroom and tackled the boxes again, managing to locate a pair of jeans without holes in them and a blouse that wasn't horribly wrinkled. She'd have to go with ballet flats because the lack of pedicure precluded sandals, but that would work.

She and Halcyon had decided that the first order of ring business would be paying Dottie a visit. Maybe they'd get lucky and she'd have the ring, and all of this could be over. At worst, Dottie would probably know other people to check with. Since other people likely meant older people, that meant wearing decent clothes and being on their best behavior.

After that, Halcyon wanted to go to a jewelry store near New Orleans and see what they'd give her for her engagement rings. Marina had protested until she was blue in the face, but Halcyon had insisted that it was way past time she got rid of them and it might solve the cash-flow problem. Worst case, they didn't find the ring and on the night before the world was set to end, they'd blow it all on one final hurrah in New Orleans. But before she could do any of that, Marina had to take care of an obligation that she'd been putting off.

Visiting her mother.

She'd told herself that she was busy getting Avery to college and then with her and Avery's exploding lives. The truth was, Marina was grateful to have a reason to put it off but would have settled for reasons with fewer long-term repercussions. She supposed she could still convince herself she had good reason to stay away, but it had been two weeks. And Marina liked to pop in regularly to make sure nothing was going on that she needed to know about—like a facility coup staged to get rid of her mother.

The thought of having Letitia out among society again was frightening for so many reasons, not the least of which being that Marina was living in the only structure her mother owned. So after getting dressed, she grabbed her keys and headed for the highway. The sooner she got it over with, the sooner she could get on with saving the world.

How many people could say that?

Thirty minutes later, Marina walked into the assisted living facility and signed in at the front desk. The nurse's aide who usually worked at the front opened the locked door to allow her inside. She forced a smile and entered. It might have been two weeks since she'd last visited her mother but emotionally, it still felt like yesterday. Which made her feel guilty and sad and angry. It wasn't supposed to be this way. You weren't supposed to dread seeing your mother, and as long as she had a breath left in her, Marina was going to make damned sure Avery never felt that way about her.

The professionals always tried to tell Marina not to take the things her mother said to heart. That Letitia wasn't quite right and she didn't mean the things she said. But Marina knew better. When doctors saw Letitia, she played the role of the feeble-minded old lady. The kindly, knitting grandma with white hair and a penchant for daytime talk shows. But Marina saw the shift in her expression when the doctors looked away. The narrowing of her eyes as she tried to figure out what angle to work. How to better her position.

She'd seen that shift all her life. Letitia often pretended to be one kind of person in front of others, but she was always herself when it was just her and Marina. So Marina didn't buy for a second that Letitia said horrible things to her because her mind was slipping. The truth was, she'd always said horrible things. Not that Marina doubted Letitia was crazy. She was absolutely batshit insane. But she was cruel crazy. Not the-aliens-are-coming-to-get-me or the-dog-is-talking-to-me crazy. Marina would be the first to point out that it was getting worse with age, but the hatefulness had always been there. People in Last Chance who had known Leticia well enough to see her true colors would agree.

As she walked down the hall to her mother's room, she was grateful once again that Letitia had played games all her life. If the doctor had known the real woman behind the innocent smile, he would have known her problems weren't caused by dementia. But Hallmark granny shooting at the postman was enough for him to seal her lockup warrant. Finally, Letitia's kindly old lady ploy had gotten her the exact opposite of what it usually did.

It was the best possible solution to a horrible situation, because as Letitia got meaner, she grew more violent. It was the violence that finally jolted Marina out of her forty-seven-year stupor and had her looking for creative solutions before her mother killed someone. The postman had been lucky she had refused to wear glasses. Otherwise, she probably wouldn't have missed.

She knocked on her mother's door but there was no answer, so she inched the door open and peered inside. Her mother sat near the window, staring outside, the bars on the window a constant reminder that she could see things outside the building but she couldn't live among them.

"Hello," Marina said as she stepped inside.

Letitia flashed her a look of disgust before turning back to the window.

"Didn't figure I'd see you this week," Letitia said. "Shouldn't you be spending your time losing weight and prettying yourself up to find a new man to support you?"

Marina held in a sigh. She should have known that news of her situation would have reached Letitia. In Last Chance, gossiping was the local pastime. Between the facility staff and visitors, word would have filtered back.

Letitia turned as she approached and gave her a more comprehensive review. "Looks like you had some work done. Guess that's why you haven't been here to see me. Too little, too late, since your man already bolted."

"I haven't been here because I was helping Avery get set up at college."

Letitia waved a hand in dismissal. "Stop coddling her. She's old enough to take care of herself."

"You mean like I was in elementary school, when you checked out of being a mother?"

Letitia flashed her a look of anger. "What the hell are you talking about? I was a great mother. It's not my fault that you didn't listen to anything I said. If you had, you wouldn't be in the situation you are now. If you can't keep a piece of shit like Harold, then there's no hope for you."

Marina knew she should ignore the words. Should turn around and leave and seriously consider whether or not she ever wanted to return. There was nothing for her here. She'd known that since she was a child but for whatever reason, she'd never stopped clinging to the hope that one day her mother might act like she loved her. Then about a year ago,

Letitia had gotten nasty with Avery and that was the breaking point. It was one thing for Marina to suck it up. She'd been trained to do it since childhood, but no way was she allowing Letitia's toxic personality to damage her daughter.

"Just like there was no hope for you holding on to my father," Marina said.

Letitia jerked her head back as if she'd been struck.

"I told your father to leave, and no way was I allowing him back after he took up with Constance. Being drunk is no excuse for taking up with a whore, even when they trick you into it."

"Uh-huh. Except that Constance was already pregnant with Halcyon when you met my dad, which means that *you* took up with *her* man, not the other way around."

"I don't have to listen to this! Nurse! Nurse!"

Marina shook her head as a nurse hurried into the room and scanned Letitia, trying to assess what the problem was.

"I want this bitch out of my sight," Letitia said. "And I don't want to see her again."

The nurse's eyes widened, and she opened her mouth but apparently, couldn't figure out what to say.

"That's okay," Marina told her. "I was just leaving."

The nurse followed her into the hall and shut Letitia's door behind them.

"I'm so sorry, Mrs. Trahan," the nurse said. "But please don't take that personally. She doesn't mean the things she says."

Marina gave her a tired smile. "Yes, she does. She's been saying those things my entire life."

Before the nurse could respond, Marina walked away, wondering how far and how long her obligation to her mother extended. Sure, Letitia had said she never wanted to see Marina again, but that was another lie. Letitia absolutely wanted Marina to come back. Not because she cared at all about her daughter but because she wanted to maintain the illusion that she still had control over her. And making Marina feel bad about herself was the one thing that always seemed to make Letitia happy.

She was in for a real surprise when she realized that the old Marina was long gone.

And the new one didn't give a damn what Letitia thought or said.

She walked out of the facility and smiled, for real this time. It was as if a spine-crushing weight had been lifted from her. She'd finally done it. She'd refused to take her mother's shit and the world hadn't fallen apart. More importantly, she wasn't leaving feeling worse about herself, as she usually did.

In fact, it was exactly the opposite.

She felt ready to conquer the world.

CHAPTER TWENTY-ONE

THE JEWELER HALCYON had in mind had a small shop on the highway to New Orleans, about twenty minutes from the city limits. A friend of hers who had moved to the city after a divorce years before said he was trustworthy and would give her a good price on quality stones. Now they just had to hope that the stones in her rings were quality and the trip might actually be worth some money.

A young, pretty saleswoman greeted them as they walked in. Halcyon explained what she needed and the saleswoman went into a back room and emerged a minute later with a small gentleman wearing a suit and thick glasses. He introduced himself as Stewart Davis, the owner of the shop, and Halcyon showed him the two rings she was interested in selling.

He nodded and picked up the rings. "Give me some time to assess them. Look around. See if there's anything you might be interested in for trade."

"Wait!" Marina grabbed his arm as he started to walk off. She reached into her pocket and pulled out her wedding ring. "This one too."

He took the ring and disappeared into the office.

"Marina, no," Halcyon said.

"Why not? You're trying to sell yours."

"But it's been a long time."

"What difference does it make? I'm not going to get back together with Harold. Tomorrow, next week, next year...the ring still represents the same broken promise."

Halcyon's eyes widened. "Yes, but..."

"That's too rational coming from me?"

"I wasn't going to put it that way, but yeah."

"I think I had an epiphany this morning when I visited Letitia."

"The only epiphany I've ever had in Letitia's presence was that I was glad I wasn't carrying."

Marina smiled. "It was something like that, but I struck back with words instead. She tried so hard to get to me and it didn't work. I turned it around, Halcyon. It shocked her and more importantly, it made her mad. And I've wanted to do that for so long. The best part is, I didn't care what she said. It meant nothing. Just the hateful ramblings of a bitter old woman."

Tears welled up in Halcyon's eyes and Marina stared at her sister, surprised. "Are you all right?" Marina asked.

Halcyon threw her arms around Marina and squeezed her so tightly it was slightly painful. When she released her, she sniffed and patted at the corners of her eyes to remove the tears, careful not to smear her makeup.

"I'm just so happy for you," Halcyon said. "I've wanted this for you all our lives. And I'd decided it was never going to happen."

Marina nodded. "This week has given me an entirely different perspective. And whether I have another ten days or thirty years on this earth, I want them to be on my terms. I'm done living my life for everyone else."

"Praise the Lord and pass the ammunition," Halcyon said. "Or whatever is more applicable."

"At the rate I'm firing off, mouthwash?"

Halcyon grinned. "Come on. Might as well look around. We're not that far from Last Chance. It's possible the ring could be here."

Marina nodded and motioned to the saleswoman who'd been standing back from them, probably wondering what kind of breakdown was occurring and whether or not to say something.

"I don't suppose you have any old rings—heirloom type stuff?" Marina asked. "We have an elderly aunt who lost a ring years ago. We keep thinking we'd like to find something similar to replace it but haven't found anything suitable so far."

"We have several older pieces," the saleswoman said. "What were you looking for?"

"A silver twisted band and a good-sized ruby," Marina said. "We don't get a whole lot of detail out of her. She's slipping, if you know what I mean."

The saleswoman gave them a sympathetic look. "My grand-mother is that way. Awful to see, isn't it? Come over here and see if any of these will work."

They followed her to a side counter and she pulled out a tray with three ruby rings on it. The stone was far too small on one, so Marina didn't even bother to pick it up, but she spent several minutes inspecting the other two. They were both pretty but unfortunately, didn't elicit so much as a finger twitch from her.

Marina shook her head. "I don't think they'll work. I think she said the band was twisted like vines, right?" Marina looked at Halcyon.

"That's what I remember," Halcyon said and looked at the saleswoman. "Thank you for showing us these."

"No problem," the saleswoman said. "I hope you find something that works. Can I get you water or coffee while you wait?"

They both shook their heads and walked over to a sitting area near a case at the front of the store. Right after they sat, the door to the shop opened and Ms. Kitty walked in. She smiled at the saleswoman who greeted her.

"Hello, Ms. Kitty," the saleswoman said. "I believe Mr. Davis has your piece ready. He's doing an assessment right now so it will be a few minutes. Can I get you anything while you wait?"

"No. Thank you." Ms. Kitty turned and caught sight of them. "Fancy meeting you two all the way out here. But then, you can't do better than Stewart for custom work."

"That's what everyone says," Halcyon said.

Ms. Kitty took a seat next to them and looked at Marina. "How are you holding up, Marina? I heard about that mess with your daughter. Is she all right?"

"She's fine," Marina said. "I mean, considering. I guess we're both fine, considering."

"Considering your husband is a no-taste-having asshole?" Ms. Kitty asked.

"That covers part of it," Marina agreed.

Ms. Kitty looked at the counter next to them and frowned. "You shopping for engagement rings? That's some fast work."

"God no!" Marina said. "I think I'd rather wear handcuffs."

"Same thing," Halcyon said.

Ms. Kitty grinned. With three husbands in her rearview mirror, she and Halcyon probably shared an opinion on the term "permanent."

"I'm looking to sell my wedding rings," Halcyon said. "In case Marina needs the money for Avery and things."

Ms. Kitty gave her an approving nod. "You're a good woman. I know some don't like it that you speak your mind, but I happen to admire that quality in a person."

"Probably because you've got it in spades," Halcyon said.

Ms. Kitty laughed. "There is that. I'm surprised you never had those rings turned into something else—a nice bracelet or something."

"I thought about it but never got around to doing it," Halcyon said.

"My daughter divorced her first husband years ago," Ms. Kitty said. "He was a piece of work, which I knew from the beginning, but you can't tell a nineteen-year-old a damned thing. So I bit my lip and paid for the wedding, even though I knew they wouldn't make it until she was of legal drinking age. They didn't. He did buy her a decent ring, though. That's about the only thing he ever did that was worth anything."

"Did she have it made into something else?" Marina asked.

"No," Ms. Kitty said. "She stuck it in a drawer and left it, probably hoping it was all a bad dream, but then she met her current husband. He came across it shortly after they were married and asked why she still had it. She said she'd just never done anything with it but she'd go have it made into a necklace or something. Well, he got all butthurt over the idea of her walking around wearing a diamond that came from her first husband, even if it wasn't on her ring finger. So she gave the ring to me and told me to get something for myself."

"And you made it into something for her, didn't you?" Halcyon asked.

Ms. Kitty grinned. "No. I had it made into a tie tack and gave it to him."

Marina and Halcyon burst out laughing and couldn't stop, even when Stewart came to see what was going on. He took one look at them and retreated back into his cubbyhole. The saleswoman had been laughing as hard as they were, so he'd probably decided it was a woman thing and he didn't want to know about it.

"I want to be you when I grow up," Halcyon said.

Ms. Kitty shook her head. "If you want to be me, you can't do responsible things, like grow up."

Ms. Kitty patted Marina's hand. "You hang in there. Any time you need to let your hair down, you come to Ms. Kitty's. Booze is on me. I got all kinds of things in my bar that will take your mind off your troubles."

She looked over at the saleswoman as she rose. "I'm going to go run a few errands and I'll be back in about an hour."

"Still want to be her," Halcyon said as Ms. Kitty walked out.

"She *is* supercool," Marina agreed.

Stewart came out of his office and over to where they sat.

"The gold on the bands is good quality," he said. "And the diamonds are better than average, but none are huge. I would appraise the entire lot at about seven thousand. I can write up separate appraisals if you need them for insurance purposes."

"And if we wanted to sell them?" Halcyon asked.

He shook his head. "I'm afraid I couldn't do better than five thousand. And that's more than you'll get anywhere else because I'll turn them into more up-to-date pieces. Others will have to sell them as-is and the designs are somewhat dated."

Halcyon looked over at Marina, who nodded. Five thousand was more than they had when they'd walked in the shop.

"We'll take it," Halcyon said.

DOTTIE DIDN'T SO MUCH AS RAISE an eyebrow when she saw Marina and Halcyon standing at her doorstep. Halcyon might want to be Ms. Kitty someday, but Marina really hoped she could be Dottie. The regal woman never appeared to be ruffled by anything. Not in appearance or in action. It must be awesome to exist in that state of calm. Either that, or Dottie was the best actress that had ever walked the face of the earth.

"Ladies," Dottie said. "What a pleasant surprise. Please come in. I just made a pitcher of sweet tea and homemade chocolate chip cookies."

"Did you know we were coming?" Halcyon asked.

Dottie laughed. "Of course not. How could I?"

"So you brew tea and bake cookies on the regular?" Halcyon asked.

"I'm old and Southern," Dottie said. "It's what we do."

"That clinches it," Halcyon said. "I'm not getting old."

"No one visits you except me," Marina said. "I think you're safe."

Halcyon did a fist pump. "Loophole!"

Dottie smiled as they walked into the kitchen and gestured toward a farmhouse table in a beautiful breakfast nook with three walls of windows looking out into a garden that appeared as if it was sculptured by fairies.

"Your garden is gorgeous!" Marina exclaimed. "Don't tell me you do all this work yourself."

Dottie nodded. "I enjoy it. It relaxes me and it's satisfying to see the result every time I step into the kitchen."

"Good Lord, why don't you win the best home garden contest every year?" Marina asked. "It looks like an arboretum."

"I don't enter," Dottie said as she slid a tray of tea and cookies onto the table.

"Why not?" Marina asked.

Dottie frowned. "There was a thing one year. Apparently, someone took offense to my string of wins and saw fit to spray the lawn with weed killer. It took me years to get the soil right again."

"What the hell is wrong with people?" Halcyon asked. "It's flowers. No one's life has ever ended over flowers."

"If I had a garden like this and someone sprayed it with weed killer, their life might end," Marina said. "Do you know who did it?"

"Oh sure, but there's knowing and there's proving," Dottie said.

"Let me guess," Marina said. "Serina LeDoux."

Dottie raised one eyebrow and Marina shook her head. Serina was Preston and Patricia's now-deceased mother and had come in second to Dottie every year that she'd entered the competition.

"Ding-dong, the witch is dead," Halcyon said. "You should totally enter again. That cow Patricia isn't going to climb over your fence to spray anything, and Preston's wife doesn't get out of the bottle long enough to walk a straight line, much less garden."

Dottie stared at Halcyon for several seconds, then burst out laughing. "You, my dear, are rather a breath of fresh air."

Halcyon shrugged. "I just say what everyone else is thinking."

"It's an admirable trait," Dottie said.

"I find that rather surprising coming from you," Halcyon said.

Dottie nodded. "My mother had specific ideas about how a lady was to behave. Then with my husband being mayor, it seemed prudent to continue along the lines of my mother's teachings. But rest assured, I'm as well versed on reality as you are."

Dottie turned to look at Marina. "Speaking of reality, how is Avery?"

"She's okay," Marina said. "Went back to school this morning. I don't see her coming back anytime soon."

"At my age, you're not surprised by much anymore," Dottie said. "But the extent to which this has been taken, and without Harold lifting a finger or even opening his mouth, is beyond the pale. I hope you're able to work this out before it causes permanent problems for Avery."

"Me too," Marina said.

"Holy crap!" Halcyon said. "Sorry to interrupt, but these cookies are the best thing I've ever put into my mouth. Will you marry me, Dottie?"

Dottie smiled and Marina could tell she was pleased by the compliment. "I think both of us have put marriage in our rearview mirror but I might be convinced to bake a batch for you from time to time."

"I'm holding you to that," Halcyon said and stuffed half a cookie in her mouth.

Marina picked one up and took a bite. "Wow. I'm coming over when you cook for Halcyon."

"It's been a long time since someone enjoyed my cookies," Dottie said. "They were William's favorite and I don't make them often. But I was feeling nostalgic today, so I'm glad you ladies came by. But I'm assuming you're not here to eat cookies and talk about my garden, so what can I do for you?"

"Since everything is a mess, we're on a distraction mission," Halcyon said.

"That sounds like an excellent plan," Dottie said. "How can I help?"

"A friend of mine has an elderly aunt who was given a ruby

ring a million years ago by some lost love," Halcyon said. "It was stolen by one of their less scrupulous family members about twenty years ago. Rumor has it, for drugs."

Dottie shook her head. "That's a shame."

Marina held in a smile. When Halcyon turned on the talent, no one sold fiction better than she did.

"It's really been a tough time for the family," Halcyon said. "Anyway, the aunt is getting to that point where things from the past are more present in her mind than things in the now, if you know what I mean. So she keeps looking for the ring but can't find it, of course. My friend was thinking maybe she could find something similar and put her aunt's mind at ease. So she's been looking for a replacement and Marina and I thought we'd go on a scavenger hunt and see if we could find anything."

"That's a very kind thing your friend wants to do," Dottie said. "So I assume you're asking me if I have any heirloom jewelry I might be willing to part with?"

"I know it's kind of a nosy question," Marina said. "But no one else in Last Chance has your taste and culture. We figured if anyone had quality pieces, it would be you."

"That's such a nice thing to say," Dottie said. "And I do have several pieces, inherited, but no rubies. The women in my family favored sapphires and emeralds."

"Oh well," Marina said, shoving her disappointment aside. "It was a long shot, but at least we got to drink tea and partake of excellent cookies while gazing at this extraordinary yard. There are far worse ways to spend time. I ought to know. I've done a lot of them lately."

"There is someone else in town who might have something like what you're looking for," Dottie said. "In fact, for all I know, they might have the exact ring."

"Seriously?" Halcyon said. "Who?"

Dottie frowned. "Preston LeDoux or Patricia Martin. Their mother was a bit of a jewelry hoarder and she acquired a lot of her pieces through dubious channels."

"She bought stolen jewelry?" Marina asked.

"Oh, she never would have admitted that any of it was stolen," Dottie said. "But when you meet someone in a parking lot and pay ten times less for an item than what it's worth, we all know the score. She had the bad judgment to force her maid into doing the exchanges, which is how that bit of information got around."

Halcyon shook her head. "Unbelievable. That family is a rash on the butt of this town."

"And a lingering one at that," Dottie agreed. "Anyway, I'm sure you don't want to cross that line—assuming they'd even let you in the door—but I thought I'd throw it out there. With the way they spend, Preston and Patricia will need the money at some point and those pieces will probably be some of the first things to go."

Marina rose. "Thank you so much for entertaining our craziness. Maybe we'll just take a girls' trip to NOLA and look at some shops there."

Dottie gave her an approving nod. "I think that sounds like a wonderful idea. But I'm so glad you stopped by. Please do it again when you have time to relax. I've been known to make a decent coffee cake."

"My favorite," Marina said. "And we'd love to visit again. I really appreciate all your support with everything lately."

"Oh, I haven't done anything," Dottie said.

"Yes, you have. Just knowing that you think I'm doing the right things makes a difference," Marina said. "I've always had a lot of respect for you, so your opinion matters."

"Thank you," Dottie said, and Marina could tell she was

flattered. "I wish I could do more. If you come up with anything, please let me know."

"I will," Marina said.

They headed out and climbed into Marina's car.

"That woman should have 'Class Act' inscribed on her tombstone," Halcyon said.

"Definitely. What do you want on yours?"

Halcyon shrugged. "'Later, bitches'?"

Marina laughed.

"What about you?" Halcyon asked.

"'Finally taking a day off'?"

Halcyon grinned. "We could always take that trip to NOLA."

"I can't. I don't have anyone to keep Snooze."

"Ask Adelaide to do it. She's made it clear she wants to help and it's not like he could damage anything in her yard by digging. She kills everything."

"And she also has five thousand cats."

"Oh yeah. I forgot about that."

"Besides, I don't think the ring will be in New Orleans," Marina said. "If Alexios is right, it will be in Last Chance."

"Yeah, but apparently, our most viable option is the LeDoux. The only way that works is if we go back to that whole breaking-and-entering thing."

"I know. And it was a sketchy enough idea before, but after this crap with Avery..."

"We might as well check ourselves into the nearest jail cell if we're caught." Halcyon held up her finger. "There is one way that wouldn't require black masks and the potential wearing of handcuffs."

"How?"

"That annual environmental charity auction thing. It's held at the LeDoux estate. The whole family lives in that fake Tara, so you'd be close to everything Patricia and Preston inherited."

"Even if I was invited—which I'm not—what am I supposed to do? Walk around the house digging in drawers for jewelry? That would get me arrested just as quickly as crawling through a window."

"No one's asking you to dig in their undies drawer. I just figured if you got close enough, you might feel something. If you don't feel anything, then we know it's not worth the risk of breaking in. Everyone wanders around a bit when it's a house party. The ole 'I was looking for the bathroom' thing but really, it's just people being nosy."

Marina shook her head. "We're still stumped at the 'I'm not invited' part. And no way could I wrangle an invitation. Especially now."

"I bet Dottie was invited. Maybe you could be her plus-one."

"Dottie doesn't go. Patricia always bitches about her not showing up but never turns down the big check she writes."

"Of course she doesn't," Halcyon said. "But Dottie said she wants to help. Maybe you could convince her to go this year."

"How? It's not like I can tell her the truth."

Halcyon frowned. "Yeah, I don't imagine too many people would go for the magical ring story."

"They'd all think I'm going down the path of my mother."

"Maybe we could pose as the gas company or the cable guy."

"This is Last Chance, not New York City. Everyone knows what we look like. And you're great with stage makeup and costumes but there's no way you're getting us past people we've known our whole lives."

Halcyon sighed. "This whole sneaky thing is a lot harder than I thought it would be."

"Which is why most criminals get caught."

"So what now?"

Marina blew out a breath. "I don't know. But it's getting late. You have the drummer tonight, right? Or the engineer?"

"Engineer."

"Then let's call it a day. I'm going to contact Alexios and see if I can drag anything else out of him. I refuse to believe that he's been walking the earth for centuries and doesn't know more than this."

"You think he's keeping things from you?"

"Not necessarily. But that last time we talked, he seemed off."

"How do you know he wasn't off the times you saw him before and this last time was normal?"

"I guess I don't."

"But what would he gain from keeping information from you?"

"Nothing that I can think of, but what do we really know about him or his world?"

"Not much, I guess. And only what he's told us." Halcyon shook her head. "I guess I hadn't thought about it that way before, which is odd because I'm usually suspicious of everyone."

Marina nodded. "I know. And he's probably exactly who he says he is, but if he can make money appear in my bank account, then how do we know he can't manipulate our feelings? What does your gut tell you? You were always a better judge of people than me."

"Unless I was dating them," Halcyon agreed. "I suppose I took him at face value. I never got the impression he was lying, even though all of this is beyond outlandish. And I know he claims his great talent is walking through locked doors but someone who can't be hurt by a gun has a big advantage in this world. If you decide to talk to him again, be careful."

"I will," Marina said.

She didn't really think Alexios was dangerous. Not that way. But then, she'd been married to Harold for twenty-eight years and clearly, she hadn't known him at all. She'd only known Alexios for days.

Her sister's caution was warranted.

CHAPTER TWENTY-TWO

MARINA COULD HEAR Snooze barking when she pulled up to the cabin. Crap. Her good weapons were all inside. She dug around in her purse and came up with cuticle scissors. They would have to do. She could always aim for the eyes.

She hurried to the front door, trying to cross the porch as quietly as possible. She slipped the key in the lock and slowly turned it, then inched the door open and peered inside. Snooze stood staring at the back door, still barking like a maniac. She hurried inside, locking the door behind her, then grabbed the pistol from the kitchen drawer and ran to look out the back window.

Nothing.

At least nothing she could see, but something was clearly bothering Snooze now as it had this morning. She went back to the kitchen and snagged her cell phone from her bag, then yelled at Snooze to stop barking. She'd never gotten a chance to call Luke, and it looked as though it was past time now. He didn't answer, but she left a voice mail, gave him a brief description of her concern, and slipped the phone in her jeans pocket. Hopefully, he'd check messages soon and call her back.

Snooze looked over at her and whined, then scratched the door.

"Do you need to go potty?" Marina asked.

Two barks.

"Is something out there?"

One bark.

Crap!

"Is it an animal?"

Please let it be a bear. Or an alligator. Or a rabid raccoon.

Two barks.

Marina drew in a breath.

"Is it a human?"

One bark.

"Do you know who it is?"

Please let it be Alexios or Luke or even Harold.

Two barks.

Marina's heartbeat ticked up a notch.

"Was it the same person this morning?"

One bark.

This so wasn't good. Someone was lurking around her cabin and they were persistent, despite the fact that she had a loud dog and they'd probably seen her on the porch with a gun. What kind of fool went up against those odds? And why? For some worn-out furniture or her collection of yoga pants? It wasn't worth being shot just to get some food, and if that was what he was after, wouldn't he have waited until she left and broken in then?

None of this made sense.

A knock sounded on her front door and she choked back a scream. Snooze turned to look at the door, then her, clearly waiting to see if he needed to spring into action or take a nap. The door was a solid slab of wood with no peephole and there wasn't a window that she could look out and see the area in front of the door, so she decided to go old school and ask who was there—standing behind the refrigerator.

Bullets couldn't go through the refrigerator, right?

"It's Luke."

A breath of air she hadn't even realized she was holding rushed out of her and she hurried over to let him in. He took one look at her and his face was filled with concern.

"Sorry," he said. "I didn't mean to startle you. I was finishing patrol in this area and figured I'd just stop by and check in. What's wrong? Did you see something? Did someone try to break in?"

"No. But someone was here. This morning and again just a few minutes ago. Snooze alerted me both times—the same bark he was using the other night."

"And you're sure he's not catching scent of a bear or alligator?"

No way could Marina tell Luke that she could talk to her dog. He'd block her number and relegate her to crazy woman status. And with her family history, she couldn't really make a case to the contrary.

"Snooze doesn't indicate with a bark when it's an animal," she said. "He usually bays. And I went out back this morning and looked. I saw someone run off in the woods. Too tall to be a bear and way too fast to be a bear on his hind legs."

Luke frowned and headed for her back door to look outside.

"Did you see anyone this time?"

"No. But I didn't go outside. After this morning and then with Snooze going off again, I got spooked."

"Of course." He unlocked the back door and headed onto the porch. Marina stepped outside behind him and closed the door so that Snooze couldn't get out.

She scanned the woods along with Luke, but this time

there was nothing running through the trees. At least, not that she could see. But then, he might have left when he saw Luke drive up.

"Where did you see the guy running this morning?" Luke asked.

Marina almost sighed with relief. No "you thought you saw" or "that you might have seen." He believed her.

"That way," she said, pointing to the left. "Just to the right of the cypress tree. I didn't get a good look, though. He was just a shadow."

Luke headed down the porch in the direction she'd pointed, leaning over the railing as he went, staring at the ground. When he got to the end of the porch, he frowned.

"There's footprints here," he said. "Too big to be yours."

She hurried over and leaned over the railing. Sure enough, two large boot prints were visible in the soft dirt of a bare patch.

"Oh my God," she said, feeling slightly dizzy. "He was right at my house."

Luke nodded. "He probably heard Snooze barking this morning and ran into the woods. Then you came out armed and he figured it wasn't the time to try anything."

"Maybe so, but what about this afternoon? If he just wanted to steal something, wouldn't it be easier to watch the cabin until I left? If he was that scared of Snooze, he wouldn't have come back at all."

Luke frowned and looked out in the woods. He didn't say anything, but Marina could tell he didn't like the way the events had lined up either.

"Let's head back inside," he said.

"Would you like something to drink?" Marina asked and headed for the kitchen. "I have soda and wine and bottled water. I'm afraid I don't lean toward beer or whiskey. Or coffee, maybe? I was just thinking about making a pot."

"Coffee in the evening? You must be one of those people that caffeine doesn't affect. Water would be great."

She nodded and grabbed two bottles of water from the refrigerator. Coffee absolutely kept her up, but she didn't want to say that staying awake sounded like a good idea given the circumstances. She didn't want him to think she was that kind of woman. The kind that needed the man on a white horse to save her. Hell, she didn't want to be that kind of woman, either.

But the situation *had* unnerved her.

"What do you think is going on?" she asked as Luke sat on a stool at the counter.

"I'm not sure."

"Could it be your poacher?"

He shook his head. "I caught him this morning. And all the evidence points to only one guy."

Okay. She moved straight past unnerved to scared.

"This cabin has sat empty for years," she said. "And no one has ever bothered it. Clearly, whoever this is knows that someone is living here now. If he wanted to steal a television or food or whatever, he's had all the time in the world during the day when I've been gone."

He nodded. "I know. That's exactly why I don't like it either."

Her stomach rolled. It was one thing for her to imagine the worst. Her mind and emotions were all over the place with everything she was dealing with. But if Luke thought the situation was bad as well, then that meant she *should* be worried.

"But it still doesn't make sense," she said. "Why would anyone be after me? And if he is, why run off the other night or this morning? I didn't think serial killers were so skittish."

"If he wanted to kill you, he'd just shoot you from the tree line when you got out of your car."

"Not helping."

"I'm sorry. I didn't mean..."

She waved a hand in dismissal. "I get it."

"I want to help. But I'm as confused as you are. Can you think of any reason someone would be watching you? I know you're about to start divorce proceedings. Would your husband have hired someone?"

"To see what? And for what purpose? He's already told me he blew all our money and he inherited the house from his mother. Even if there was some leverage he could get on me, it wouldn't matter. There's nothing to fight over."

"What about the LeDoux? Leverage is their MO, right?"

"Sure, but they don't need any on me. At the moment, they're holding all the cards. Besides, that first night this guy was lurking around—the night I met you—was before Avery got into a fight with Chastity."

"But you'd already caught Chastity with your husband."

A blush crept up her neck. It was one thing to discuss her superbly failed marriage with other women, but rehashing the gory details with a man—a good-looking, single man—wasn't something she was comfortable with.

"Maybe Chastity was trying to get something on you," he continued. "Give herself something to fire back with in case you took her to task publicly."

"Everyone in Last Chance already knows exactly what kind of person Chastity is. And besides, she's not smart enough to prepare that way. Preston paid off her teachers to get her out of high school."

"Smart and clever are two different things. I've known plenty of people who couldn't add two and two but could screw you out of two hundred before you knew what was happening."

"That's true, but still, I don't see where she'd have anything to gain. She already has leverage against me with Avery."

"Okay, but I still think you should keep an eye on them. I haven't been in Last Chance for very long, but it seems that most of the problems in this town all stem from the same place."

Marina frowned. Was it really that simple? That one of the LeDoux had paid someone to get some dirt on her, just in case she protested her divorce or pursued charges against Chastity for stealing Avery's clothes or some other unpleasantness they might be anticipating? It seemed too simple. And for whatever reason, she felt as if something more sinister was going on.

Then a horrible thought occurred to her and she sucked in a breath.

"Are you all right?" Luke asked.

"Yes, sorry." She coughed to cover up her loss of control. "Sucked water down the wrong pipe."

He stared at her silently for several seconds, almost as if he was studying her, and she began to feel somewhat uncomfortable with his scrutiny. What was he thinking? Was he sorry he'd given her his number? Or sorry he'd helped Avery? God knows, most people wouldn't want to step into the middle of the mess she had going on and if he wanted to ghost her, she wouldn't blame him.

"Uh, I was thinking," he said. "I have this thing tomorrow night. A charity thing and it's at the LeDoux estate. I can bring a guest so if you wanted to go with me, it might be an opportunity to see how they act around you. Maybe they'll give something away."

Marina stared, all ability to speak completely gone. Was he asking her out on a date?

She wasn't even sure what that looked like anymore. Or felt like. Was she supposed to be this confused? This fearful? Of course, technically she was still married and had thought she was going to remain so until a few days ago, so there was that weighing in. And then there was all the current drama in her life. Why would Luke want to step further into that mess than he already had? And taking her to a party at the LeDoux estate would be jumping in naked and feet first. Besides, it wasn't as though she was a hot-bodied twenty-year-old. She was an overweight, past-her-prime, jobless, essentially homeless woman with limited funds to her name.

Why in the world would he risk aggravation to go out with her? What was the draw?

Luke must have sensed her apprehension because he launched into an explanation. "I hate those sort of things, but I don't have a choice in going. It's for the environment and I'm the game warden, so there's expectations. And since I buried myself in my work as soon as I got here, I haven't really taken the time to get to know people. Unfortunately, the ones I do know—mostly poachers and trespassers—are less than stellar. As are the LeDoux. So I really don't want to show up alone at an event at their house."

He alternated looking at her and glancing at the wall as he spoke, and Marina could tell he was as uncertain as she was. When he finally came up for air, she smiled.

"So you want to use me as your human shield?" she asked.

"Guilty as charged. I asked Adelaide if she'd go with me but she said she'd rather wrestle a bear."

"My money's on Adelaide."

"Mine too."

Marina looked at him, the anxious expression, the way he was bouncing one leg up and down. He was nervous. Guys got nervous? She'd always thought they held all the power, but here was this attractive, gainfully employed, full-head-of-hair guy, asking her to an event and looking worried that she might say no.

Which is exactly what she should say. For so many reasons.

"Do you think that's a good idea?" she asked finally. "I mean, you know what I've got going on with the LeDoux. I already put you in their sights by asking you to help Avery. Showing up to their house with me might have them all taking aim."

"You're worried about my reputation?"

"Well, yeah. And your job. Besides, if people see you there with me, what will they think?"

"I hadn't thought about it, but I suppose they'd think I was the smart one and Harold's an idiot."

She felt the blush creep up her neck and onto her face. Good Lord, she felt as though she was back in high school. Except no one had ever made her feel this way in high school. But if they had, then she was going to guess it would have been exactly like this. Her palms were sweating and for the first time in forever, it wasn't because of a hot flash. And she knew, with certainty, that come tomorrow, she was going to regret what she was about to do.

"And honestly," he continued, "if showing up with you on my arm makes the LeDoux mad, then that's just a bonus. They can't kick me out. I'm the game warden. And sorta the guest of honor."

"Yes," she said, before she could change her mind. "I'd love to be your human shield."

His shoulders relaxed and he smiled. "I can't think of anyone better to have in front of me."

Her face felt as if it were on fire and she was certain he'd noticed the color display. So embarrassing, and yet she was too excited to care. Which was troubling.

"Are you going to be okay here tonight?" he asked. "Maybe you should stay with your sister."

His words broke her out of her post-date-acceptance haze. "Halcyon is allergic to Snooze, and I don't want to leave him alone again. I did that last night to be with Avery. Snooze will alert me if my non-serial killer stalker returns, and Halcyon lent me a pistol and a shotgun. I know how to use both, in case you were wondering."

"This is Louisiana. Kinda goes without saying."

"We'll be fine. Whatever this guy is up to, he doesn't seem to be on a direct attack. Like you said—if he wanted to hurt me, he could get me coming out of my car."

Luke nodded and gave her shoulder a squeeze. "Then I'm going to head out. I'll pick you up at six tomorrow, if that's okay. And if you hear anything tonight, call. No matter the time. I'll have my phone with me."

He headed out of the cabin and she engaged the dead bolt behind him. Then she reached up and touched her shoulder where his hand had been.

Good Lord Almighty. Forty-eight years old and she was having her first official schoolgirl crush.

CHAPTER TWENTY-THREE

MARINA WAITED until her flushed skin had returned to normal before sending Alexios a text. The LeDoux were definitely gunning for her but there was another party who had an interest in her fading into the sunset. It took several minutes for Alexios to show up, and she began to worry that things had taken a turn for the worse and Alexios and his condo were long gone.

She could tell by his slumped shoulders and the tightness of his expression that things were still wrong. His movements were stiff as he crossed the living room and sat on one of the kitchen stools, and his red T-shirt was wrinkled. She looked down and almost gasped. His socks didn't match. Whatever was going on in his world, it was bad.

He noticed her gaze and sighed. "My dryer is on the blink. These were the only two clean ones I had left."

"You wash your clothes?"

"I have to if I want them clean."

"Of course. I was just...I guess I thought you just imagined what you wanted to wear and it was there. Or you walked into a closet and came out clothed. I never thought about gods doing laundry."

"Demigod," he corrected. "Gods *don't* do laundry. They have underlings for that."

"And your appliances break just like ours? This is all so fascinating."

"Our equipment doesn't work exactly as things do on earth, although the dryer eating one sock is a regular occurrence, hence why I had loose singles left in my drawer. But the method of power is different and since my connection to my world is sketchy, so is everything else. My television cut off right in the middle of *A Godwink Christmas* this morning, and I've never seen that one before."

"They end up together and they're still running the Charlotte Inn."

"Good to know in case things don't improve."

"Which is what I wanted to talk to you about. That and something else. So I take it things are still off for you? Have you been able to communicate with your world at all?"

"No. I've tried all avenues of communication, but everything is blocked. I finally got a message from Zeus that said simply to wait."

"Wait? On what?"

Alexios shook his head, clearly frustrated. "I have no idea. On the one hand, I'm happy that he responded at all. It means he's still up there and handling things. But that one word didn't tell me anything. Not about what is happening there or what could happen here."

"Do you think he's getting your messages and just can't risk answering?"

"I'm certain. But I hate being in the dark. It's unsettling."

Marina nodded. Unsettling was putting things lightly. If Zeus lost control of the other world, would having the ring make a difference? Or would all of humanity end up doing laundry for an invading species? Marina had just finished a twenty-eight-year stint waiting on other people. She'd been looking forward to wrinkled clothes and leaving dog hair on the floor for more than a day.

"Well, I'm afraid I have more unsettling things to discuss," she said and told Alexios about her stalker.

He listened intently, frowning the entire time, and sat silently when she was finished.

"Do you think someone from the invading world could be watching me?" she finally asked.

He slowly shook his head. "I can't say it's a certain no, but it doesn't seem likely. It's not easy to transport between worlds. It's what keeps them safe. And if our enemy had figured out how to access Earth, we wouldn't be having this conversation. It's like your famous scientist Stephen Hawking said—that an advanced civilization arriving never turns out well for the lesser one."

"I see. So you don't think this creep has anything to do with the ring?"

"I didn't say that. In fact, I think it's highly likely that he does."

"But how or who?"

"Remember I told you that Drakos had aligned himself with a small faction in our world that aligned with the invaders to overturn Zeus. My guess is it's one of our own who is here watching."

"Am I in danger?"

"I don't think so. I'm sure he's hoping you'll find the ring and will attempt to steal it before I can get it back to my world. Then they can use the power to overthrow Zeus."

"Oh. If I find the ring and he realizes it before you get here to collect, will he kill me?"

"I can't imagine why he would. You're no threat to our world."

"I'm no threat to *this* world unless I eat too much garlic."

"Yes, well, if only our world were being attacked by vampires, I'd take you back with me."

"I don't think I'd be very popular there. Not with your boss, anyway. I've developed this habit of saying what I think."

He gave her a small smile. "My guess is that is long overdue."

She nodded. "Are you sure there's nothing else you can tell me about the ring? In all this time, you've never formed an opinion on how to find it? On how it hides? On what might prompt it to give a signal?"

He was silent for several seconds, his brow scrunched. "I've been going over my notes—trying to find something that would help. There was one incident that was a bit off, but it was prior to my being placed on this assignment, so the information I have is secondhand."

"Secondhand is better than nothing. A lot of facts can be carried in gossip."

"That's true. Well, the story as I heard it is that one of the Seekers started feeling odd—dizzy, short of breath, flushed— but only when she was at home. It never happened elsewhere."

"But she couldn't find the ring?"

"No. And given that she died of heart failure shortly after my predecessor met her, we can't be certain she was even in proximity of the ring. It might have been a medical condition."

"But she had no symptoms outside her house? Unless there was something toxic in her home, that doesn't track."

"Correct. My predecessor checked for toxins but found nothing. However, she'd had a young child die shortly before he arrived. Remember, this was years before competent medical care was readily available so it wasn't uncommon.

Because of that, the argument was made that being in the home and seeing her daughter's belongings triggered the failure of an already-weak heart, but that when she was away from her home, it was easier to block from her mind."

Marina sighed. "Yeah, that makes more sense than the ring causing it. What about Aphrodite?"

"What would you like to know?"

"What does she like? I know she likes dogs, but what else? If the ring contains her blood then it might be attracted to the same things she is. What does she love the most?"

He gave her a rueful smile. "Herself. Aphrodite is very self-indulgent. I assume you gathered that from the way she treats her husband and her dismissal of her sexual partners, even those she shares a child with."

"She doesn't sound like a very nice person...um, goddess."

"There are worse, but there are better."

"And there's nothing else you can think of? Nothing at all that might send me to the right avenue of investigation?"

He shook his head. "I wish there were. I've gone over everything a thousand times—literally—but I can't come up with anything."

She nodded. It was disappointing, but she figured that would be the case. Alexios had nothing but time and if there was anything that had stood out to him, he'd had plenty of opportunity to notice and document it. It was beyond troubling to her that this situation had carried on for so long and through so many Seekers and yet they still knew next to nothing. Maybe it was as simple as the ring was no longer on earth.

"So given that I have a stalker, what's the plan if I find the ring?" she asked. "Do I text you that instant? Or should you just follow me around in case this guy is trailing me other places besides just my house?"

"I wish I could go everywhere with you. Two days ago, I

could have. But along with my inability to communicate, I've been cut off from my power supply. Hence the issue with my television and my dryer. I can't run my condo on electricity or any of your other fuels, so right now, I'm on what you would refer to as a backup generator."

"That doesn't sound good. What happens if you run out of juice?"

"Then all my ties to my world are severed and I have to hope that someone comes looking for me. That someone is *able* to come looking for me. In order to prevent cutting off all access to communication, I have to ration my power, which means I need to stay in the condo. Leaving and reentering takes a good amount of 'juice' as you call it, so I need to stay put until you find the ring."

Marina liked how Alexios said "until" and not "in case," but then she guessed if the alternative was remaining trapped in another world in an invisible condo with no power, she'd be optimistic too. At least her dryer worked.

"So basically, don't call unless I have something," she said.

"I'm afraid so. I'm really sorry about this. I wish I could hang around and look out for this man. I know it must be unnerving knowing that someone is watching you."

"I'm less than thrilled about it. But what about you? Is there anything I can get you for your condo? I have clean socks. Do you need food or something to drink? A book maybe, since you're on television hiatus?"

Alexios stared at her for a moment, clearly surprised. "You'd do that for me?"

"Of course. If I have anything that can help, it's yours."

He leaned over and kissed her on the cheek, then sniffed, and she could see the tears pooling in his eyes. "That's the nicest thing anyone has ever said to me."

"That's a shame. Manners are free. So is kindness."

He smiled. "You're an incredible person, Marina Trahan. I am rarely surprised but you've surprised me. And since I can tell you're sincere in your offer, I would love a pair of matching socks and if you have a couple of good romance books, that would be great."

She grinned and headed into the bedroom, dug around in the boxes for a minute, and came back with a box of socks and a stack of romances.

"These are new," Alexios said as he opened the box. "And so soft!"

"I'm on my feet all day. The one thing I do *not* scrimp on is footwear."

He gathered the socks and books and looked at her.

"I have great faith in you, Marina. That's never been the case before. You're not at all like the others, but in the ways that I believe will ultimately count the most, you're so much more. Believe in yourself and the ring is yours."

He headed out the door and Marina drew the dead bolt. Her heart clenched for the strange man from another world, who would be sitting, invisible, in a box, while a stranger held his life in the balance. Cut off from his world, he didn't even have the ability to make final declarations to his loved ones.

She couldn't even begin to imagine how he felt.

Everything she cared about was at risk as well, but it was all at her fingertips. She could pick up the phone and call Avery just to hear her voice. She could be at her sister's house in ten minutes, drinking wine and bitching about her day. She could sit in her recliner, watching television and scratching Snooze's head.

She wasn't alone.

CHAPTER TWENTY-FOUR

HALCYON STARED AT MARINA, then pinched her own arm. She frowned and walked up to Marina and put her hand on her forehead.

"What are you doing?" Marina asked, batting her sister's hand away.

"I'm trying to see if you're running a fever."

"Why would I be running a fever?"

"Maybe you're ill?"

"I'm perfectly fine."

Halcyon leaned in and studied her face closely. "Show me your boobs."

"What? No! What the hell is wrong with you?"

Halcyon took a step back and crossed her arms across her chest. "I don't believe you're my sister. Those gods have taken the real Marina and replaced you with something else. You have a birthmark below your left boob. I figure they wouldn't get that detailed with a clone. So...Mardi Gras up. Show me your boobs."

"Oh, for Christ's sake," Marina said, and yanked her tank and bra up so that Halcyon could see the heart-shaped birthmark under her left breast. It used to be right below her left breast, but after the day gravity happened, it became underneath.

Halcyon gave the birthmark the side-eye.

"What's your favorite food?" Halcyon asked.

"I tell everyone it's pizza but it's really Reddi-wip, straight out of the can."

Halcyon's jaw dropped and she sank onto a stool. "It's really you."

"Of course it's me."

"But you showed up at the crack of dawn and told me I have to help you with clothes because you have a date tonight. Do you realize how that sounds?"

"You thought I was an imposter because I have a date?"

"Marina, this is *you*. You and Harold sort of fell into a relationship in high school without any romantic dancing beforehand. As far as I know, you've never been on an official date in your life. And now, you waltz in here and tell me you're going out with a man you met a couple of days ago *and* you need something to wear."

Halcyon threw her hands in the air. "I had an easier time believing the magical ring story."

Marina considered. "I guess it is a bit out of character."

"More like out of this universe."

"I thought you'd be happy."

"As soon as I get over being dumbfounded, I'm going to be ecstatic."

"I haven't even told you the best part."

Halcyon sucked in a breath. "You test-drove him already?"

"What? No! Of course not. He asked me to be his date to the charity event."

Halcyon's eyes widened. "Oh! At the LeDoux estate."

"Why do you think I said yes? This is my only legal opportunity to search for the ring there. Good God, I'm not ready to start dating and I'm definitely not ready to test-drive someone. But they can't kick Luke out without looking bad so they'll tolerate me because of him."

Halcyon tilted her head to the side and studied Marina for a bit. "You might not be ready to start dating but you're attracted to Luke."

"Well, yeah. Sort of. I mean, he's an attractive man and he helped Avery. It's hard not to like him."

"I like him too. But like has nothing to do with attraction."

"Can we please not talk about that now? There's another situation I need to tell you about."

She filled Halcyon in on her stalker and her sister grew more agitated as she explained. When she was done, Halcyon threw her hands in the air.

"What the hell were the gods thinking? Aren't they supposed to have everything figured out? They're doing a crappy job of running all of this if they didn't anticipate this happening."

"*We* didn't anticipate it happening."

"*We* didn't know the enemy could pop down to earth like Alexios."

"True. So they're behind the eight ball, which isn't good, but it doesn't change reality. This guy is probably lurking everywhere, just waiting on me to find the ring. And when I do..."

"He's going to make his move."

"And if he gets the ring, then it's all over."

Halcyon frowned. "How do we know that Alexios is the good guy? I mean, we only have his word. What if he's working for the enemy?"

"I don't think so. Unless any of the others can send lightning down to earth, I have the singed carpet to prove that

Zeus was listening to Alexios when he first met with me. Besides, you've met him and you're a human lie detector. Do you think he's working with the enemy?"

"I would first like to point out that Alexios is only half human, so that might imply that my detector is only half effective. But you're right. I think he's exactly who he says he is. All that stuff with the condo and the socks and reading romance books is just too in-depth to be playing a role. Besides, I know acting when I see it."

Marina nodded. "So I need a plan. For if I find the ring, I mean."

"Right, because Stalker Boy will be lurking. Okay, what we need is a decoy. You'll have it with you at all times and when you find the real one, you hide it under a boob and have the decoy in your purse. No one will look under your boob."

"Except you, apparently."

"That's different. I once hid a joint under my boob and even made it past pat-down at the jail. Traded it to Deputy Franks for a turkey sandwich and a sugar cookie. I was *so* hungry."

Marina stared. "There is so much wrong with that story, I'm not even sure where to start."

Halcyon waved a hand in dismissal. "Later."

"Here's another sticking point—Alexios said the gods can't see the ring, remember? So if I pull out basic jewelry and they can see it, won't they know it's a fake?"

"Maybe once you find it, the ring becomes visible again."

Marina considered this. "I suppose that's as plausible as everything else, isn't it?"

"All you have to do is try not to give Stalker Boy the ring, and when he threatens violence, then cough it up but be all weepy and sad and shit."

"And I am supposed to just whip up a batch of weepy and sad? I don't have your abilities."

"Think about *Old Yeller*."

Marina stared at her sister in dismay. "That book sucked so hard. I had nightmares for weeks. Why on earth is it in the elementary school library?"

"Exactly my point. There's no way you can keep from crying if you think about that poor dog."

Marina sniffed. "Okay, maybe that will work."

"Maybe?"

"Stop talking about it or I'm going to cry."

Halcyon grinned. "I think I have the decoy thing covered. Give me a sec."

She headed down the hall for her bedroom and Marina walked over to the kitchen window to look outside. The lady who lived across the street was out deadheading her flowers. Her husband was on the porch making fishing lures. Two houses over, a harried mother wrestled two young children into her car. That was it. All completely normal. But somewhere out there, Stalker Boy had to be lurking.

Or was he?

If Alexios had lost power, did that mean Stalker Boy was working without ties to their world as well? It would make sense. She assumed the use of power could attract attention. So if Stalker Boy was trying to fly below god radar, then he probably wasn't zipping around Last Chance in an invisible condo. Which meant he was on foot unless he'd stolen something to get around. Or unless he could fly.

She sighed. These were things that it would have been nice to go over with Alexios. But with him on lockdown, all she had was supposition and her own creativity to go on. And at the moment, her creativity was in overdrive.

Halcyon hurried back into the room and handed her a ring.

She lifted it to get a closer look. It was a single silver band with a large ruby framed by diamonds.

"This is nice!" Marina said. "I can't let Stalker Boy steal this. It's got to be worth some serious cash."

"It's fake. A good fake, but a fake, nonetheless. It was a prop for one of the plays we did last year. I have a bunch of stuff for the theater group stored under my stairs."

"What if he can tell it's not real?"

"Do you think they're all jewelers? If you refuse to hand it over right away, Stalker Boy will think he's getting the real deal once you do."

"You think so?"

"I don't see why not. I have a velvet jeweler's pouch I'll get you. That will make it look more legit and will be easier than a box."

"Okay. One problem solved. Now, about my wardrobe..."

Halcyon blew out a breath. "I'm afraid that one is going to take a bit longer."

"Thanks."

"Just being honest. You've never needed that kind of wardrobe since Harold wasn't exactly the type to rub elbows wearing a tuxedo. And given that I'm a good four inches taller than you and all my evening wear is made for high heels, everything I have would be granny length on you."

"Not to mention you're thinner than me."

"That's spandex. I'm a size 14, just like you."

"You're wearing spandex right now?"

"No, I'm wearing black jeans and shirt, and the shirt is loose enough and long enough to hide a bunch of stuff that doesn't need to be seen."

"If only my inherited skills applied to weight loss."

"Tell me about it. I'd have you rubbing my fat butt every day, even if you didn't want to. Dieting sucks."

"I tried South Beach for a couple weeks this spring."

"How did that go?"

"I gained two pounds."

Halcyon shook her head. "That's why women stop trying. I did that keto thing that everyone is raving about. Tracked everything I put in my mouth. I even skipped a cough drop when I had an allergy attack because of the sugar in it. One week later, I'd lost half a pound. The engineer was supposed to be doing it with me. He cheated with hamburgers, chips, cereal, and regular sodas and lost four pounds."

"How is that possible?"

"I have no idea. But it's the exact reason women quit dieting and why there's no excuse for a guy with a roll around his waist. All they have to do is give up one beer a week and the weight falls off. Things like this, hot flashes, and pantyhose are why I'm certain God's a man."

"Truth," Marina agreed. "Could we hem something of yours?"

"One of us might be able to, but it wouldn't be me."

Marina sighed. "Sewing isn't exactly my gift either. Working with fine fabrics probably isn't the time to try my hand at it again."

"Do you have an iron?"

"Yes. You don't?"

"The rare garment of mine that needs ironing goes straight to the dry cleaner."

"But how do you get the wrinkles out of your sheets?"

"I don't. Why in the world would I care about wrinkled sheets? I'm sleeping on them. You know, adding more wrinkles, especially if I have company. We really need to work on your priorities."

"If I start sleeping on wrinkled sheets would that make you happy?"

"It would be a start. How much time do you need for hair and makeup?"

"Including shower? Forty-five minutes, maybe."

"Okay, then get that done by five and then I'll come to get you in a dress."

"It's going to take an hour to get me in a dress?"

"Potentially. Just get everything else done beforehand. It's hard to breathe well in the spandex, and sometimes it hurts a little to lift your arms."

"It sounds like you're going to give me a heart attack."

Halcyon shook her head. "We're going to give *him* a heart attack."

CHAPTER TWENTY-FIVE

ADELAIDE BANGED on Dottie's door, tapping her foot as she waited for an answer. It was too early for house calls, but when it was an emergency, basic Southern manners didn't apply. And this was definitely an emergency. When Dottie finally opened the door, she peered out at Adelaide with a frown.

"What on earth are you doing banging on my door before nine o'clock in the morning?" Dottie asked.

"You know you've been up since five. Can't sleep late with an old bladder."

Dottie closed her eyes and sighed. "That is beside the point. Get inside before the neighbors see you standing there all disheveled."

"What are you talking about?" Adelaide said as she walked inside and followed Dottie back to the kitchen. "I just took these out of the dryer."

"Really? And when did the dryer cycle finish?"

Adelaide shrugged. "Yesterday maybe. Monday. I don't know."

Dottie waved at the breakfast table. "I just made a fresh pot of coffee and cinnamon rolls. I assume you're interested?"

"Hot damn! I came at the right time."

"I'm sure it wasn't planned," Dottie said as she sat the tray of cinnamon rolls on the table then poured two cups of coffee. "So to what do I owe the pleasure of your company?"

Adelaide stuffed half a cinnamon roll into her mouth. "I need a favor," she said as she chewed.

"That's both intriguing and frightening."

"I know. That's why I'm here. Are you invited to that charity shindig at the LeDoux's?"

"Of course. I'm one of their biggest contributors. Preston never misses an opportunity to attempt to kiss my butt. He thinks, incorrectly of course, that he can convince me to support him in his bid for mayor."

"Ha! You'd vote for me before you'd vote for Preston."

"Unfortunate and also true."

"Are you going alone?"

"I'm not going at all. I never do."

"I need you to go this year and take a plus-one."

"Given that this isn't my scheduled week for resurrecting my dead husband, I'm not certain how I'd manage a date."

"Don't give me that. You could have a date. You keep yourself up."

"I keep myself up for me. I don't want a relationship with a man. That part of my life is over. Once you've had a great one, no one else would ever measure up."

Adelaide nodded. "I can see that."

Dottie studied her for a bit. "You actually mean that."

"Of course I do. William was one of the rare good ones. I don't like most people and even fewer men, but William was an exception. You picked well, Dottie. I don't blame you for quitting while you're ahead."

Dottie looked pleased and then gave her a curious look. "And there was never anyone who tempted you?"

"Once. I was barely eighteen. He swept into town and swept me off my feet, if you can believe it."

"So what happened to him?"

"He went back to his wife."

"Oh." Dottie frowned. "I'm sorry."

Adelaide waved a hand in dismissal. "Like I said. William was one of the rare good ones."

"Wait—you never took another chance? You were only eighteen."

"I was old enough to know what I didn't want, and that was it. Watched my momma put up with too much crap. It didn't seem like a good fit for me. Figured I'd end up in prison while the cops dug up my backyard looking for a body."

Dottie sighed. "Why do you have to take everything to the extreme?"

"Because then I can be pleasantly surprised when things don't go poorly."

"There's a certain dismal logic in that. Anyway, what is this favor?"

"I want to be your date for the charity thingy."

Dottie shook her head. "Absolutely not."

"You didn't even hear my reason why."

"There is no reason good enough for me to risk taking you as my guest to the LeDoux's."

"What if Christ was returning?"

"He wouldn't go to the LeDoux's."

"Fair enough. You know my cousin Luke is the new game warden, right?"

"Of course. He's one of the guests of honor, although I'm guessing Preston isn't overly happy about that now, given that he helped Avery get out of jail."

"Yeah, well, he just added insult to injury. He's taking Marina as his date."

Dottie's eyes widened. "You're lying."

"I'm a lot of things, but a liar isn't one of them."

Dottie covered her mouth with her hand. "Good. God."

"I told you I had a reason."

"Christ returning would have been easier to manage. What in the world is he thinking?"

"Maybe he's thinking that Marina is pretty and the LeDoux suck."

"Well, what is *she* thinking?"

"That Luke is hot and Harold never was?"

Dottie wrinkled her nose. "He's your family and at least twenty years your junior. You can't go around calling him hot. It's unseemly."

Adelaide shrugged. "I got eyes, don't I? Him being younger just means he looks better cause he's still got his teeth and hair. And he's like a fifth cousin or even further down the line. I probably share more blood with you."

"I don't know why I bother."

"Neither do I."

"Well, you have to tell him that he can't do this."

"Already did. He said pissing the LeDoux off was just a bonus."

Dottie threw her hands in the air. "Then we have to talk to Marina. Explain to her what a horrible idea this is."

"Did that too. She told me she had her reasons and nothing I said would change her mind."

"What in the name of all that is holy is going on in this town? When sane, low-key women like Marina Trahan start acting this far out of character, I have to wonder what's in the water supply."

"Maybe she's on drugs, or maybe she's following in her mother's footsteps, or maybe she's just reached that state of not giving a damn that I was born with. Regardless of the reason, she's going to that party and I'll bet money there will be trouble."

"And you think by being there you'll prevent it?"

"Not a chance. But if things go south, Marina will need help."

Dottie blew out a breath. "Okay. Because this is a real emergency, I'm going to do something I never do and not only go to that party but bring you as my date. *But* I expect you to wear something appropriate. And you're not bringing that shovel. I'm also patting you down beforehand."

"There's so much trust in this room, it's overwhelming."

"What's overwhelming you is all the reality."

Dottie rose from her chair and motioned to Adelaide. "You need to go. I have things to do to get ready."

"Like what? It's not even midmorning."

"For starters, I'm going to church to pray."

———

WITH HALF of the morning and most of the afternoon stretching in front of her, Marina decided to try a different tactic and search for the ring by computer. Halcyon had some appointments that would eat up most of her day, so Marina was on her own. With Stalker Boy probably lurking somewhere nearby, she didn't feel like sticking to her cabin, so she grabbed her laptop and headed into town. The café had free Wi-Fi and excellent breakfast, so she figured she'd spend a couple hours there, then decide what to do next.

The early breakfast crowd had cleared out and gone to work and the seniors were usually long gone by midmorning as well, so only one other table was occupied. Marina headed to a booth in the corner that sat in front of the big picture windows that faced Main Street. That way, if Stalker Boy was lurking somewhere, she might be able to get a good look at him.

A girl Avery had gone to high school with popped over, chewing gum and smiling at the same time. "Morning, Mrs. Trahan. What can I get you?"

"Coffee and the breakfast special, please."

"Do you want pancakes or waffles? Oh, and chef made some vanilla croissants this morning. You can have that instead."

"That sounds great."

She nodded. "I had one myself. How's Avery doing at school?"

"She's getting settled in and likes it so far. Classes start next week."

"I heard about her problem with Chastity. That girl is nothing but trouble. Chastity, I mean. Not Avery. I'm really sorry she had to deal with that. You too."

A wave of embarrassment rushed through Marina and she struggled to shove it down. Would she ever be able to accept these expressions of sympathy without feeling awful all over again?

"Thank you," Marina said. "What are you planning to do now that you're done with high school?"

"Oh, I start nursing school in January. I'm working here until then, putting together some spending money, you know?"

"That's great. Well, good luck."

"Thank you, and tell Avery hi next time you talk to her."

"I will."

Marina looked up and down the street but didn't see anyone she didn't recognize. If Stalker Boy was around, he was out of sight, but he couldn't stand in the bushes forever without someone having a problem with it. If she kept checking, she might get a peek.

The server brought her coffee and Marina opened her laptop and googled Aphrodite. Might as well start with the source, right? If the ring held Aphrodite's blood then maybe it was attracted to other things that she liked as well as to the Seeker. Maybe she had a penchant for vanilla croissants and the ring was right here in the café in the lost-and-found box. It was just as reasonable a theory as anything else. She scanned several sites that offered up information on the goddess but ultimately, it was all legend and speculation.

She picked up her coffee and took a sip. Of course it was all speculation. What else could it be? Humans didn't believe that those gods actually existed. Plenty believed in a god, but probably not a lot worshipped at the altar of Zeus. These were legends. The stuff tall tales and sometimes interesting movies were made of.

But the other Seekers were real.

They hadn't been successful, but maybe there was a common thread among them that would give her a hint. Cleopatra, Lady Godiva, and Marilyn Monroe. She started searching again and stopped ten minutes later when her breakfast came out.

Well, they were all women. And all were considered beauties of their time. All had power of some sort. Cleopatra was married twice with many lovers. Lady Godiva married once and had no known lovers. Marilyn Monroe married three times and the lovers part was sketchy as hell. Cleopatra had four kids. Lady Godiva had nine. Marilyn never had any, although she'd tried. One lived in Egypt. One in England and one in the United States. All lived in opulence.

Marina was never considered a great beauty and certainly not "of her time." The only power she consistently displayed was over Snooze and since she fed him, that wasn't really anything to brag about. She'd been married once and her husband had a lover, but that probably didn't count. She had one child, who might be destined for prison if she couldn't straighten things out, and she currently lived in a shack on a mosquito-infested bayou where her only bathroom sink desperately needed a plumber.

Her life and theirs couldn't have been more different.

Unless you counted Lady Godiva riding naked on a horse to get lower taxes. Marina had never ridden a horse sans clothing, but there was that one jaunt on a four-wheeler. Unfortunately, it hadn't been a financial boon to anyone except the doctor who'd treated the grass burns she'd gotten when she wrecked. She'd be willing to do it again if someone would lower her taxes, although she suspected that the government would be more inclined to give her a break if she agreed to always ride clothed.

"Here you go." The server slid her breakfast on the table and Marina smiled at the eggs and bacon and practically salivated over the vanilla croissant.

"This looks great," she said. "Thanks!"

"I'll be back with more coffee in a sec."

Marina mulled over what she knew about the ring while tackling her eggs and bacon. Since she had more breakfast than facts, mulling took her about four bites in. She held in a sigh. When she'd agreed to do this, she hadn't thought it would be so difficult. She'd thought it would be more like hide-and-seek for adults.

And she hadn't really bought into the whole end-of-the-world scenario. She'd thought Alexios was just being dramatic. And in all fairness, he did strike her as someone who Avery would label "extra." But now, with communication cut off from his world and the way he looked yesterday, Marina convinced that Alexios had been telling her the truth. It wasn't just a story to get her to move faster. Things were really dire.

How in the world was she supposed to accomplish in a matter of days what others hadn't managed over the course of their lifetimes?

But somehow, she had to do it. Because in few days—give or take—the world as she knew it might end. No more Avery, Halcyon, or Snooze. No more breakfasts at the café. No more opportunities to ride naked on a four-wheeler. Granted, there would also be no more Harold, her mother, Chastity, Patricia, or Preston, but that wasn't the way she wanted to rid her life of those people. The price was too steep.

"Are you out celebrating your newfound insanity?" Adelaide's voice cut into her thoughts.

"Maybe," Marina said, and motioned for her to sit.

Adelaide slid into the booth and snagged a piece of her croissant before she could protest.

"If you're going to try to talk me out of going to that charity thing with Luke, don't waste your breath," Marina said. "My mind is made up and nothing short of death is going to change it."

Adelaide nodded. "I figured as much. I don't pretend to understand why you want to walk into the lion's den, but if it's something you've got to do then I can respect that. You're not a woman who does things by the seat of her pants. You said you've got reasons. That's good enough for me."

Marina studied Adelaide for a bit. "Why are things so easy for you to accept? I almost never see you flustered, unless it's over your cats."

Adelaide shrugged. "No point in making a fuss over things I can't change."

"You can't change cats."

"God, isn't that the truth. My one weakness, I suppose."

"I wish I could do it. Stop worrying so much, that is. It's exhausting."

"It's easy enough to do."

"Is it really that easy for you? How?"

"Because I don't care what people think of me and I don't have to consider anyone else when I make decisions."

"I guess that is a big advantage of never marrying or having kids."

"Among others. I know what most people think—that I'm the lonely, crazy cat lady who should be pitied. They couldn't be more wrong. I love my life. Have loved every day of it, even the crappy ones. And I've had my share. But every single minute—good or bad—I only had myself to congratulate or blame. It's easier to compromise with yourself than with others."

"You've never wanted a relationship? Someone special to share your life with?"

"Maybe once, as a young girl. But that dream passed and reality set in."

"Trust me, I'm full on reality at the moment and being alone is looking better than ever. But still, there's times when it would be nice to have someone help you pull the weight."

Adelaide raised one eyebrow. "What weight, exactly, did Harold help you pull? You took care of the house and did a good job trying to remodel that tacky hunk of lumber. You cooked the meals and tended the garden. You raised that girl. And you did it all while still contributing to the household finances."

Marina stared down at the table. "I've been thinking a lot about that lately."

"And you know I'm right. That's no slam against you. Good Lord, I'd bet that's life for 90 percent of women with a family."

Marina looked at Adelaide. "Being overworked, taken for granted, and marginalized?"

"Yes."

"Well, it's crap."

"Of course it's crap but...there's that reality thing again. You can't change the past, but you can damn sure choose your future. You've taken control of everything that has been flung your direction. Where was Harold when Avery was being arrested? When she was in jail? When she was in court? You've always been the strong one. You just bowed down to centuries of outdated thinking and deferred to the man of the house, when the truth is, there *was* no man in your house. There was only you."

Marina flushed a bit, both pleased and embarrassed by Adelaide's words.

"It wasn't always that way," Marina said. "Harold and I, I mean. We got together in high school probably because we were both too shy to force ourselves into situations where we might become the center of attention. Harold was sweet then. We both loved music and he took me to every concert we could scratch up the money for. On weekends, we'd pack a picnic basket and head out in his boat to fish but we usually ended up reading books or talking and napping."

Marina shook her head. "Even when we were first married, it was fun. I suppose, in the beginning, we were nothing more than two kids playing house but it was an adventure every time we scraped together the funds for something extra. The decision for Harold to open his own business was made jointly and we celebrated every new client with dinner and wine. I've never seen anyone more excited than Harold when I told him I was pregnant with Avery."

Marina sighed. "And then..."

"Life has a way of taking the joy out of living if you let it," Adelaide said. "I've seen so many couples just like you two get beaten down by responsibility and tragedy. And unfortunately, it's usually only one of them that keeps it all together. Then the one who got off easy complains about the lack of attention while the one who's been juggling all the balls resents having no help."

"I guess that pretty much sums it up. I hate that my life has been reduced to a cliché."

"Only a small piece of it. But the rest of it is what you choose to make it and my money's on you having a better future than Harold. You can handle anything life tosses at you. Harold, not so much."

"I wish that were true. But at the moment, even plumbing is getting the best of me. I have a leak in my bathroom sink and can't get Bucky to return a phone call."

Adelaide waved a hand in dismissal. "He's paid his utility bill and has beer money for the next week. You won't hear from him until he runs out."

"This town could really use another plumber."

Adelaide narrowed her eyes at Marina. "Maybe."

"What? You think I should fix it myself?"

"Why not? In the time you spend waiting on Bucky to put down his beer and return a phone call, you could probably figure out how to do it yourself. You did plenty of home improvement stuff before. Besides, you young people have the YouTube. It's probably on there."

Marina smiled. "You really don't like depending on other people, do you?"

"I passed introvert somewhere in my teens and moved straight to hermit when my parents died and I inherited their house and investments. After I quit my teaching job, I stocked up on groceries and didn't leave my house for a month. It was a glorious thirty days."

"I can see that."

"But you and I are very different people. Humans drain me

so I try to avoid them as much as possible. But you're good with people and perhaps more importantly, good *for* people. That's a calling that I'm afraid you'll never be able to shake."

"So you're saying I'm doomed to a life of socializing?"

"You're doomed to a life of being surrounded by people who care about you. There are worse things."

"Like being surrounded by buttholes?"

"Ha. Yeah, you've had your share of that lately. Going to get another taste of it tonight. I know I can't talk you out of going, but I want you to be careful. The LeDoux are smarting over Luke getting Avery out of jail, and the threat of pursuing a theft charge for their little angel has them more than a little ruffled. They won't tell you to leave. Not as Luke's guest. But the passive-aggressive behavior will be full force."

"I'm not looking to make more trouble for Avery or for myself. But if my being there diminishes their joy, then there's no place I'd rather be."

Adelaide snorted. "You and Luke share the same thoughts on that one. You like him, don't you?"

Marina struggled to keep her expression normal. "Of course. Why wouldn't I, after what he did for Avery?"

"Yes. He really came through on that one. Still, that's not what I meant and you know it. But don't worry. I won't pry. The only advice I have concerning romantic entanglements is to avoid them, but that doesn't work for everyone."

"We're not entangled. I'm not even divorced."

"The heart doesn't know anything about our legal system."

"But I—"

Adelaide rose and reached over to pat her hand. "You're a good woman. Better than you know. Stronger than you ever thought. You'll figure out the rest. I'll see you tonight."

"What? Tonight?"

Adelaide just waved over her shoulder as she walked out of

the café. Marina blew out a breath. Luke said Adelaide refused to be his plus-one, and she didn't think he was lying. And there was absolutely no way the LeDoux had invited Adelaide to their house. Since she wasn't financially indebted to him and didn't care if everyone knew everything about her, Preston didn't have anything he could use to keep her in her place. So who was she going with? And why?

Her cell phone rang and she saw it was Bucky. About time.

"You called about your sink, right?" he said. "I can probably get to it in a week or so. Can't give you an exact day or time. Might not even be that week."

Marina stared out the window as Adelaide crossed the street, walking right in the middle of traffic and fully expecting they'd all stop.

"You know what—don't bother. I'll fix it myself."

CHAPTER TWENTY-SIX

MARINA STARED at the tiny black garment Halcyon was holding, her feeble recollection of physics and geometry rolling through her mind.

"That looks like a hair band," Marina said. "There's no way that will fit around my waist or hips. Heck, even my head might be stretching it—literally."

"I wore this last spring for the engineer's company party."

Marina grabbed the offending item and dangled it from her pinkie. "This? You wore this swatch? Where? On your ankle?"

"It fits from under your chest to just over your hips. Smooths everything out and gives you an awesome waist. Just makes things disappear."

Marina shook her head. "No. It can't make things disappear. All those things that appear to be gone have just been shoved somewhere else. Like into a kidney or, God forbid, into a bra. I don't have any more room at that inn."

"Let's just try it. If it doesn't work, then you don't have to wear it. The dress has a little room in it, and it's stretchy material."

"Great. If this doesn't work, I can look like a lumpy mess."

"This will work. Trust me."

"I'm having trouble understanding how you even got in this."

"Crisco and water pills. We don't have time for the water pills so we'll just have to make do. Although if you'd told me you were going to spend the day playing plumber, I would have gone ahead with that plan. You were already in the bathroom most of the day."

"You want me to lather up with cooking oil? Won't the hair band slide around? I don't want to be that woman pulling at her undergarments all night."

"The Crisco sinks into your skin after a bit. Makes it really smooth, so added bonus in case things progress beyond your claim that you're doing this to find the ring and Luke's claim that he's doing it to make the LeDoux mad."

"Things will not progress. I'm not in a place to progress. This is a non-progressing sort of deal."

Halcyon shrugged. "Suit yourself, but you realize that if you don't find the ring, you've only got so many days left to get in some really awesome sex. And I'd really like for you to have some before you die."

"How do you know...you know what, never mind."

"How do I know when it's really awesome? Or how do I know you haven't had any? I think the second question is self-explanatory given that I know Harold is your one and only and, well, Harold. As to the first, when your entire body tingles, then catches fire—but in a good way, not a hot flash way—then it explodes in wave after wave of ecstasy that feels so incredible that you don't even care if it was your last moment on earth. Your mind is empty of everything but pleasure. You're too weak to move. All you can do is breathe and with every breath, your body tingles all over again."

Marina sighed. She'd definitely never had an experience

like Halcyon described. With some coaching, she'd taught Harold how to get her to the finish line, so to speak. But she'd never flamed from pleasure and her mind had never gone blank. It had usually made a mental note to change the bedsheets.

Had her entire life been about settling?

Halcyon squeezed her arm. "Oh, honey, I'm sorry. I wasn't trying to make you feel bad."

"You didn't do anything. It's just that lately I view my life different from how I did before. And I don't like a lot of what I see."

"You still have time to change all that."

"Do I?"

"Absolutely. You're going to find that ring and save the world and collect all that money. Then you and I are going to spend at least a year traveling to exotic places with even more exotic men."

Marina nodded, but she knew that what Halcyon wanted was a dream. A great big glorious dream, but such a long shot. And even if she found the ring, there were so many other things going on in Alexios's world that she worried it might be too late. But she couldn't think about any of that now. With so many things overwhelming her mind, it was better if she just concentrated on one at a time. She needed to attend the party and figure out a way to wander around and see if she could sense the ring. Assuming wandering was possible wearing a hair band around her waist.

"Let's get me stuffed in this thing like boudin," Marina said.

"Now you're talking." Halcyon reached into the tote bag she'd brought with her and handed Marina a tin of Crisco.

"You were serious about that?"

"Get naked and slick."

Marina cringed. "Words you never want to hear directed at you from your sister."

"C'mon. You're burning daylight and I've still got to address the hem."

Marina pointed at Snooze, who was lounging in the corner of her bedroom. "Out. I'm not willing to embarrass myself in front of more living beings than Halcyon."

Snooze rose from his spot and headed for the living room. She could swear he was looking at her as if she'd lost her mind. Refusing to be shamed by her dog, Marina shrugged off her robe and dug out a gob of the Crisco. She hesitated for a moment, then slapped the goo on midthigh where Halcyon had indicated and rubbed it up to just under her chest, giving a silent thanks that Halcyon was busy digging shoes and purses out of the tote bag rather than watching her. She'd already turned her back to the mirror, not even wanting to see the debacle herself.

"How's it going?" Halcyon asked and looked over at her.

"All done on the front and sides. I can't reach all of my back."

"I'll get that. Turn around."

Marina faced the wall and got a full-length view of her naked, greased self and frowned. Yes, she showered every day —sometimes more if it was a particularly bad hot flash day— but she usually toweled off and pulled on clothes of some sort. She didn't really spend time staring at herself naked from head to toe.

At first, she wanted to tell Halcyon to forget everything, pull on her robe again, and destroy all the mirrors in her home. Then she looked again. This time taking into account the last twenty-eight years of her life.

There were stretch marks, of course. She had Avery to thank for those and for the loose skin around her middle.

Well, it used to be loose. In the past five years, she'd packed on enough pounds to fill it out. And the cuts she used to have in her thighs and biceps were rounded out now, disguising the muscle beneath that she knew was still there.

She smiled. Honestly, she looked pretty damned good.

"Let's do this," Halcyon said.

"What the hell," Marina said and stepped into the hair band.

"I'll get the back. You work the front. It's better if we pull at the same time."

Marina bent over and grabbed the top of the hair band. "One, two, three."

Both she and Halcyon pulled at the same time and managed to get it past her knees and onto her thighs, where everything came to a halt.

"Okay," Halcyon said. "This is where we start inching it up. The top is touching the Crisco, so if we can get it all over the grease then we'll be good."

Marina wiggled her toes, pretty sure blood flow had stopped to her feet, then regripped the top of the hair band and gave it a hard tug. It inched up a bit and Halcyon followed with a pull on the back. They continued this method of coverage until they reached her butt.

"This is the hardest part," Halcyon said.

"Because it's the widest part, and shoving it into my intestines won't work. And don't even suggest any orifices. I'm going to a party, not prison."

"Just keep the front from moving and try to keep from lifting."

Before Marina could even ask how one kept from lifting, Halcyon gave the hair band a huge pull and Marina went up on her toes like a ballerina.

"Flat feet," Halcyon said, and gave it another yank. This one managed to get it over the bottom of her rear.

"Don't move," Halcyon warned. "We're in that precarious zone where it could tip over the edge."

"Then why did you stop?"

"Because I have a hand cramp."

"That's valid."

"Stop talking. Don't move. Maybe don't breathe."

"I suppose it's too late to tell you I have to pee."

Halcyon pulled again and this time the hair band flew up in the front as well.

"Yay! The butt is done," Halcyon said. "Now we just have to pull it up to your chest and back down over your thighs and you're ready for the dress."

Marina winced as the top of the band rolled and dug into her stomach. "Then let's hurry before this pushes out my breakfast."

"Okay, joint effort again. One big pull and we should get it. One, two, three!"

Marina yanked the hair band as hard as she could and it flew up, coming to rest beneath her boobs.

"Touchdown!" Halcyon yelled.

Marina lowered her arms and tried to respond, but she was out of air. She tried to suck in a breath but there was no room in the hair band. She lifted her boobs with her hands and tried again, but still nothing.

"What's wrong?" Halcyon looked at her in the mirror.

Marina opened her mouth and pointed to it.

"Now you're hungry? You're like a three-year-old."

Marina shook her head. "Air," she managed.

A pain shot through her left side and continued through to the right and down to her privates. Everything inside her was in a bind. This was never going to work.

"Off," she croaked.

"Are you kidding me? I think I sprained my wrist."

"Can't breathe. Something wrong."

Marina swayed and Halcyon popped around her and stared at her face, her eyes widening.

"Oh my God, you're ghost white. Don't pass out! Pull!"

She moved to Marina's back again and they both yanked at the hair band, but everything ground to a halt when they reached her waist. There, the entire thing clenched in a rolled-up ball. Pain ripped through Marina's stomach and she doubled over.

"You have to stand up to get it off," Halcyon said.

"Cut it."

"I paid forty dollars for that."

"I'll give you a hundred to cut it off of me."

"Fine. Where are your scissors?"

"No scissors. You'll never get them underneath this and if you move wrong or I have a gas pain, you'll stab me. Get the utility knife from the kitchen drawer."

"You want me to use a razor?"

"I want you to use a razor very, very carefully. Just cut at it from the outside until it's weak enough to break."

Halcyon grabbed the utility knife from the kitchen and walked back into the bedroom, wearing an apprehensive look. Snooze poked his head around the door, then immediately turned and fled. Marina couldn't blame him.

"Okay," Halcyon said. "Here goes."

Marina heard the fabric tear as the razor sliced through it and with every cut, she felt her internal organs sigh with relief. Finally, only a narrow strip remained and Halcyon hesitated.

"It's so small," she said. "I don't want to cut you but I can't pull it out any."

"Just cut the outside folds. It has to rip sooner or later."

"Okay. Here goes. Don't move."

Marina sucked in, trying to give Halcyon more space to work, and concentrated on tightening her core so she could be absolutely still. She was moderately successful. She heard the tiny rip of fabric once, then again, then a final cut and the rest of it tore apart and shot out the door and into the living room.

Snooze yelped and she heard him scramble.

Marina ran out of the bedroom and spotted the old hound standing at the back door, the hair band draped across his neck. He looked both confused and offended. She couldn't blame him.

She walked over and grabbed the wrecked garment, then dug a hundred bucks out of her wallet and took them both back to Halcyon, who was sitting on the bed, laughing so hard she was crying.

"Take both," Marina said, and handed her sister the hair band and the money. "I don't want to ever see that thing again. My insides haven't hurt this bad since we ate burritos at that truck stop last month."

Halcyon shoved the scrap of fabric into her tote bag. "Keep the money. I owe you a massage or spa day or maybe a bottle of painkillers."

"How the heck did you wear that and breathe? Walk? Or did you just put it on for show and stand in one place until the guy of the week helped you out of it?"

"Oh, I never let them see the hardware under the dress. I take it off in the bathroom first."

"You managed to get this off alone? In a small room?"

"Yes, but that was about six months ago. I'd had the flu the week before so I think I was lighter then. And there was the whole water pill thing."

Marina narrowed her eyes at her sister. "Didn't you 'fall' in the bathroom six months ago and sprain your wrist?"

Halcyon blinked. "Maybe."

Marina shook her head. "Where's the dress? And it better not have a corset or even a full-length zipper or I'm dragging out slacks and a silk blouse."

Halcyon pulled the cover off the dress and showed it to Marina. It was basic black, straight line, and sleeveless. The top plunged down a bit low for Marina's usual style but it was dressier wear and this situation was hardly usual. Unfortunately, the length would leave it looking like a pilgrim costume on Marina.

Halcyon saw her assessing the bottom and shoved the dress at her. "Put it on. I'll take care of the length."

"You don't sew."

"I have a plan."

Marina pulled on a bra and underwear—to hell with panty lines—then pulled the dress over her head. Halcyon took care of the small zipper on the back and Marina studied herself in the mirror. Except for the length, it wasn't bad. Halcyon knew how to pick a cut that was flattering for a little more baggage. It probably would have looked even better with the hair band, but Marina was happy with her overall appearance.

"That bra is great," Halcyon said. "Really pushes the girls up into the neckline. Don't wear a necklace. Highlight your assets. Between the awesome chest, your younger-looking face, and your hair, which I swear has grown another inch, you'll be the talk of the party."

"I have a feeling I would be the talk of the party even if I wasn't attending."

Halcyon pulled duct tape out of her bag and sat on the floor. "Okay, hold still for a second. I want to mark the length."

"You're going to hem the dress with duct tape?"

"It works great. Half of my skirts have duct tape on them. I need to get them in for repair but never remember until I want to wear them. Anyway, I'll tape it up and iron it on the hem. This plan has the added advantage of allowing me to let it out and still wear the dress. If this was permanent, I'd be arrested for wearing it at this length."

It seemed a little short even for Marina, but she wasn't about to argue with Halcyon. When her sister went to finish taping and press the hem, Marina touched up her makeup and hair, which had gotten a little tousled in the Great Hair Band Struggle of the Twenty-First Century. By the time she'd sprayed and tweaked everything she thought could use improvement, Halcyon was ready with the dress. She slipped it over her head, careful not to touch her hair or face, and Halcyon zipped her up. When she looked down and saw the amount of thigh exposed, the automatic desire to tug it down coursed through her. But before she could take action, Halcyon sighed and put her hands over her heart.

"You look so gorgeous," her sister said. "Oh my God, Marina. You're so beautiful. You always have been but just look. Let me grab my phone. I've got to get a picture."

Marina looked in the mirror and blinked. Was that really her? She moved closer and saw the uneven hips and the bulges on her back created by her bra. Her thighs were still too big and too white, and her biceps had seen tighter days.

She didn't just look pretty damned good.

She looked fabulous.

And she wasn't just telling herself that. She really felt it. Not just because of the skin or the hair or the push-up bra that had probably been designed by engineers at NASA, but because something in her own mind shifted. She was forty-eight years old. She wasn't supposed to have a twenty-year-old body or skin. She wasn't supposed to look smooth in a stretchy dress. Her boobs weren't supposed to stand at attention without serious hardware giving them a boost.

And she was perfectly fine with that.

No.

She. Was. Happy.

To hell with the media and society and commercials and magazines telling women they were supposed to look eternally young. Not only was that impossible, it was a lie. That didn't mean she shouldn't take care of herself, and she hadn't done a great job of that the past several years. Putting everyone's needs in front of her own had taken a toll. But that was all about to change. And loving herself didn't mean she wouldn't wear makeup or style her hair or wear clothes that suited her body type. You could love yourself and still like things to look a certain way. But it would all be within reason.

For the last several years, she'd watched a handful of senior women in town, and had always admired how attractive they remained, even though they were in their sixties and seventies. Dottie was one of them. And certainly, she was always impeccably turned out, which helped. But it struck Marina now that the reason those women were so attractive wasn't because they were what would be considered traditionally beautiful. It was because of the way they carried themselves. It was because of the way they felt about themselves. Their confidence made them more attractive, just like neediness and uncertainty could make a naturally beautiful person look less than what they were.

It was so simple. Yet so difficult to achieve because it meant embracing all her "flaws."

Marina was ready.

It was her time.

CHAPTER TWENTY-SEVEN

MARINA KNEW she was gawking like a teenager, but the man standing on her doorstep was so handsome in his custom black suit. He'd been dressed well in court but had looked the part of the lawyer then. Now he was totally Bayou James Bond—sexy and dangerous. But more important was how he was staring at her.

There was no disguising his appreciation. The long lingering gaze, the slow smile.

"You look fantastic," he said.

Marina blushed. "So do you."

He offered his arm to her. "Then let's go piss some people off."

"I thought you'd never ask."

Cars lined the street and the circular drive to the Southern mansion the LeDoux called home. Luke offered to let Marina out in front of the house, but she was too nervous to stand there alone. Not because she was afraid of a confrontation. She was kinda expecting one of some sort, even if it was conducted quietly. She was more afraid of what she might do if there was no one else there to rein her in.

Her attitude over the last six days had changed so drastically, she wasn't even sure she knew herself anymore. But she liked what she saw, and she was really hoping that the world wouldn't end so she could explore more of the new and improved Marina.

It was a bit of a hike from Luke's truck to the house and Marina said a prayer of thanks that she didn't let Halcyon convince her to wear that awful Lycra thing. Of course, the fact that she would have been passed out after another minute of wear would have probably prevented her from leaving the house in it, but still.

As they approached the front door, Luke slowed and looked over at her. "Are you ready for this?"

"I've been looking forward to it all day."

"Okay. But before we enter, if anyone starts trouble with you, how would you like me to handle it? And I don't mean how I would handle it *for* you. I have zero doubt you can handle things on your own and quite frankly, I'm looking forward to seeing it. But I need to know at what point or in what situation you would like backup."

Marina felt her chest tighten for just a second. This strong, confident man believed in her. Believed she was strong and confident, too. And by God, she wasn't about to prove him wrong.

"If I'm about to cross a line that will make our current legal situation worse, then intervene," Marina said.

"And if things get physical?"

"Good Lord, they're assholes, not thugs. They're not going to throw down in front of witnesses."

"You'd be surprised at the things I heard during my time working the legal system."

She blew out a breath. Before this week, she wouldn't have

thought Avery capable of launching at someone either, but everyone had their breaking point.

"No. I probably wouldn't be surprised, come to think of it," she said. "I suppose if things get physical, then try to break it up before I punch someone. My dad was a big boxing fan and taught Halcyon and me how to box from the time we were little. I might look all made of sweetness and light but I have a wicked right hook that would get me into a lot of trouble."

He stared at her for a moment, then grinned. "The more I know about you, the more I like you. I don't suppose you taught Avery that right hook."

"Guilty."

"Ha! Let's do this."

She took his arm and they rang the doorbell. One of the caterers answered and invited them inside, pointing toward the back of the house. Down the hallway, she could see into a large living room where people stood holding drinks and napkins with finger food. She tightened her grip on Luke's arm as they stepped into the room.

And then, as people caught sight of Marina, they stopped talking and began casting nervous glances between her and Preston, who was standing near a huge fireplace, talking to Patricia. His deputy lackey, Kyle Pitre, was standing nearby, as always, and leaned over to whisper something to Preston.

Preston's head yanked around and he stared at Marina, first in disbelief, then it all shifted to anger. He started to walk forward, but Kyle put his hand on Preston's arm and said something again. He must have been pointing out Marina's date, because Preston looked over at Luke, his mouth forming a scowl before he turned back around to face a clearly livid Patricia.

"Apparently, we've made an entrance," Luke said.

"Like that wasn't what you were trying to do." Adelaide's

voice sounded behind them and they turned around to see her grinning. Marina did a double take when she saw that the grouchy senior was actually wearing a dress.

"I didn't even think you owned a dress," Marina said, taking in the long, silky navy garment with a sparkly silver collar.

"I have one," Adelaide said. "This is it. Take a good look. Maybe even a picture. You'll see it about as often as Halley's Comet."

"I thought you said you wouldn't even attend one of these events if you were bound and gagged," Luke said.

"Well, that was before I found out you were bringing Marina as your date," Adelaide said.

"And you were afraid you'd miss the show?" Luke asked.

Adelaide gave him a slightly disgusted look. "Boy, please. I'm here in case she needs backup. There's only a handful of people in this town who will stand up to the LeDoux and most of them aren't at this party."

Marina smiled. "Do you have your shovel?"

"Dottie wouldn't let me bring it." Adelaide grinned.

"You're here with Dottie?" Marina asked. "Did you drug her?"

"Thought I might have to," Adelaide said. "But she's a good sort. Got off her high horse and came because I thought you might need more support than you'd have otherwise."

Marina's heart warmed that the two older women had come to an event they usually avoided strictly because she might need them. She'd always been on good terms with both women, but Marina had never known that they liked her that much. It was a good feeling. And when all this mess was over with, she was going to spend some time getting to know the two of them better.

"Well, I appreciate both of you," Marina said.

Adelaide nodded. "Tonight, I have something better than the shovel."

Luke's eyes widened. "You're not packing, are you?"

"Of course I'm packing," Adelaide said. "I'd leave home without a bra before I'd leave my gun. Doesn't mean I'm going to shoot people. The LeDoux aren't even worth the cost of a bullet."

"I'm almost afraid to ask," Luke said.

Adelaide dug into her purse, pulled out her cell phone, and waved it at Luke. "This little piece of electronics has taken down more people in the past decade than cancer. All you have to do is capture the wrong moment, put it up on YouTube, and it's all done but the crying."

"Genius," Marina said. "Except for the part where I have to be the poster child for propriety or I'm just as guilty."

"You're way closer to that mark than me," Adelaide said. "And yours is sincere. Since the LeDoux are faking class, they'll crumble. Mark my words."

"I hope they last long enough for me to get a tour of the house," Marina said.

Adelaide frowned. "Why on earth would you want to see more of this garish pile of crap?"

Marina shrugged. "Basic curiosity. Not like I get invited up here on my own."

Adelaide motioned to someone across the room and before Marina could ask what she was up to, Dottie walked up.

"We've been talking to your date," Marina said.

Dottie sighed. "I know. It appears hell has frozen over. But she convinced me we might be needed."

"And you're up," Adelaide said. "Marina would like a tour of the house and since neither Preston nor Janice is likely to offer that up, I need you to ask."

Dottie's expression never changed, nor did she ask a single

question. She simply headed off in Janice's direction. Marina felt her chest tighten just a little. These were two of the women she respected the most in Last Chance and they were trying to help her, no questions asked. It was both humbling and somewhat overwhelming.

Marina watched as Janice's face lit up at the chance of showing off her home to Dottie. Until Dottie waved for Adelaide and Marina to join her. Then she looked as if she'd been sucking on lemons, but she did her best to hide her dismay when Dottie looked back at her.

"Do you want me to come with you?" Luke asked.

"No," Marina said. "I've got this. Janice is a coward. No way would she try anything. And definitely not in front of Dottie. Go mingle with all the people you need to talk to. In case this goes south soon, I'm going to need a ride home."

"Or to the sheriff's department," Adelaide said.

"Yeah, I'm trying to spend less time there," Marina said as they crossed the room to where Dottie was standing with the unsmiling Janice.

"Oh, great," Dottie said as they stepped up. "Now we can get going. I just love what you've done with this wallpaper, Janice. Did you pick the pattern yourself or did you use a decorator?"

Marina could tell Janice was struggling with being angry that she had to host Marina directly and wanting to bask in Dottie's praise. The wallpaper looked like something that belonged in a bordello owned by the color-blind, and Marina was certain Dottie hated it as much as Marina did, but that just showed the first lady's ability to work a crowd.

As they walked through the six bedrooms and bathrooms upstairs, Marina made a point to sidle close to any furniture that looked like it might hold jewelry. But nothing tugged at her. Well, except for the fact that the place looked like it had been furnished by children. The decor and furniture were so mismatched, it almost made Harold's mother's taste look exquisite. Preston and Janice's room was all red and shiny gold and made her wish she was wearing sunglasses. The suite Patricia and her husband shared was shiny silver and bright pink. It looked like a room in a cheap Vegas hotel. But Chastity's room was the worst. Despite the fact that the "girl" was in her twenties, her room was decorated with unicorns. It looked like a preteen occupied it.

Dottie fed Janice a steady stream of questions, so all she had time for was to glance back occasionally with a quick frown at Marina before she plastered on her fake smile again for Dottie. Adelaide elbowed Marina in the side every time Janice played split personality and Marina was fairly certain she was going to bruise.

"Is there an award for the worst acting job ever?" Adelaide asked as Dottie pulled Janice into a closet for a minute.

"If there is, Janice wins, it. Hands down. And Dottie wins the best."

Adelaide nodded. "I don't know how she does it. And all with that serene smile. I'm pretty sure every time I look at Janice I appear as if I have gas."

Marina nodded. "Or smelled a port-a-john."

"That perfect-face ability has got to be in the DNA. No way can you learn that. I know I couldn't."

"I don't think I could either."

"Oh, you're plenty gracious enough to pull it off."

"Not lately. I think I finally reached that stage you were born into."

"Welcome to the best years of your life."

Marina nodded but she wondered if she only had days rather than years to enjoy her newfound attitude. So far, the house tour had yielded nothing, and if the ring wasn't here, then where else would it be? Few people in Last Chance had a lot of disposable income and even fewer had inherited assets, especially of the giant ruby kind. And if they had inherited that kind of stone, it probably would have been sold off long ago. Dottie and the LeDoux were two of the only families that had the money to let something like that sit around.

Marina had conjured up a theory earlier that day that maybe everything that had happened recently had been the ring working to get her to the right place. But that didn't appear to be the case. The ring had brought her closer to Dottie and Adelaide, but Adelaide's family wasn't rich and she would have never held on to something that valuable. She was too practical and not at all sentimental. Dottie had already said she didn't own anything with a large ruby, so that really only left the LeDoux. Preston and Patricia were the last of the family line and they all lived in this estate along with their children, so unless they had it in a safe-deposit box, it would be in this house. But unless it didn't want to be found, Marina was convinced the ring wasn't here.

She must have sighed without realizing it because Adelaide gave her a hard look.

"What's up with you?" Adelaide asked. "Coming to this party is out of character enough, although I'm thrilled if being this perverse is part of a new you. But touring this god-awful place is enough to make a person constipated. Why in the world would you want to do it? It can't be just to hack Janice off, although I will admit, that part has been fun."

"I don't know how to explain it," Marina said. "I guess I was just hoping to get an answer that I don't think is here."

"I hope the question wasn't 'why are the LeDoux assholes' because that one might need some time to answer."

Marina smiled. "Come on. They're headed back downstairs. There's catered food and an open bar. Might as well make gluttons out of ourselves and make them even madder."

"Now you're talking."

They followed Dottie and Janice back toward the staircase that led into the living room. About midway down, Marina paused as she saw Chastity enter the room—with Harold. Adelaide sucked in a breath.

"Wow. He's got some serious balls showing up here with her," Adelaide said. "He's lost his damned mind. Maybe that facility will put a bed for Harold next to your mother."

"They'd kill each other."

"Bonus plan."

Marina heard Adelaide's words but they didn't register. So many emotions were overriding them—disbelief, anger, sadness, grief. How in the world had the man she'd spent thirty years with gone that far off the rails? How could someone just dump their family and never look back?

And here he was, only days after Marina had caught him with his child sidepiece, and Avery probably hadn't even gotten the stench of sitting in jail off of her, and he was trotting around in an ill-fitting suit like he'd done nothing wrong.

And that was when it hit her. He didn't think he had.

Harold had always put himself first. Marina had known that, but she'd been raised by a woman who put men on a pedestal, no matter how many times they hopped off and rolled around in the mud. Harold was the primary financial support, so it was Marina's job to make sure that income was protected and that meant giving Harold more time to dedicate to his career, which meant less responsibility for their home and their daughter. But somewhere along the line, everything had become Marina's job and Harold had merely sat back and enjoyed the spoils.

She'd updated his mother's hideous house and kept it clean

and repaired. She'd done all the shopping, cooking, and laundry. She'd raised their daughter. And she'd still gone back to work after Avery started preschool.

Harold put himself first because he could. He didn't care about fair or equitable or partnership. He didn't care about promises or vows, either. And he certainly didn't care that he was making a fool of himself with Chastity LeDoux. But with his huge opinion of himself, he probably didn't see things that way.

Adelaide elbowed Marina. "Look at Preston," she said. "He's mad enough to spit nails. I don't think he likes Baby Precious with Harold."

"Why would he?"

Adelaide shrugged. "I would never have a useless twit of a daughter like Chastity, but if I did, I'd be looking to pawn her off on the first guy who would take her off my hands."

"He probably thinks all this doesn't look good for his election bid."

"You're probably right. God knows, any objection he has wouldn't be about what's best for that girl. It will always be about what's best for Preston."

"He and Harold have that in common."

"A lot of men in Last Chance do. If it makes you feel any better, I don't think Luke is that type at all."

"Oh, this isn't a date. I mean, not that kind. Jeez, I'm still married."

"To that." Adelaide pointed to Harold, who was standing with his hand on Chastity's back and grinning like an idiot.

"Still, I'm not ready for a relationship. I don't know that I ever will be."

Adelaide waved a hand in dismissal. "You're not the kind who winds up alone. Someone will sweep you off your feet. You're a good woman, Marina. Better than Harold ever deserved. And I have to say it tickles me that makeup can't cover those bruises Avery left on Chastity's face. That girl has a great punch."

"I'm afraid I might have taught her that," Marina said.

"Even better."

Preston glanced up at them and then hurried across the room toward Chastity. Marina assumed to warn the happy couple that things weren't going as expected.

"Uh-oh," Adelaide said. "Big Daddy LeDoux is going to tattle to Baby Precious."

"Maybe we should get downstairs and blend."

Adelaide nodded and they headed into the crowd in the living room and sidled down the far wall toward the bar when Marina spotted Luke talking to the owner of the hardware store. They were halfway across the room when Marina almost walked right into Harold. She glanced around but Chastity was nowhere in sight. Probably off getting an earful from daddy dearest.

"Marina." Harold's eyes widened. Clearly he hadn't expected to see her there. "You look great," he said.

Marina felt a wave of dismay wash over her when she realized that he actually meant it. Talk about too little, too late.

"I'm going to puke," Adelaide said. "I need alcohol. Stop talking, Harold. You're creeping people out."

"Thanks," Marina said. "I see my date has a drink for me."

Harold whipped around and spotted Luke holding a drink up and smiling at Marina. She flashed him a seventy-five-watt smile back and gave Harold a little wave and a glance. The look of shock on his face made the entire night worthwhile.

"It was worth putting on this dress just to see his expression," Adelaide said as they approached Luke.

Luke smiled and handed her a glass of wine. "Looks like Harold was surprised to see you here."

"The surprise was that I had a date," Marina said, and laughed.

"He said she looked great," Adelaide said. "It was all I could do not to kick him in the crotch."

"Don't do anything that can get you arrested or sued," Luke said. "Especially in this house."

Adelaide waved a hand in dismissal. "Do you know what the biggest advantage is to being the grouchy old lady?"

"Elastic-waist pants?" Marina guessed.

"That's second. The biggest advantage is that I can just pass things off as nerve damage or losing my balance. Who's going to argue?"

Luke's smile turned to a frown and Marina realized he was looking over her shoulder.

"Trouble is headed our way," he said. "Stay calm, Marina."

"You!" Chastity LeDoux yelled as Marina whirled around.

CHAPTER TWENTY-EIGHT

"You have the nerve to show up at *my* house," Chastity ranted. "After what your daughter did?"

Marina stared at the girl, whose black eyes showed through the makeup. Her nose was still swollen to twice its normal size. And she felt the room tip just a little. How had things gotten this out of control?

"Maybe if you hadn't been stealing from her, she wouldn't have tried to stop you," Marina said.

Chastity's face flashed with anger. "I wasn't stealing. Harold gave me those clothes."

"Harold has no right to give away the property of another adult. But then, you have a habit of trying on other people's clothes. Maybe you should talk to your daddy about upping your allowance so that you can buy your own."

"You bitch!" Chastity yelled and leaped at Marina, grabbing her around the neck. Marina fell backward into the table stocked with glasses for the bar and the whole thing collapsed, sending them both crashing down. Marina could feel broken glass pressing into her back and pieces nicked her arms and the side of her face as she struggled to pull Chastity's hands from her throat. She was just about to let go with a solid right hook when Chastity flew off of her.

Adelaide and the hardware store manager helped Marina up and she saw Chastity dangling in the air as Luke clutched her around the waist. She was kicking and screaming like a small child. The entire crowd of partygoers was staring at her in horror, including the love of her life, Harold.

Dottie rushed up to Marina, clearly distressed. "Are you all right? Do you need the paramedics?"

"No," Marina said. "I'm just a little banged up and have some glass cuts."

"Unbelievable," Dottie said and whirled around to look at Chastity.

"What the hell is wrong with you?" she asked.

The fact that the question had come from Dottie, including a curse word uttered in her completely serene voice, rendered everyone silent.

"It's not me!" Chastity screamed. "It's all her fault."

Dottie shook her head. "Your parents ruined you. It's pathetic."

There was a sharp intake of breath from those standing around and everyone froze when Preston came running up and demanded that Luke put his daughter down.

"I'll do that when she's in handcuffs," Luke said. "Not a minute before, and you really don't want to try to make me. I'm done with you people."

"Handcuffs?" Preston stared at Luke as if he'd lost his mind.

"Your daughter attacked Mrs. Trahan," Luke said. "She's cut from the glass and has marks on her neck. There are about twenty witnesses, so don't even think you're going to weasel out of this one."

Preston's expression shifted from outrage to calculating as

he glanced around at the potential witness pool. "We'll just see about that, won't we?"

"Clear the way," the sheriff yelled, and people moved aside for him to walk through. He took one look at Marina and the collapsed table, then at the still-screaming Chastity, and Marina could tell he wished he were on a long vacation.

Time to fish or cut bait.

"What happened here?" he asked.

"This thing attacked Mrs. Trahan," Luke said. "Mrs. Trahan will be pressing charges, so I suggest you put the problem in handcuffs before she launches at anyone else."

"You can't do that," Preston said to the sheriff.

"I don't see that I have a choice," the sheriff said and motioned to Luke. "Flip her around and I'll cuff her."

"What?" Chastity screamed, completely outraged. "You're arresting me? What about her? She shouldn't even be here. Are you arresting her too?"

The sheriff looked over at Marina. "Mrs. Trahan, were you invited to this event?"

"Yes," Marina said. "I'm here with Luke. He's one of the guests of honor."

He looked her up and down and Marina knew he was taking a mental inventory of the torn dress, the nicks and cuts from the glass, and the marks on her neck.

"I'll need you to come down to the sheriff's department and file a statement," he said.

"Now?"

"I think that might be best," he said.

"Works for me," Luke said. "This party sucks."

The sheriff walked off, pushing Chastity, who'd shifted from screaming to wailing, in front of him. Preston hurried after them, still arguing, but the sheriff just kept walking without responding.

"Don't worry," Adelaide whispered. "I got you."

"Can someone please get me a damp towel for Mrs. Trahan?" Luke called out.

A caterer rushed up with the request and Luke blotted her face and arms.

"I'm afraid this won't do a lot of good," Marina said. "I can feel cuts on my back as well."

He nodded. "Then let's get this over with and get home."

"Can we stop and pick up my sister on the way home?" Marina asked. "I'm going to need some help with my back and even though you've seen me partially clad, I'd prefer to keep the rest confidential."

He smiled. "I prefer to call it 'saving it for later,' but I'll go with whatever you'd like. And yes, we can stop and get Halcyon. Probably best that she stays with you anyway. To keep *her* out of trouble."

Marina blushed at his "saving it for later" comment. Was he really interested in her? She'd thought his invitation was because he felt sorry for her and held plenty of dislike for the LeDoux. It hadn't occurred to her that he might really be interested and she wasn't sure, at all, how she felt about that.

On the upside, she didn't have to make a decision about it tonight and since she still hadn't a clue where the ring was located and her time was almost up, that decision might never require pondering.

"Wait up front with Adelaide and Dottie. I'll get the truck," he said.

Adelaide gave him a nod and the three of them headed for the front door. Dottie was shaking her head the entire time.

"I just can't believe it," she said. "I know the LeDoux are white trash who conned their way into money, but this is beyond the pale."

"Doesn't surprise me in the least," Adelaide said. "Why do you think I bullied you into bringing me?"

"Well, you were right on that one," Dottie said. "I thought maybe some snide comments and at worst, someone flinging a drink at someone else. But this? This is unacceptable on every level."

Adelaide shrugged. "You know what they say—you can give people money but you can't give them class."

"Clearly," Dottie said, and Marina could tell she was genuinely upset.

When they got to the drive to wait on Luke, Dottie put her hand on Marina's arm. "I am so sorry."

"For what?" Marina asked. "You didn't do anything. In fact, you've helped me."

"I think I could have done more," Dottie said. "I never expected things to go as far as they did, but I should have known after that business with Avery that Preston was going to double down on stupid. If you want to file a civil suit, I would be happy to pay for your attorney. I know one in New Orleans who specializes in such things. Normally, I loathe that sort of thing when it's personal business but the LeDoux have taken things entirely too far. They're ruining this town."

"Thank you," Marina said. "Right now, I just want them to go away, but if I change my mind, I'll let you know."

"Please do," Dottie said. "And I'll be making some changes myself. Come tomorrow morning the people of this town are going to have to choose a side. No more riding the fence."

"What are you going to do?" Adelaide asked.

"For starters, I'm going to pull my donations to every organization that has a LeDoux on the board."

"That only punishes the organizations," Marina said. "Don't do that."

Dottie raised one eyebrow. "Do you really think people will

choose Preston over me and my money? I don't care what he has on them or how low the average IQ here is. No one is that stupid."

"She's right," Adelaide said. "Worst case, anyone who really feels they can't go up against Preston will simply abdicate their position on the board or committee."

"I don't know what to say," Marina said. "I can't tell you how much I appreciate the support you two have given me. It was totally unexpected, and yet I feel like we've been in the trenches together for years."

"You're a class act," Dottie said and then pointed to Adelaide. "And Lord knows, this one can make me cringe like no one else, but her values are solid. That's more important than social graces."

"You heard her," Adelaide said. "Next time she's telling me to act right, remind her of that."

Marina smiled at them as Luke pulled up. "Thanks again."

Adelaide opened the door as Luke hurried around to help her, then he jumped back in and they headed off. As he pulled out of the driveway, he looked over at her.

"Are you okay? Do you need to go to the hospital first?"

She shook her head. "I'll be okay. Ask me again tomorrow after my back has had a chance to process everything."

"Lumbar?"

"Yeah, how did you know?"

"You live long enough and well enough, you have lower back problems."

"How old are you, anyway?"

"Forty-five."

She nodded. "You're not going to ask me how old I am?"

"Noooooooooo."

She laughed. "Forty-eight. A very exhausted forty-eight."

"Most people would already be prone if they'd had the week you have."

"Prone sounds really good about now."

"Let's get this thing with the sheriff over with, then you can go home and lie around for a whole day if you'd like."

She nodded but her mind was already whirling. Another visit to the sheriff's department. Was the sheriff going to kowtow to Preston again? Would she somehow end up taking the blame for this too? And what would that mean for Avery?

"Can I ask you a question?" Marina asked. "It's kinda out of left field but it's something that's been nagging at me."

"Sure."

"You said you've owed Adelaide a favor for a long time, but Adelaide said she didn't know you well."

Luke frowned and nodded. "Both those statements are true. I have faint memories of Adelaide from when I was young, maybe five or so, but then I didn't see her again until I contacted her about applying for the game warden position. I wanted to get her take on things."

"Why did you go so long without seeing her?"

"Because my mother and I moved out of state. My father was a cruel man and he took his failures out on her. The last time left her in the hospital. Adelaide heard about it through some family and drove straight there and wrote my mother a check. That money helped us get away. Probably saved our lives."

Marina shook her head. "That's incredible. It's amazing all the wonderful things you never know about a person."

"Marina?"

"Yes?"

"I just want to say that this has been the most interesting date I've ever been on."

She smiled. "That's me. Bringing creativity and visits to the sheriff's department into the lives of others."

———

PRESTON'S CAR was parked outside the sheriff's department when Marina and Luke arrived. Marina blew out a breath. The sheriff's arm was probably twisted all the way behind his back by now. Luke reached over and squeezed her shoulder.

"The fact that he left his own party and raced to get here before us says everything," Luke said. "He's scared because he knows how bad this is."

"But he's probably in there blackmailing the sheriff. The truth won't matter. And the people who saw what happened probably won't have the backbone to say anything."

"Adelaide and I will."

"Neither of you will matter to the prosecutor or the judge. That's why Preston gets away with everything."

"Not this time."

Marina nodded and climbed out of the truck but she didn't feel very optimistic as they made their way to the front door. She could hear yelling as soon as they got close.

"You can't be serious!" Preston yelled. "You can't allow her to press charges. It's her word against Chastity's."

"I'm afraid not," Sheriff Owen said. "You see, someone took video of the entire thing. It's up on YouTube and already has five thousand views."

Marina looked over at Luke, who shook his head. Video? YouTube?

Then she covered her mouth with her hand to keep from laughing.

Adelaide.

"It just happened!" Preston continued to rant. "There

aren't even five thousand people in Last Chance."

"Apparently people outside of our little town are interested as well. I can't help you with this, Preston. Chastity attacked Marina Trahan without any provocation. Marina didn't even defend herself. She only tried to pull Chastity's hands from her neck. You best see about getting her a good lawyer. This is going to be ugly, especially given the situation with Avery."

"That's our cue," Luke said and walked inside.

"I agree with the sheriff," Luke said. "You should get a very good lawyer for your daughter. That video is irrefutable evidence. I don't care how many people you've got dirt on. They're not going to put themselves out there when there's no loophole. You might need to adjust your methods now that everyone has a smartphone ready to go."

"I'll find out who took that video," Preston said. "They'll take it down and then they'll pay."

"I seriously doubt it," Marina said. "But I'd love to see you try."

"You can't threaten me," Preston said.

"It's not a threat," Marina said. "Just simple facts. Look at my injuries, which I will be photographing as soon as I get home. Or maybe I'll go ahead and make that trip to the ER. You know, just to get everything on record."

"It appears you've reached an impasse," Luke said. "Both of you have daughters facing assault charges. I could make a suggestion that clears the slate for everyone."

Preston's face flashed with anger. He knew exactly what Luke was suggesting and he wasn't having any of it.

"No way," he said.

Luke shrugged. "Suit yourself, but we both know Chastity has no defense against video. Avery, on the other hand, was being robbed. Which case do you think is stronger? And while you might be ruler out here in the sticks, this sort of corruption has a way of finding itself into news stories in bigger cities. News stories tend to bring scrutiny. *Unwanted* scrutiny, if I'm sitting in your seat."

"Listen to the man," Sheriff Owen said. "The prosecutor won't have any issue dropping the charges if Chastity says so and, given the circumstances, might do it anyway. This could be a big mess for everyone—Chastity, you, me, the prosecutor, the judge. You push this and you risk alienating everyone for good. No one is going to stick their neck out over this one. They can't. Video trumps everything and you know it."

If Preston had been packing, Marina was fairly certain he would have shot them all right there. His face was so red and his body so tense that she wondered if he might just have a heart attack on the spot. He'd never been in a situation he couldn't control and he was having a huge problem admitting defeat.

"What do you say, counselor?" Luke said. "Either we all put this behind us or we all move forward and let the chips fall. You want to roll those dice?"

"Fine!" Preston spat out. "I'll have the charges against Avery dropped."

Marina nodded. "As long as that happens and remains the case, I won't press charges against Chastity. But I will be requesting a restraining order. Fair is fair, right?"

"Whatever," Preston said, and stormed out.

"I still want to give my statement," Marina said to Sheriff Owen. "I don't trust him and quite frankly, I don't trust you either. So this will all be by the book. The two of you aren't going to sweep things under the rug this time."

Sheriff Owen had the decency to look embarrassed. "I'll take your statement now. Do you want your lawyer present?"

Marina looked over at Luke and smiled. "No. I want my date present."

CHAPTER TWENTY-NINE

"I STILL CAN'T BELIEVE THIS," Halcyon said as she dabbed Marina's backside with peroxide.

Marina jumped at the sting. "I know. It's sorta out there."

"'Sorta out there' describes your entire life lately. How can someone who has gone overboard trying to keep her life on the down low have so much drama in such a small amount of time?"

"Beats me. It's not like I asked for any of this."

"Oh, honey, I'm not blaming you. I'm just dumbfounded by it all. I mean, if outrageous things happened to me, no one would bat an eye. But you've always been the straitlaced one. The nice one."

"I'm still the nice one. To people I like, anyway."

"Yeah. How long is that list?"

"Not very and getting shorter by the day."

Halcyon laughed. "I can't believe Adelaide posted video on YouTube."

"We don't know for sure it was her."

"Really? The YouTube handle is KissMyOldButtPrestonLe-Doux. Who else would it be?"

"I'm just glad she did it. Now Preston has no choice but to drop everything against Avery or he's going to watch his precious go down the same path he was trying to send Avery down."

Halcyon shook her head. "Quite a night. Okay, I'm done with the peroxide. None of these are deep, but I can put Neosporin on them if you'd like."

"No, thanks. They'll be okay. Will probably itch like crazy more than anything."

Halcyon sat on the barstool next to Marina and took a sip of the wine she'd poured them earlier. "I hate to bring this up given everything else that happened, but did you find out anything on the ring front?"

"No. I even got Dottie to wrangle Janice into giving us a tour of the house."

"Really? I bet that pissed her off."

"Oh, I'm sure, but she was too afraid to say no to Dottie so she tolerated me. But we went through every tacky room in that house. I even touched the furniture when Janice wasn't trying to sneak a glare at me, but I didn't get anything. Not even a twinge."

Halcyon sighed. "I don't understand how anyone expects you to find this ring with so little information."

"And so little time."

"Yeah. We can't forget that part."

"It's hard to when the world could literally end tonight."

Halcyon stared. "I thought Alexios said a week."

"He said 'give or take' a week."

"Oh. That's not good. I love you but I don't want the most exciting thing I did on my last night on earth to be rubbing peroxide on your butt."

"I was kinda hoping for a better finale as well."

"Then why didn't you have one? Instead of picking me up, you could have played doctor with the hunky game warden."

"My luck, I'd find the ring after playing doctor and then I'd never be able to face him again after being so easy."

"Good Lord, what century do you think we're in? It's okay to enjoy sex with a hot guy—even one you don't know that well. It's not like you need to remain pure so our father can get more cows in exchange for your hand in marriage."

"I know. I guess it still feels too strange for me. Harold was the only one. I never did this whole sexy-dance thing."

Halcyon gave her a sympathetic look. "I get it. And I swear I'm not trying to push you into doing something you're not comfortable with. I'm just reminding you that it's not only okay to want sex with a man you're attracted to, but it's expected. I'm not saying you have to act on anything but you should at least stop denying your feelings."

Marina pursed her lips. "That's fair and really wise. Okay. I'll admit that I'm attracted to Luke. A lot. But I'm also afraid that some of that might be—what do you call it—rebound?"

"That's possible although I don't think so. Luke is a good-looking guy and he's smart, confident, and nice to top it off. It would be harder to *not* be attracted. And I know that him helping with Avery might seem like something that could cloud your better judgment because of all the emotions wrapped up in it, but I just don't think that's what's going on here. He's a good guy, Marina. I would bet my alimony on it."

"That's huge."

"You know what you have to do, right?"

"Get sluttier?"

"That's one solution but I was actually thinking you needed to find the ring. The only sex you have cannot be with Harold. That's just not right. And you're just not a one-night-stand sort of girl. You need more time to get comfortable with the idea."

"Trust me, if I knew where to find the ring, I'd go grab it right now. For a lot of reasons. Not just being destined to have spent my life with only okay sex."

Halcyon sighed. "I wish I had an idea. Good Lord, I'm the creative one. I always have ideas. But this time...nothing."

"I know. But this isn't exactly a normal situation. I mean, it's not like we have experience with magical objects or saving the world."

"Nothing beyond Disney and all those Marvel movies."

"Somehow, I doubt that applies."

"Speaking of superheroes, did you call Avery?"

"Oh yeah. As soon as I got done giving my statement. I knew someone would send her that YouTube link. Sure enough, she'd just played it right before I called."

"What did she say?"

"Plenty. Some of it I didn't understand but the things I did understand, I probably wouldn't repeat."

"That's my girl. Did you tell her about Preston dropping the charges against her?"

"No. I don't want to put that out there until I'm sure, and I think I want it in writing. It was hard enough to keep her from coming home to take on Chastity again. If Preston reneges on his promise, I don't want her to know about it."

"Yeah, a murder charge would be way harder to defend than an assault. So what are we going to do about the ring?"

Marina shook her head. "I wish I knew."

———

MARINA SAT in the rocking chair on her front porch the next morning with a thermos of coffee. Snooze lay next to her, enjoying the tiny breeze that would probably disappear soon. Her back ached from the fall she'd taken the night before and some of the nicks from the glass smarted a bit, especially those on her rear. But there were no other lasting physical effects.

The emotional effects, however, were huge.

So many things had happened to her over the last several days that sometimes Marina felt as if she had whiplash from it. She'd spent more time reacting than making qualified decisions, and that didn't sit well with her. Granted, all of this didn't exactly fit under the banner of rational, so she needed to cut herself somewhat of a break. But she also needed to get things under control. She needed to take some time to think. To process. To consider all the possibilities. All of this drama was clouding her mind, making it harder to concentrate on finding the ring. She needed to clear things out.

Some of the decisions she'd made were rock solid—like leaving Harold. Others might not have happened if she hadn't been in the thick of a personal crisis. Like quitting her job or going to a party at the LeDoux estate, which was essentially inciting a riot. Granted, that riot would lead to the charges against Avery being dropped but it was still so out of character for her.

So was this really the new Marina? Or was she so emotionally charged that she was doing things she otherwise wouldn't do?

It was a hard question to answer, especially when she was still in the thick of things. She'd thought about talking it through with Halcyon but she knew her sister. Halcyon's response to every decision she'd made would be to give her a high five. As far as her sister was concerned, Marina's newfound attitude was long overdue.

And maybe it was that simple.

Maybe it was time to stop overthinking everything. Given that she wasn't even sure she'd wake up this morning and Earth would still be the same, there was probably no better time to stop overthinking than the present. Why waste precious minutes?

She sighed. It was all so confusing.

She heard a vehicle approaching and looked at the dirt road. Halcyon probably wasn't even awake yet and even Adelaide would have given her a heads-up before driving out. Avery darn well better be at school, so the only person she could think of who would drive out this way, this early, was Luke. And she wasn't sure she was ready to see him, because she still hadn't worked out how much of her attraction to him was genuine and how much was because of the emotionally charged situation he'd stepped in the middle of.

She was shocked to see Harold's car round the corner.

What the hell did he want?

She deliberated between walking inside and locking the door behind her or walking inside to get the shotgun. Finally, she decided he wasn't even worth the walk and she would just tell him to leave. If the past week had shown her anything, it was that Harold was a coward before anything else.

He pulled into her driveway and sat there for several seconds, not moving. Finally, he climbed out of the car and trudged her way, hands in his slacks pockets and staring at the ground. When he got close to the porch, he looked up at her.

"Is it okay if I come up there?" he asked.

"Suit yourself."

He hesitated for a moment but finally walked up the steps and took a seat on the bench next to her. Snooze gave him the stink eye, farted, and went down the steps and under the house. Marina had the overwhelming urge to follow suit.

"What do you want, Harold?"

He blinked, clearly not expecting her to be so abrupt.

"I wanted to talk to you," he said.

"Then do it. I've got a lot of things to do. As you can well imagine."

"That's why I'm here. I want to apologize."

"Seriously?" Marina didn't know whether to laugh or simply slap him.

"I know I've caused a lot of trouble. Chastity was a really bad decision."

"She dumped you, didn't she?"

He flushed a bit and Marina figured she'd hit the nail on the head. Not that it surprised her. Harold was never the great love of Chastity's life. There was only room for one person there and Chastity had inserted herself in that slot a long time ago.

"We agreed that the relationship wasn't going to work," Harold said.

"Ha! You just now realized that? You're just another middle-aged cliché, Harold. Thinking a woman half your age is interested in anything but the size of your wallet. Did she find out we're broke? Or did she finally get tired of you not jumping in to help her beat up your wife or daughter?"

At least he had the good sense to look embarrassed, but Marina didn't even care. She'd given this man everything and he'd repaid her by destroying all their lives. And over what?

Nothing. Nobody.

"I made a mistake," he said. "I fully admit that. I don't know what I was thinking. Chastity could never be you."

"Got that right. There's not enough class in the world to get her to my level."

He shook his head, clearly frustrated. "Marina, I'm trying to tell you that I'm sorry for everything and I don't want a divorce. I want you to move back in. I want to be a family again."

"You mean move back and clean *your* house and cook *your*

dinner and do *your* laundry? No thanks. I paid my dues. I'm done."

He blinked. "It's our house. I never should have said the things I did."

"No. You shouldn't have. I didn't deserve them, but since you knew you were dead wrong, you spouted a bunch of crap because you felt guilty. Well, you know what? Live with it. I hope you go to your grave knowing that you pissed away the best thing that ever happened to you."

"I already know that," he said, his tone now pleading. "I love you, Marina. I want us to be together."

"What's in it for me?"

His eyes widened and he stared.

She nodded. "Don't have an answer, do you? You know why? Because there's nothing in it for me. I gave everything and took nothing. You took everything and cheated. Why on earth would I want to go back to that? I'm so much better off on my own."

His jaw twitched and she could tell he was angry. This wasn't the way he'd expected the conversation to go.

"It's that game warden guy, isn't it?" he asked.

She laughed. "I figured you'd go there. You can't wrap your mind around the fact that I'd rather live in this shack in the middle of nowhere than be married to you another day. And that *guy* is the reason your daughter isn't still sitting in jail. So the next time you see him, instead of sneering, you might want to try saying 'thank you.' He cleaned up your mess. And did it for no reason other than he hated what was happening to Avery, whom he'd never even met before that day. Doesn't it tell you anything, Harold? That a perfect stranger had to defend your daughter against *your* crap decisions? Do you see how far off the rails this has gone?"

He opened his mouth to speak but Marina put her hand up.

"You know what, don't say another word," she said. "I don't care about any of them. Get off my property or I'll get my shotgun. And if you think I won't open fire on you for trespassing, take a second to remember who my mother is."

It was probably the comment about her mother that got him because he jumped up and hurried down the steps.

"And Harold," she called after him. "I still expect to receive that twenty grand you agreed to. So I suggest you look into a mortgage on that hideous house you love so much. I'll have my attorney contact you."

He didn't even look back at her when he jumped in his car and tore out down the road. Marina watched the dust collect behind the Mercedes as it rounded the corner and felt her chest tighten just a little. She'd done the right thing. She knew that. But it still wasn't as easy as she thought it should have been. She'd never know for sure if Harold had ever loved her but she knew she'd loved him once. She just didn't anymore.

And all of that made her sad.

She slumped back in her chair and pondered the scant number of relationships she'd had over the course of her life. The best one, of course, was with Halcyon. The sisters had been tight from the first moment their father had shoved them into a playpen together, and it had always been the two of them against the world. But even though she loved her sister with all her heart and was certain Halcyon felt the same, Marina had been surprised lately to realize all the things they'd never said to each other. That they rarely talked about the most serious things they were dealing with.

She supposed it was because neither wanted to create friction or lower morale within the only great relationship they had.

But for Marina, it was also because she didn't want Halcyon to know how much she struggled with certain things. She'd always been the calm, strong one when it came to just dealing with day-to-day life. She didn't want her sister to know that some days she'd taken a drive in her car just to cry without anyone seeing her. Or that sometimes she went days without sleeping because an overwhelming feeling of restlessness nagged at her.

Then there was Letitia. The problems Marina had with her mother had embarrassed her so badly that she didn't want anyone to know the extent of the issues. Sure, some things got around but few people would have had the balls to go tattling to Halcyon about Marina. So she'd remained ignorant on the extent of Letitia's bad behavior. And when they were kids, Halcyon wasn't allowed to visit Marina's house, so she never saw firsthand how Letitia treated her.

Constance hadn't liked Marina and she'd hated Letitia, but she'd let the girls play together at her place because it was what their father wanted. Now that she was older, Marina understood that Constance hadn't really loved their father, either. She wasn't capable. But she'd wanted him and that desire had kept her doing his bidding. By the time he passed away, the sisters' relationship was cemented so strongly it would have taken dynamite to blast them apart.

Mostly, when she and Halcyon got together, it was to have a good time. Share some drinks and some gossip and generally escape all the things they were forced to deal with. Even when it was a bitch session, it was something fairly innocuous, like how big a butthole Patricia was or how Halcyon kept having to tell the local busybodies to butt out of her theater productions. So maybe it was as simple as neither of them wanting to drag their serious baggage into the only escape time they had.

And then there was Avery. She loved her daughter to pieces but they were still at a somewhat awkward place—where

Avery was trying to be an adult but wasn't really there yet and Marina was trying to let her be an adult and sometimes failing. She supposed that was the normal dance of any mother and daughter, especially at this stage of life. And Marina knew she'd always be Avery's mother and would never be able to stop the desire to make things better, but she was also looking forward to the time when they could be friends.

Then there were her parents. And boy was that a load.

Her father had died when she and Halcyon were only ten but she remembered him as being fun. Also irresponsible. He went months without acknowledging he had kids, then he'd show up one day with presents and play for an afternoon only to disappear again right after. Marina was fairly certain he had loved her but she was equally certain that he had no desire to be a parent. She'd cried when he died and still missed him sometimes, but her day-to-day life hadn't really been affected by his death.

Her mother was the first and biggest of her relationship failures, and Marina had spent so many years thinking that was her fault. That's the way Letitia had conditioned her to think. If only she'd been prettier or taller or quieter or smarter or whatever the adjective of the day was, then her mother would have loved her. Her entire childhood had been overshadowed by her attempts to gain her mother's approval, and even once she'd gotten old enough to realize that was never going to happen, she'd never been able to completely cut the umbilical cord until recently.

As Letitia had gotten older and nastier, Marina had finally admitted to herself that she'd never been anything to her mother except the scheme that hadn't worked. Letitia had lied about being on birth control so that she could get pregnant, figuring a baby would woo her father away from Constance and turn him into the white-picket-fence guy. It was the worst plan ever. For anyone. But especially for the children who only existed as a strategic move by a selfish adult.

Marina knew all of this because Letitia had told her the story when she was a teenager. Repeatedly. And in great detail. Her mother's point was that Marina didn't want to make the same mistakes she'd made and be saddled with a whiny kid for all the good years of her life. That's exactly how she'd put it. "Saddled." Letitia had never let Marina doubt that the best years of her life had been stolen from her because she'd had to raise a child.

So that relationship was finally where it needed to be. As shallow as a teaspoon of water.

Marina would see to it that her mother had care until she passed but she wasn't going to pretend any longer that there was any love there. Letitia wasn't capable.

Her mind flashed back to one night when she was maybe six years old. Letitia had taken her to the fair. Not because she intended for Marina to enjoy the rides and food and games but because there was a band playing that Letitia liked and she wanted to hit on the guitar player.

LETITIA DRAGGED her past the snow cones and funnel cake and all the cool gaming stations and the rides and headed straight for the tent where the band was playing. There was a single seat left close to the front and Letitia took it and told Marina to sit on the ground next to her.

Marina asked if they could play a game or ride the Ferris wheel when the concert was over but Letitia frowned and told her that they hadn't come for Marina and if she'd been able to find a sitter, then Letitia wouldn't have brought her at all. Marina slumped on the ground, holding her hands over her ears when the concert started. It was loud and she didn't like the music. Despite taking the chair, Letitia stood the entire time, waving her hands and trying to catch the attention of the guy on stage. Finally, Marina got so bored, she wandered off.

She walked down the midway, gawking at all of the flash and glitter. The smells were overwhelming—both good and bad. And the rides whirled past with people screaming with excitement. She stopped in front of a booth that was selling cheap toys. A bored-looking man with tons of tattoos and very little hair stood behind the booth, but he barely gave her a glance.

She gazed at the items on the shelves and a magic princess set caught her eye. It had a tiara with sparkly multicolor stones all around it, a ring with a big plastic stone, and a magic wand covered with silver glitter. It was the prettiest thing Marina had ever seen. She stood there gazing at it, thinking about how it would feel to wear that tiara and to be not just a princess but one who could do magic.

Magic would fix everything.

"You got money, kid?" the man behind the booth asked. "Because if not, move along. You're blocking my display."

Marina's heart dropped. Maybe if she could just stand there a bit longer, her mother would come looking for her and would buy it. But even as the thought rolled through her head, she knew it wasn't true. Her mother wouldn't even notice she was missing unless the band stopped playing and she wanted to leave.

"Which one do you like?" A lady's voice sounded above her.

She looked up and saw an old lady with silver hair that seemed to shine. She was wearing a purple pantsuit and bright pink lipstick. And she was smiling. She had a nice smile.

"The magic princess set," Marina said.

"That's a good choice," the lady said and handed the disgruntled man some money.

He shoved the bills in his pocket and the lady took the princess set off the shelf and handed it to Marina.

Marina's breath caught in her throat. "For me?"

The lady laughed. "Of course. I already have a tiara. It's at home on my dresser."

Marina clutched the princess set and looked up at the lady, who looked as if she were glowing under the midway lights.

"Thank you," Marina said, so overwhelmed that the words came out as a whisper.

"Every little girl deserves to be a princess," the lady said. "And everyone should have a little magic in their lives."

Then the lady touched her cheek and walked away. Marina held the princess set close to her chest, her young heart overwhelmed with the kindness of a stranger. In fact, that single act of kindness had affected her so much that it had probably shaped her into the person she was today.

"HOLY SHIT!" Marina bolted up from her chair.

No way. It couldn't be that easy.

CHAPTER THIRTY

SHE RAN INTO THE CABIN, grabbed a box off the bedroom floor, and sat it on the bed. She started yanking clothes out of the box and tossing them left and right like a madwoman. At the bottom of the box she found what she'd been looking for. An old wooden chest that her father had given her one year for her birthday. She'd painted it several times as her favorite color changed with age, and now it was flecked in spots, showing five different colors on the top alone.

She placed it on the bed and said a silent prayer. Then she slowly opened the box and reached for the princess ring in the bottom corner. The princess ring with the big red stone. As soon as she touched it, she knew.

This was it.

The ring shimmered and then began to glow. Inside the glow, the appearance shifted and for just a moment, she saw its true shape. It was the ring Alexios had shown her. The ring of power. It had been right there in her possession the entire time.

Snooze began to bark, breaking her out of her trance.

The stalker!

If he was outside then he'd try to steal the ring.

She ran into the kitchen, trying to find something to hide the ring in, and grabbed the first thing she saw on the counter. Banana nut bread. She parted it a bit on the bottom, then shoved the ring inside and wrapped it back up in Saran Wrap. Then she pulled the decoy ring out of her purse along with her cell phone and sent Alexios a text.

He walked through her front door seconds later, looking more haggard and more anxious than she'd ever seen him.

"How's the generator holding up?" she asked. If Alexios didn't have any power left, he couldn't even attempt to contact Zeus.

"Hanging in there," he said, giving her an expectant look.

She nodded and put one finger to her lips, then motioned to the barking dog.

Alexios's eyes widened but she could tell he was thrilled. She handed him the bag with the decoy ring and he stared into it at the cheap bit of jewelry and frowned. Then she thrust the banana nut bread at him and he looked even more confused.

"Even though you can see it now, I put the ring in a velvet pouch for transport," she said, making sure her voice was loud and clear. "And I added a little something for you—for your journey home. I know how you love sweets."

He stared at the banana nut bread for a moment, confused, then his face cleared in understanding. Marina knew he was on a diet. She would never give him something loaded with sugar. He threw his arms around her and squeezed her as tightly as he could for a man holding bread.

"You are my hero," he whispered before kissing her on the cheek.

He released her and headed for the door. She could see the tears pooling in his eyes as he looked back at her and smiled.

Then the door burst open and a man wearing a mask

stepped inside. He held something in his hand that was round and kinda looked like a stress ball, but whatever it was had Alexios taking a few steps back. Alexios had told her that earthly weapons couldn't harm him but clearly whatever the stalker was holding could.

"Give me the ring," the stalker said.

"And seal my death warrant?" Alexios asked.

"You're dead if you don't," the stalker said. "It's either me or Zeus. I wouldn't expect mercy from either."

The stalker lifted his arm, moving the object closer to Alexios, who cowered a bit and shook his head as if in pain.

"Stop!" Alexios yelled. "Take it."

Alexios thrust the velvet pouch at the stalker. He took it and loosened the drawstring to peer inside. Then he smiled and Marina felt her blood run cold. Until this moment, it had all been an adventure. A child's game almost. Except that it wasn't a game. And these men weren't children.

For the first time since it had all begun, she realized that this was really a war. A war that someone would win and someone would lose. Where people would die. And gods. Both. She clutched the counter as she started to sway. This was it. The stalker was going to kill her and Alexios, and the ring would never get back to Zeus. The world would end.

She'd miscalculated.

She'd thought by giving Alexios a decoy that if the stalker intercepted him, he'd take the bait and run. But it looked like he was going to take the bait, kill them, then run. She wouldn't even have an opportunity to warn Halcyon or Avery. Or more importantly, tell them how much she loved them one last time.

This was how her life ended.

And despite all the awful things that had happened the past week, Marina still loved every moment of every day she'd been on earth. Even the bad ones. Every second had shaped her into the person she was today. And finally, after forty-eight years, she thought she knew exactly who that person was.

More importantly, she really liked her.

The stalker punched his fist with the weapon toward Alexios and the demigod crumpled onto the ground. Marina rushed over to him and crouched down, figuring at least they could die together. She looked back at the stalker and he laughed. Then he ran out of the cabin, slamming the door behind him.

Marina pressed her fingers against Alexios's neck, checking for a pulse. Did demigods even have a pulse? Surely they did, right? He was half human. She sucked in a breath when she felt nothing, then moved her fingers a bit and went perfectly still, as if willing his heart to beat.

Then she felt it. Faint but there.

A couple seconds later, his eyes fluttered and he moved a bit. Then he sat up and blinked several times, his watery eyes trying to focus on her face.

"Can you hear me?" Marina asked. "Can you breathe? What can I do?"

Alexios smiled. "You already did it. But if you wouldn't mind helping me up..."

"Of course!"

Marina stood and reached down, gathering Alexios in her arms and pulling him up. He was wobbly but managed to stand upright as long as he was touching the wall.

"Is Zeus really going to kill you?" Marina asked, just in case the stalker or someone else was listening.

"I honestly don't know," he said, playing along.

"You could stay here."

"If he had to come looking for me, it would only make things worse. It's best to face my failure now. Thank you for everything you've done. I'll try to lobby for your reward, but I can't make promises."

"I'm not worried about it. I'll pray for you."

The corners of his mouth twitched. "To whom?"

She followed him to the front door and watched as a shimmering white door materialized on her front porch. Alexios walked through the door, turned around, and raised the banana nut bread in the air and smiled.

"Good luck, Marina Trahan."

The door disappeared in a blink of light and Alexios and the ring were gone.

Marina slumped down into her rocking chair. Her decision was final.

She was taking the rest of the day off.

CHAPTER THIRTY-ONE

ONE MONTH *later*

MARINA STOOD in the middle of the downtown building and smiled at all the old wood covered with dust. It was perfect. Absolutely perfect.

"Are you sure about this?" Halcyon asked, wrinkling her nose. "There's that new strip mall on the highway to New Orleans. Everything is shiny and clean."

Marina shook her head. "I don't want shiny. I want something with history. Something that's old and still beautiful."

"Well, you certainly have the old part covered. But I have to admit, the location is great."

The building was located right in the heart of downtown Last Chance, across from the café and next to the bakery. Advertising wouldn't even be necessary. In a matter of two days, most everyone in town would visit the bakery or café and they'd see her signs. Everyone would know she was there.

"I can't believe Dottie bought this place," Halcyon said. "And everything between you guys is cool, right? It's all legal?"

Marina nodded. "I signed the papers yesterday. I'm leasing the space with the intent to purchase. No set purchase date, and I don't start making lease payments until the shop is open and in the black."

"I love her," Halcyon said. "And the fact that she swept this building up before the LeDoux got their grubby hands on it is awesome."

"I think it really pleased her. It's a huge thumb in the LeDoux's faces, but Dottie style."

"Classy."

"Exactly."

"Preston and company have been keeping a lower profile ever since Little Miss Chastity turned the charity event into a street brawl."

"I think they're hoping people will forget and Preston can still become mayor."

"I think that ship has sailed. More and more people are starting to speak up about their bad behavior. I think your situation, Dottie pulling her donations, and Adelaide posting that YouTube video have unraveled their carefully laid plans."

"I'm still getting messaged about that video. But it's a small price to pay to get the charges against Avery dropped."

"How's Avery doing?"

"Good. Relieved. I think she's finally letting all of this go and focusing on her studies. She's still not speaking to Harold, but I promised her I wouldn't bring it up. It's her decision. If she wants to talk, she knows I'm always available."

Halcyon tapped her fingers on an old countertop and studied Marina for a moment. "Have you heard from Alexios?"

She already knew the answer, of course. But Marina knew Halcyon was as worried for their friend as she was.

"No," Marina said. "I don't know what to think, really. I mean, the world hasn't ended, so that's great, but I wish we knew what was happening. Is the war still going on? Is Zeus winning?"

"If he wins, do you think we'll ever hear from Alexios again?"

"I don't know. I hope so. I really liked him. But he gave up so much of his life trying to find the ring that I wouldn't blame him if he didn't want to come here again."

"That's true. I kinda miss him, though."

"Me too."

"So what's the story with you and the hunky game warden?"

"He has a name, you know."

"First name Hunky. Middle name Game. Last name Warden."

Marina grinned. "You're impossible."

"No. You're impossible. Are you going to go out with him or what?"

"I *have* gone out with him."

"I'm not talking about hanging out like friends. I'm talking about taking that man for a ride."

Marina closed her eyes and shook her head. "I'm not ready for a ride. My divorce isn't even final. We're taking things slowly. Friends first. Then if we both think things should move forward, they will."

"Uh-huh."

"What?"

Halcyon sighed. "That man is waiting on you to give him the go-ahead. He made up his mind a long time ago. Men like that don't spend time with a woman unless they're attracted."

"She's right." Alexios's voice sounded behind them.

Marina whirled around and practically sprinted across the room, then threw her arms around the thin man and whirled them both around in a circle, laughing and crying at the same time. Alexios was laughing too, and when she finally ran out of breath and released him, she saw him wipe the tears from his eyes. Halcyon came over and gave him a hug and kiss.

"You don't know how happy I am to see you," Marina said.

"I have an idea," Alexios said.

"We were afraid..." Marina's voice trailed off.

He nodded. "It was rough. By the time I got back, I was afraid it was too late. But you did it, Marina. The ring made the difference. Zeus defeated the enemy. Our world is safe. Your world is safe."

Marina's chest clenched. "Oh my God. That's incredible. I'm so happy for you. For us. For everyone."

"And the stalker?" Halcyon asked.

"Was one of our own, as I'd suspected," he said. "I would have liked to have dealt with him myself, even though that's not normally how I handle things. But Zeus was in a mood and all that negative energy needed somewhere to go."

"Yikes," Marina said.

Halcyon grinned. "I think Zeus and I would get along. There's something I need to grab out of my truck. I'll give you guys a minute but don't leave before I get back."

As Halcyon slipped out of the building, Marina reached out and gave Alexios's hand a squeeze. They had shared something that most people never did—they'd been tasked with the impossible and had prevailed even when it didn't look good right up to the very end. He was her friend, her brother...family.

"The banana nut bread was genius," Alexios said. "I've told that story so many times and gotten so many free drinks because of it. You have quite a fan club in our world. The bakery is even selling 'Marina Bread' now. It's a huge hit."

"It's a shame you couldn't have any of it," Marina said.

He grinned. "I ate the entire thing. It was glorious."

"What about your diet?"

He waved a hand in dismissal. "I wanted new clothes anyway."

"I think you've earned them."

He frowned and leaned closer, studying her face. "Your skin?"

"I know. I'm aging again. It didn't just sprint back to where it was but everything is starting to come undone. I saw a couple strands of silver in my hair yesterday, and I'm extremely disappointed to announce that my chin hair has returned for a second act."

He frowned. "I don't understand."

"I just figured it was the ring. Maybe the ring was where the power really came from and once it was gone..."

"I'm sorry."

"I'm not. This is me. It's who I'm supposed to be. And I'm gloriously happy with that."

He smiled. "You should be. You're the most awesome woman I've ever met. So what is all this?" He swept his arms out.

"I'm opening my own beauty shop. I'm calling it A Touch of Magic."

Alexios put his hand over his heart. "I love that."

"I thought you might."

"Well, if you're opening up shop, you're going to need some capital."

Marina stared. "You mean the money?"

"Of course. We made a promise. And you killed it on your end of things."

"Oh, but my divorce isn't final. I know you don't understand our laws, but if that money appears now, I might have to give half of it to Harold."

"Don't despair. My people researched all of this." He

handed her a folder. "That's all the information concerning your inheritance from a very distant cousin. Inheritance is not community property, so no sharing required. You will, however, have to pay taxes on it or risk trouble with your IRS, so we added a bit on top to cover that end of things."

"Seriously? You did that?"

"I don't think you understand how happy Zeus is."

"Probably not as happy as me right now."

Marina threw her arms around Alexios and hugged him, bouncing them both up and down.

When she stopped bouncing, she blew out a breath. "That's incredible."

"Incredible is an understatement. It's literally out of this world."

Halcyon walked back in, carrying a large square package covered with brown paper.

"What's out of this world?" she asked.

"I'm getting the money!" Marina yelled, and Halcyon let out a loud, "Whoot!"

He laughed. "I thought you might be excited, especially after the splurge on that trip to Mexico the two of you took."

"How did you know about that?" Marina asked.

"Zeus has this way of rewinding the view, so to speak."

Halcyon narrowed her eyes. "I hope he doesn't view everything."

"Unfortunately, no," he said. "Was that surfer as good as he looked?"

Halcyon grinned. "Better."

"We thought things might end," Marina said. "Soooooo..."

"It was a really good choice," Alexios said. "Maybe next time you can bring Hunky. You know, once you go ahead and admit you want him."

"Thank you!" Halcyon said.

"I'm not discussing this with the two of you," Marina said.

"Talking is the last thing this situation needs," Alexios said.

Marina smiled, then grew serious. "Do you think I've had the ring my whole life? Or did it turn into that toy when I came into my power?"

"I don't know," Alexios said. "I don't think we'll ever know. But it does give me pause. To think that all those before you might have had the ring just sitting in a drawer all their lives."

"But if it was there the whole time, why didn't I feel it?" Marina asked. "I mean, I did when I took it out but before then, nothing. And I packed that box myself."

"I'm afraid I don't know the answer to that either," he said. "My historians have been over everything, including the moment when you realized you knew where the ring was. They wanted to know if you'd tell me what you were thinking about. There was a particular expression on your face that they felt was powerful emotion attached to a memory."

"It was," Marina said, and she told him the story about the fair.

Alexios shook his head. "It's an incredible story, and I have to wonder if that moment of contemplation along with coming into your power so late in life and all the emotional stress and hard choices you faced that week all culminated in your success."

"You think that finding myself allowed me to find the ring?" Marina asked.

"Why not?" he said. "It's as good an explanation as any."

Marina nodded. Maybe he was right. Maybe he wasn't. But none of that mattered. The only important thing was that Zeus had won the war and earth was safe. With luck and a set of good doctors, Marina could live to play with her grandchildren. Or maybe grand-animals if Avery stuck to her newfound all-people-suck stance.

Alexios gave her a hug and kiss. "I have to run."

"Another assignment?" she asked.

"No. A much-needed vacation. There's this cute barista that I met in a neighboring star system."

"Will we ever see you again?" Marina asked.

"I don't know," Alexios said. "But I wouldn't count it out."

He gave Halcyon a kiss and headed out the door, then disappeared.

Marina stared out the glass storefront, then sucked in a breath. "I just realized something."

"What?" Halcyon asked.

"That woman—the pretty lady who bought me the princess set—it was Dottie's mother."

"You're sure?"

Marina nodded. "There was a picture on Dottie's fireplace when I went over to sign the papers. I kept thinking she looked familiar but it just clicked."

"That's so cool. And it makes total sense. First the mother, then the daughter. It's a fairy godmother family."

"It kinda is. Do you ever wonder if some things are fate?"

"You mean that we're destined to do or become whatever due to some preassigned set of parameters?"

Marina nodded.

"I don't think so. I think things are put in front of us and our life becomes what we make of those things. Some people turn dust into gold. Other people sprinkle water on it and roll around in the mud."

"So you're a believer in free will."

Halcyon grinned. "Of course. So what are you going to do with all that money? Pay for the building, right? And get it decorated to the nines. What about a trip to Italy? No! Bora-Bora."

"Let's not get ahead of ourselves. I can't just fling money everywhere or someone will tell Harold, or worse, the IRS."

"But you have paperwork for everything."

"And would still have to put up with a bunch of auditors crawling up my butt, which could also result in freezing the funds until they're satisfied."

Halcyon sighed. "I hate it when you being right spoils my fun."

"But some of it will go into the shop for sure. And I'll keep plenty set aside for Avery's schooling and expenses."

"And a new house."

"I don't think so. Not yet anyway. I like the cabin."

"You have mice living in the attic."

"Adelaide is giving me one of her cats."

Halcyon stared. "Wow. She must really like you. But what is Snooze going to think?"

"I suppose he'll think I'll stop harping on him to catch the mice."

"At least get some new furniture."

"I will definitely do that," Marina said. "And I really need to fund my retirement. I'm not getting any younger."

"So true."

"Neither are you. In fact, you're getting older before I do. By six months anyway."

"So rather than journey down that dismal path, why don't you take a look at your gift?" Halcyon handed Marina the package.

Marina sat it on the dusty counter and as she tore the paper wrapping off of it, a picture frame came into view. She pulled the rest of the wrapper off, then gasped.

It was a photo of her. But one like she'd never seen before. She was standing in her bedroom, wearing the dress she'd borrowed from Halcyon. But the background was blurred and the entire picture had been rendered in black and white. Marina was touching a lock of her hair and had her other hand on her hip. It looked like one of the old pinup girls' pictures.

"I thought you could hang it in the shop," Halcyon said, shifting nervously. "But if you don't think it's good enough..."

"Are you kidding me? It's incredible. How did you— Oh my God, Halcyon. This is gorgeous. I've never looked this good. Not even at that moment, but this picture..."

"I just played around with it a bit in Photoshop. It's no big deal."

But it was a big deal. Marina didn't pretend to know fine art, and Photoshop looked as hard as preparing a tax return, but she knew quality when she saw it. And the photo was simply beautiful.

"That picture you have hanging in your living room," Marina said. "The one of the sunset over the bayou. Did you take that?"

Halcyon nodded.

"Wow." Marina shook her head. "I thought you'd bought it somewhere. I knew you were a talented artist, but this... Halcyon, you have to do something about this."

"Like what?"

"Take some more classes. Get some cool camera equipment. I have the money for it. Put up a website and sell these."

"I don't know..."

"Listen, you have a gift and you're bored. The theater here doesn't keep you busy enough and we both know you're not going to move to a larger city. You have to find something more to do with your time and talent."

"Sleeping and daytime TV are something to do," Halcyon protested, but Marina could tell her sister was thinking about what she'd said.

Halcyon reached over and took Marina's hand.

"You and I are going to take on the world," Halcyon said. "Sisters—Act 2."

Marina shook her head. "The Final Cut."

For more hilarious stories by Jana DeLeon, check out her website for more information janadeleon.com.

ABOUT THE AUTHOR

Jana DeLeon grew up among the bayous and marshes of south-west Louisiana, and she loves writing about the unique setting and the people that make Louisiana special.

If you enjoyed her humor, please check out her USA Today, New York Times, and Wall Street Journal bestselling Miss Fortune Series.

https://janadeleon.com

CPSIA information can be obtained
at www.ICGtesting.com
Printed in the USA
LVHW041549181021
700767LV00002B/168

9 781940 270715